I0524612

SEERS' MOON

KAREN WOLFE

Published in 2009 by New Generation Publishing

Copyright© Karen Wolfe

First Edition

The author asserts the moral right under the Copyright, Designs and Patents Act 1988 to be identified as the author of this work.

All Rights reserved. No part of this publication may be reproduced, stored in a retrieval system or transmitted, in any form or by any means without the prior consent of the author, nor be otherwise circulated in any form of binding or cover other than that which it is published and without a similar condition being imposed on the subsequent purchaser.

Published by New Generation Publishing

Also by Karen Wolfe:

'Seers' published in 2008 by Legend Press

To my father, who opened the Library door and led me in.

To my mother, who read to me so beautifully.

To my Gran, victim of a less enlightened age, whose

writing died with her.

PROLOGUE

Snitty Bedford peeked in the bus-shelter to see if anybody was looking.

When he'd made sure they were, he whipped his mack open, and gave them an eyeful.

Ooh, but them piercing, girly screams made him feel good. *Powerful.* That and the moonlight shining on his manhood. He was off his own patch tonight: different village, same thrill. They screamed again. Trapped, weren't they, nowhere to look but straight *at* him, and couldn't get past without touching…they'd got that really gobsmacked look, all round mouths and big, frightened eyes…over-awed, the silly cows. He swelled with pride. Weren't they the lucky ones, sharing his excitement…and then it dawned on him they weren't looking at *him* at all, but goggling at something over his shoulder…he swung round, which was a mistake considering there was a walloping great dog…no, not a dog, a wolf!…only six feet away, sizing up his assets with yellow eyes, and slavering.

With a scream louder than anything his audience had managed, Snitty bundled himself into his long grey mack and ran for his life, bare feet slapping painfully on the uneven pavement. And huddled together in the bus-shelter, three young girls and Miss Agnes Dean, retired florist, watched in disbelief as Mrs. Lazenby's ginger tom, hissing and spitting, sprang over the fence and chased an enormous wolf the length of Brimwold High Street.

Miss Dean wiped her steamed-up glasses with an embroidered handkerchief, and sighed. 'I know I'm an old silly,' she remarked. 'But I always thought that wolves were a lot, well, *bigger* than that.'

*****

1

SEERS' MOON

Granny took her teeth out, and put them in to soak with her corsets.

Squirt of lemon-juice and a few drops of Old Maid's Prayer'd bring 'em up good as new. Then she took her shoes off, sank her throbbing feet into a bowl of warm beetroot-mash, and poured herself a cup of strong tea.

What a day! She'd been on the go since sun-up, and everything ached...specially her face, what with all that smiling and being sociable. Still, she had to admit, it wasn't every day you was Invested first-ever Grandmistress of the Bartlesham Guild, or *any* Guild, come to that...and all in all, she thought everything'd gone off pretty well.

Her sister Mariander had been going to stay the night, but she'd shot off home because Her Bernard'd took ill that morning. Off his food, they'd said when she'd rung 'Heaven's Gate' to see how he was, so it must've been serious because he only ever woke up at mealtimes...not that she minded, really. It was nice to be by herself after being on show all day.

Course, officially Hom'd been there to help but, Highmaster or not, you couldn't get no sense out of him because he'd gone and Fallen In Love, and with her own niece Statia, if you please.

Least she hadn't been lumbered with them awful Ceremonial Robes Old Tukesley, the last Grandmaster'd favoured; making Festa Bough her Undermistress had been a good move.

All right, the girl might be short on soap, water, and social graces, but them things'd come, and it had to be said, she couldn't half sew. She'd knocked up something Black and Dignified in no time, which even, Granny felt, made her look a mite thinner and more In Charge.

It was a lovely evening: Summer on the way at last, and about time, too. And a clear sky, after weeks of rain. She really oughter go and have a look round the garden...but then, it'd still be there in the morning.

She pushed her mind out, over the valley, but it hadn't got more than a few hundred yards before she felt it letting go, switching off...Thomas wound himself round her legs, miaouwing plaintively. The moon was full, and he could feel it, smell it...a perfect hunting night...but would Granny wake up and open the door?...would she Rats!

He tried one of his green-eyed glares, to no avail. Once she started the purring noise down her nose, that was it for the night. With practised ease, he pawed the back-door latch, and slipped out into the moonlit garden. Halfway out, he froze, hackles up and tail splayed like a bottle-brush. He stood motionless, ears flat and eyes slitted, for a full five minutes, before creeping, belly-down, under the hedge. Shadow on shadow, he skirted the Beechwood, emerging cautiously into the water-meadows, his favourite hunting-grounds. Wind rustled the tall grasses, and moonlight shone on the river.

But it was no good, there was nothing doing...not so much as a shrew. Something had frightened all the prey off, and the whole outing was a disaster. Added to which, Thomas' nerve had gone, along with his timing. He was stiff, clumsy and couldn't've caught a grounded moth...he gave up after an hour, and slunk disgustedly home with that sound still ringing in his head.

Thomas looked after himself. Dogs worried him not at all...nor even what had sounded exactly like a wolf howling at the moon. Dogs, geese, wolves...no problem. But something else stalked the night, something that sent him bolting home with his whiskers curling...something much, much worse.

Bevis Tate put a thick black line across the chart. Then he screwed up his Acceptance-speech...(jokes highlighted in yellow)...and rammed it savagely in the bin.

He should have been Midmaster by now, and, Texacum Powell's internal plumbing being what it was, well on his way up to Highmastership. He was still seething about that outrageous Investiture. Grandmistress Beamish, indeed! What the Sight had Tukesley Meredith been thinking of, nominating a *woman* to lead the Guild?

Granted, the man *had* received a severe blow to the head, and, as they'd discovered before his Passing, had harboured some silly crush on Bryony Beamish...but was that any reason to change things? Why meddle with a perfectly satisfactory hierarchy? And why deny those on the way up a chance?

Self-pitying tears filled his eyes. When he thought of the Agendae he'd slaved over! All the hours he'd spent on those immaculately-produced Minutes! The organisational skills he'd expended on the revolutionary filing-system and the colour-coded charts! The Sub-Committees and Steering-Groups he'd formed without even being asked! All the Get-Well cards and hospital visits he'd arranged for incapacitated Guild-members! So why, then, would nobody take him seriously? He recalled the collective groans whenever he raised a point of order in the Guildenhall, the reluctance of others to attend his Extraordinary Meetings, the derision aroused by his graphs, and the way people always seemed to be out when he called.

Then there was the wholesale mis-use of his paper-clips, marker-pens and correcting-fluid...and now that whippersnapper Highmaster Hewitt was talking of putting all the Guild-records on a *computer*!! Well, he wouldn't get away with it.

He, the one with the skills, had no intention of being reorganised by a callow youth or, worse, a woman...particularly that Beamish person.

He knew, from their mind-slips, that there were others who felt the same about the old order of things...Ritro Bowers, for instance, Basil Worthenshawe, and even a surprising number of women, notably Acacia Barnsdown. He'd bide his time...but when he was ready, they'd be sorry they'd under-appreciated him. Taking a fresh piece of paper, he began drawing up a list of names for inclusion on a possible sub-committee. There weren't very many, but Guildwilling, enough...thank the Sight he had his Project to turn to in times of stress. It was something to lose himself in...a precision job, demanding the skills of an artisan.

Frowning with concentration, he began chiselling delicately at the minute stone fragments he'd collected during his afternoon walk. The trick was, of course, getting them exactly angled...one slip, and his life's work would be lost.

Not one of Them, he reflected, would be up to constructing a scale-model of a matchbox, built from bits of Bartlesham Cathedral...

Granny's garden was not a thing of beauty...more of a homoeopathic repository. It boasted nothing that didn't earn its keep: if it couldn't be eaten, infused, made into a poultice or used as a skin-preparation, it wasn't allowed in. The whole area was an horticulturalist's nightmare: a seemingly chaotic jumble of fruit, flowers, weeds and vegetables, absolutely teeming with wildlife. Granny was an incidental conservationist.

She also subscribed to her old Dad's theory that a garden was a means of filling your belly, not a showplace for useless, fancy indulgences. So side by side grew roses and radishes, damsons and daisies, beetroot and buttercups.

She was very fond of nettles, too, along with chickweed and bindweed, thistles and dandelions, cow-parsley, dog-daisies and stinkweed...the things most gardeners uproot, but all of which she found a use for.

And one of those uses was her skin-preparations. She'd dabbled for years; had a few successes and her share of failures as well. The Bilgewort eye-bag remover, for instance. Worked a treat--if only she could've got the colour right. Because, for some reason, folks didn't take kindly to slapping slimy black stuff under their eyes... She'd been waiting weeks for the rain to stop and the sun to ripen things in her garden, and now at last she'd got the ingredients she was after. She boiled up a pan of water, and got chopping.

Rog. and Steve, of Bartlesham Constabulary, pulled up outside Granny's cottage.

They'd enjoyed cruising through Brimwold, because the warm weather had brought the girls out. There'd been a gang of them hanging about outside the 'Rat & Pitchfork', none of them wearing very much. Perhaps, Rog thought, they'd go back that way, just to check on under-age drinking...

It was also their first day back on panda-patrol following the drugs-bust fiasco up on Brim Knap that'd brought about their demotion. Six months of Road Safety for Infants' Schools hadn't been a lot of laughs, specially having to wear those itchy Harry Hedgehog suits, and it had been good of the Sarge to put a word in for them...

'*Looks* all right.' Rog. studied the thatched cottage squashed in amongst the trees. 'Bit isolated, though. Well, let's get on with it.'

'You reckon it's safe?' Steve peered over the dashboard. 'Just a sweet little country cottage, not a crack-dealer's den or anything? After all, this *is the* same scary old woman. P'raps we ought to, like *raid* her...'

'Look, will you *shut* up about sodding drugs,' Rog. snarled. 'Anyone can make a mistake, all right?'

'Fine, fine.' Steve unfastened his seatbelt. 'Just don't accept any funny little cakes, O.K? Or anything with mushrooms in!'

Granny's brew had just reached a critical stage when she heard someone knocking. Moving the pan off the heat, she grumbled her way to the door.

All right, she supposed a rhubarb face-pack *did* take a bit of getting used to, but there'd bin no call for them policemen to scream and radio for an ambulance, had there? And then one of 'em'd rushed her into the kitchen, shoved her face under the cold tap, and held it there!

They'd both kept going on about 'third-degree burns,' although what being educated had to do with it she couldn't fathom.

By the time the ambulance arrived, frightening Thomas and every living thing for miles around with its siren, the face-pack had washed off, all that precious rhubarb down the sink and her neck!-- but then, it'd never really had chance to set properly. And when she'd spluttered her way out from under the tap, them policemen's faces were redder than hers had ever been.

Funny thing was, the ambulance-crew didn't seem to mind being called out on a false alarm: couldn't stop laughing, in fact.

For some reason, they kept shaking their heads and saying: 'Rog. and Steve. Wow! Living Legends of the Emergency Services! Do you do autographs?'--and they were still laughing when they drove off.

Luckily for the policemen, they rallied round Granny before she could get her own back. One of them fetched her a towel, and the other one brought her a cup of tea. She didn't recognise them, even with her glasses on, because she never gave a thought to Outsiders, who all looked exactly the same to her. But they recognised *her,* all right, and something told them apologies were very definitely in order, even if they had meant well.

And their minds told her what'd brought them before one of them stammered: 'Message from your sister, Miss Beamish. We were asked to come because you're not on the phone. I'm afraid it's bad news about your brother-in- law.'

Full moon again tonight: try as he might to deny it, it's all happening again, and he's feeling very, very sorry for himself.

P.L.T's s terrible thing--one whole sodding week of irritability and biting things and sleeplessness and that terrible, restless longing—he'd do anything to beat it he's that desperate, and, you name it, he's tried it. Hypnosis, meditation, acupuncture, aromatherapy, vitamins--none of 'em the slightest use. He knows only too well how it will be.

That hair, well, fur, really, and the whiskers--too much for any razor, and waxing'd brought tears to his eyes--and them great, pointy ears he can't do a thing with. Hats are impossible, and the balaclava he bought just isn't him--and then what's he supposed to do with that zonking great plumed tail? Have his trousers tailor-made to accommodate it?

Even worse, he'll get the urge to cock his leg, leave his mark, and she'll go spare about dribbles on the carpet. She oughter try living with his problems!

She'll do her best to keep him in when the time comes; beg him, like she always does, not to go out....because, sooner or later, they're going to start hunting him.

7

But how can he resist the call of the moon? Like it or not, he's caught and held in its relentless cycle, exactly like the tides. It's just that he could do with a month off now and then, because he's thoroughly pissed off with this whole Werewolf Syndrome.

Rog. and Steve came out of Granny's cottage congratulating themselves on a job well done. All in all, they thought they'd handled that old woman like pretty sensitive guys.

Rog. reckoned he'd make ideal Samaritan material, and Steve was trying to decide between Bereavement Counselling and an Agony-Uncle column in the 'Police Gazette', when they spotted the Panda. Five minutes' silent study of its battered bonnet and splintered headlights didn't improve it one bit.

'Bloody ambulance-drivers,' Rog. said eventually. 'Not that anyone'll believe us.'

'Oh, well.' Steve said gloomily, 'I was getting bored patrolling, anyway, dunno about you, but I'm just about ready for another stint as Harry, the unsquashable bloody hedgehog.'

'It was awful, Bryony,' Mariander sighed. 'He'd been gone two days before anybody realised.'

Poor ole Mari, Granny thought, That Bernard might not've been much company but it's really hit her hard. 'What, er, gave it away, then?' she asked gently, 'Him not snoring, was it? Or missing his meals?'

'Well, no.' Mariander went suddenly pink. 'Just--the flies, really, round his chair. So the Matron said. Well, there *has* been a heatwave,' she added defensively.

'I'll put the kettle on,' Granny said carefully, 'and then help you sort things out for tomorrow.'

Granny sat at the front, with Mariander and her daughters, Thuja and Statia.

She'd never been to an Outsider's funeral, and decided she hadn't missed much, because it wasn't a patch on a Seer's Passing-

Ceremony. This place, for a start--talk about dismal! Nasty plastic chairs instead of proper pews, hardly any light coming in through them tidgy little windows--and *artificial flowers* everywhere! Not a bit like the Guildenhall.

And they wouldn't allow dogs in! Granny could hardly believe they'd had to leave Grufty at home. Passing-ceremonies always had as many pets as people coming to say goodbye! Brontine Clegg's widow'd even lugged his old donkey into the Guildenhall, and a fair fight she'd had to get it through the door, as well--and out again, come to that--then there was that sad, dreary music. Seers always enjoyed a nice singalong to the Deceased's favourite tunes, however rude, because, after all, it *was* their Send-Off party. But these Outsider-songs didn't mean a thing, far as she could tell--and the weeping and wailing!!

Bernard's relatives, all looking as if they'd been carved from the same block of lard, plonked themselves down opposite, glared at her and Mariander, and then let rip into their hankies. Funny, Granny noticed, that they couldn't squeeze out a single tear between them.

Then there was the Vicar. Never set eyes on Bernard, Mariander said, but he didn't let a little detail like that stop him going on and on about what a great man he'd been. Granny tried hard to recall anything saintly about Bernard, but all she could come up with was that ring he always had round his forehead where his cap'd rubbed...not that he'd been a *bad* person, it was just--Outsiders was different, and shouldn't mix with Seers, let alone wed them--still, she supposed, if the Vicar's words cheered everybody up, what did it really matter?

She'd nicely settled herself to rifle through the assembled minds, when everybody suddenly stood up. She got to her feet just in time to see Bernard's coffin, to the accompaniment of some *really* miserable music, slide behind a little velvet curtain, and disappear! Granny was outraged...fancy taking him away before they'd finished! That couldn't be right, could it?

She glanced at Mariander and the girls, but they stood blinking like rabbits caught in a lorry's headlights. Up to her, then, to Do Something.

Concentrating hard, she fixed her mind, got the thing stopped, and even managed to drag it halfway back through the curtain before the Vicar, after several increasingly desperate prods at the starter-button under his dais, leaned over and, with a sickly smile at his congregation, shoved it back.

Whereupon Granny, gritting her teeth, lugged it out again.

'Bryony, STOP it!' Mariander hissed. 'Let him GO! It's what he wanted!'

'Only trying to help, I'm sure!' Granny said huffily, releasing her mental hold so suddenly that Bernard departed with unseemly haste, and they all heard the unmistakable sound of splintering wood. The Vicar buried his head in his hands...praying, probably.

Afterwards, Thuja took her aunt on one side, and explained about cremation. Granny was appalled. She couldn't see the point of it at all, and thought it the saddest thing she'd ever heard. Being *burned*! It seemed so...lonely. And useless, too, not to be snug in the ground, rotting down with all the others and helping the worms turn the soil. That was how it should be...bodies returning to the earth, same as minds going back into the Pool...

Outside the crematorium, three hefty women were huddled under the yew-trees, looking uncomfortable. Bernard's sisters hurried forward to greet Mariander. Zinnia, Poinsettia and Begonia. Once seen, Granny thought, never forgotten.

'Mariander!' Zinnia, the youngest, mashed her sister-in-law into her formidable bosom. 'We couldn't bring ourselves to go in--you know, Outsiders and that--did it go off all right?'

'Oh, it *would've* done,' Mariander glared at Granny, 'if *certain people* hadn't started meddling with things they didn't understand.'

Granny, standing her ground, glared right back. 'Well, how was I to know?' she snapped. 'Anyway, I still don't think any of it's right and proper!'

'Why, what happened?' Begonia, the eldest, eyed Granny from a safe distance, knowing full well what Bryony Beamish was capable of.

Mariander told her. There was a stunned silence, and then the sisters all started laughing, and carried on as if they'd never stop.

'Bryony, you're priceless!' Poinsettia gasped eventually. 'Being Grandmistress ain't calmed you down one little bit!'

'You haven't heard the end of it, neither,' Mariander said grimly. 'That there Vicar's waived all the funeral-fees because he thinks his conveyor-belt's broke and he's caused Unnecessary Distress to the Bereaved! Well, how could we tell him?'

Bernard's Outsider relatives filed past, nodding stiffly in Mariander's direction.

Funny the way it went, Granny mused. What a lot of trouble Mixed Marriages caused! Two Seer parents, all the kids'd be Sighted, but get one Seer and one Outsider, and your girls'd always inherit, your lads only sometimes.

That'd been the way of it with Bernard--and what a lot of upset there'd been! All of which went to prove that you shouldn't put chitterlings in game-pie, as her Dad used to say, whatever *that* meant.

'You coming back for a cupper tea, then?' Mariander asked. 'There's one or two things of Bernard's you could have.' The sisters hesitated, until she added, 'I've got some cake in.'

Thuja and Sepia drove them home. It was a bit of a squash, even in two cars, owing to the size of Bernard's sisters, but there were only the seven of them. Mallon, Thuja's husband, had opted to look after Quinnie and Christom, because it wasn't done for Seer children to attend an Outsider's funeral; and Ran, Sepia's husband was on call at the Infirmary.

Grufty, sulking because he'd been left out, waggled his eyebrows and briefly waved his misshapen tail, then pointedly turned his back until the cake came out.

Sham the starling, however, loved having visitors because it gave him chance to Show Off and do his Noises. His Car-Alarm was well-received, likewise his Squeaking Bicycle-Brakes, and even his Yowling Tomcat--(his latest Impression, but not, for some reason, everyone's favourite)--went down quite well. But

11

his Rumbling Gastric Medley with Accompanying Flatulence and Background Snores undoubtedly got the best reaction.

'Oh, Mari, listen!' Begonia had tears in her eyes. 'I'd know them noises anywhere! He's Doing Our Bernard!' A reverential hush fell as they listened intently.

'Isn't that lovely?' Zinnia whispered. 'That's him to a 'T'! It's...a kind of a tribute, really, isn't it!'

'Well,' Granny said, when Sham had progressed to his Traffic-Jam with Horns and Revving Engines, 'What'll you do now, Mari? Can't stay in this great big place on your own, with empty houses all round.'

Mariander hesitated, gazing round the shabby old kitchen, as though seeing it for the first time, every crack and chip and cobweb.

'I've lived here too long.' she said at last, 'This house was all right once, nice neighbours, good area, too...til they started flattening it to build on. Now it's all tramps and vandals and kids shouting through your letterbox and worse...' she shivered at some uncomfortable memory...and now I can't keep on top of the cleaning, there's too many stairs and corners, and too many noises in the night.'

And too many ghosts Granny thought. *Poor Mari. What a way to live.* Into the shocked silence, Thuja said: 'Oh, Mum. We'd no idea it was *that* bad.'

'Well, it was your Dad.' Mariander went on sadly. 'He wouldn't hear of moving, and once he retired, he just give up, til I thought the house'd fall down round our ears...I'm sorry, Sepia, but it's true--he took to his chair years ago...matter of fact, it went with him into 'Heaven's Gate'...and this week was the first time he ever got out of it.'

She blew her nose again, and said firmly: 'So now's me chance to get out while I still can. I've had a good offer from one of them property-developers.'

'You decided where you're going?' Granny asked.

Mariander shuffled her feet, frowning at the worn lino Bernard'd never got round to replacing. 'Well, er, sort of.' She gave her sister one of those you're-not-going-to-like-this smiles.

'Oh?' Granny's hackles went up. Curse Mariander's mindblock.

'Yes, I…thought I might move out your way. Back Home, so to speak.'

'*My* way?' She hadn't expected *that*.

'Brimwold,' Mariander said bravely, 'is where I grew up. I've had enough of city life. I want a garden and neighbours and a community, but most of all…'

'Yes?' Granny saw her precious privacy evaporating like mist over the water-meadows.

'I want central heating!' Mariander announced. 'Because, let me tell you, this place has been an absolute pig to keep warm.'

The sisters went off bearing a carrier-bagful of Bernard's effects, and threatening to descend on Mariander when she got moved. Thuja and Statia, who were coming back in the morning to start clearing the upstairs rooms, had already gone.

Mariander closed the door behind them and went back in the kitchen to face her sister.

'See, Bry, I want to be part of things again,' she explained over a fresh pot of tea. 'And I want to start Practising. Join the Bartlesham Guild, mebbe get my Lower Levels…what's up, you think I'm too old?'

Granny stared disbelievingly over the teapot. 'Ain't *that* ,' she said, 'it's just…you mean Bernard didn't like you Seeing? *And you put up with it*? I dunno, Mari, straight I don't. Call yourself a Beamish?'

Mariander smiled uncertainly, like the sun coming out after a storm. 'Well, mebbe now I can go back to being one,' she said.

Moonlight on the Weald of Bart, lingering over the Stonebury Valley and the Healing-Stones.

Moonlight bathing the Ampleway, slipping over Brim Knap, lying quiet across the river-dykes and water-meadows.

Moonlight ghosting the Beechwood, lifting and fingering its shadows. Moonlight, nightlight, coldlight--and, somewhere, the terror of the wolf pursued.

Mariander sat herself down beside Granny's suitcase and said: 'Er.'

Granny sighed. 'What now?'

Mariander shuffled a bit. 'Well, you know when you get home? Couldn't do us a favour could you?'

'What sort of a favour? Already lumbered me with Sham and Grufty, haven't you?'

'You know I ain't got time to look after 'em proper, what with all the clearing-out and paperwork--don't mind, do you?'

'Hmmph.' She didn't, of course--just so Mari didn't take her for granted. 'So then what else you got me lined up for?'

'These.' Mariander produced a large envelope, from which she extracted several sheets of paper. 'House-particulars,' she explained. 'Brimwold area. Thought you might give 'em the once-over on my behalf.'

'You don't muck about, do you?' Granny squinted at the details, adjusted her glasses and squawked '*How* much? For that poky little place? You made of money or what?'

'Well,' Mariander folded Granny's cardigan and laid it in the case. 'I suppose they *are* a bit pricey...p'raps I'll just come and live with you instead.'

'Eh? No, you're all right,' Granny spluttered, 'don't worry, I'll find you a good 'un, count on me. Well now, time we were off. Where's that Thuja got to?'

Selfish bugger'd gone off again: never a thought for her.

Oh, he'd be out there somewhere, playing, while she stayed in and fretted.

Moonlight illuminated the chewed-up remains of his latest football: and he'd had another go at the window-sills, and even, God alone knew how, what was left of the pelmet. Wearily, she fetched the dustpan and brush, and then wondered why she

bothered. She was just so tired *of it all...she'd go tomorrow,*
straight she would. If only he didn't need her so much.

At the far end of Brimwold stood a former pigman's cottage,
now home to Aubrey and Hilary Bottomley.

It was cramped, low-beamed and built, as Aubrey often
observed after banging his head yet again, for undernourished
agricultural peasants, not *human beings.* It was a cliché of a
cottage, lifted from a fairy-tale age that never was. Visitors
pointed it out, and locals, according to their age, sniggered or
shook their heads at what it had become. The Bottomleys had
painted it sugar-pink, adding stable-type doors and double-glazed-
(to exclude those annoying country noises)...mock-leaded
windows. It was rose-clad and honeysuckled, and, for greater
authenticity, boasted a frontage cluttered with ancient domestic
and agricultural objects...a boot-scraper, a plough, a blacksmith's
anvil and a restored water-pump.

Re-painted cartwheels rested against the walls, and a
craftsman-made dovecote, studiously avoided by all self-
respecting birds, stood in the front garden. The meagre building
cowered beneath a ridiculous, top-heavy thatched roof, done in a
day by passing Cowboys...('Mornin', Missus. Tired of them ole
slates? Do you a thatch in no time!')...who were a lot quicker and
cheaper than Gobber Watts.

All of which pleased Gobber no end. Because who else got
all the spin-offs when the leaks started, when folks who'd made
false economies swallowed their pride, and came grovelling to a
real craftsman--?

Long ago, the place had been known as Clematis Cottage,
but the Bottomleys had, rather wittily they thought, re-named it
BOTTOM LEA. Whereupon the postman, who didn't like
incomers, had promptly dubbed it BUTTOCKS' END, and the
name had stuck.

Hilary Bottomley, who'd been scourging her windowsills,
was shocked to see a ghastly old woman prowling round the
empty dormer-bungalow next door.

15

Despite the heat, the old hag was wearing a long, black coat, and carrying a quite disgusting holdall, probably clanking with sherry-bottles...obviously one of those Bag-Persons looking for somewhere to sleep.

Hilary dithered. Could she shout loudly enough to penetrate Aubrey's bathtime oratorios, or ought she to phone her Neighbourhood Watch Co-coordinator, using the Pyramid System?

On the other hand, why should she be intimidated on her own doorstep? Snatching up a spray-disinfectant gun, because You Never Knew, she wrenched the door open, and called sharply

'Yes? Can I help you at all?'

The bag-woman's gaze swept over her, lingering particularly on the fresh perm and the pink rubber-gloves, and seeming to look right inside her mind. It was not a nice feeling.

After a long, uncomfortable moment, she snorted disparagingly, said 'No, ta,' and bent to look through the letter-box.

'But look! Here! You can't just...' The old woman marched off round the back, and Hilary found herself following.

'Now you listen to me!' She said sternly, 'you can't sleep here! There are Refuges for people like you...'

But the old woman wasn't listening: she was frowning over some sort of leaflet, now and then glaring through the kitchen window hard enough to dissolve the glass.

'Split-level cooker!' she muttered. 'Ex-tractor fan! Lot of newfangled nonsense!' She squinted ferociously.

'Plum..for...here, what's this say? I've forgot me glasses!' She thrust the crumpled paper at Hilary, who, after reading a few words, said weakly. 'Oh! You've got Details!'

The old woman gave her a Look. 'Yes, and why shouldn't I have? Place is for sale, ain't it?'

'Yes, but...' Hilary felt faint. Surely this dreadful person couldn't be contemplating buying the bungalow? She felt the old woman Looking at her...no, *into* her again, as if reading her mind. Then smiling evilly, she said: 'Well, I quite like it. Think I just might move in. Says here...'snatching the Estate-Agent's particulars from Hilary's hand, 'Key by arrangement with next-door neighbours. That's you, is it? Good, you can show us round, then.'

'But!' Hilary squawked, 'You can't just Turn Up! There are Proper Channels! And, anyway...who's US?'

At that exact moment, something stuck a wet nose up the back of her skirt. Hilary let out a loud scream, and whirled round like a western gunslinger, disinfectant at the ready, to find the thing *leering* at her.

It was, as she might have expected, a small mongrel of the worst possible kind. It had something horrible matted into its beard and eyebrows, and judging by the smell of it, had been rolling in something even worse...which was, presumably, why she hadn't noticed it in the overgrown grass. That, and its *extremely* short legs.

She couldn't *remember*, as she told Aubrey afterwards, fetching the bungalow key or handing it over. But she supposed she must have done, otherwise how had she come to find herself banging vainly on the locked back door, while the terrible old crone and her unspeakable dog rampaged around inside?

Another lane, another home, a deeper despair .He'd had four aspirins, a Bob Martins, a pot of tea and a lie-down in a darkened room. But it's not going away, and it's no use. Why fight it? Come moonrise, he'll be out there again, doing that old werewolf-thing.

'Dear me, what a carry-on.' You'd've thought she'd've had better things to do....the woman's shouting face had followed her from window to window, and Granny was getting plain fed-up with it.

'Come on, Grufty.' She turned her back, 'let's have a look upstairs.' Not that it'd be any better'n downstairs, but she had promised Mariander. She'd already bin round two places looked exactly the same to her; poky without being cosy, but this one was worse because it was empty.

Come to think of it, the folks in the other places had acted none too pleased when she'd turned up, just like the woman outside...funny, that. She hadn't asked 'em to stop what they were doing, had she?

Quite happy to potter round on her own--and how was she supposed to know that ole man was dozing in the tub?--Mariander'd told her specific to check the colours of bathroom-suites, it was something she was very particular about--and this one. Avocado, the leaflet said, but she recalled nursing that poisoned mallard with the runs, and his droppings, before he got better, had been *exactly* the same colour!

Pleased with herself, she explored the bedrooms, which didn't take long because they were so small, and the biggest had...she squinted at the paper again...a *ensuet shower-room!*...Mariander was getting very grand, she thought, for someone who'd grown up with an outside privy and a bathtub on a nail!

She heard Grufty's claws clicking on the bare wooden stairs, and he came waddling in with a mouse in his mouth. Granny sighed: she'd been vaguely aware of skittering noises downstairs.

'Give it here,' she told him. Sulkily, he spat the creature into her hand, where it lay trembling. She ran her finger along its spine, touched and calmed the small, panicked mind--*all right, little girl.* It was only a fieldmouse, scared but unhurt, prob'ly got in through an airbrick and nested.

'Shame on you, Grufty,' she told him, 'that was plain bad manners. Put her back, and mind you don't hurt her...she's got young 'uns down there.'

Taking the mouse in his gums...(useful teeth being but a distant memory)...Grufty slouched off down the stairs and let it go. But he lifted his leg against the wall it'd disappeared into. All right, Granny had said he couldn't keep it, but she hadn't said he couldn't *drown* it...

Tarrill Posskenway's Passing-Ceremony was the first she'd ever taken as Grandmistress, and she wanted to get it right.

Course, she'd *assisted,* many a time, but that wasn't the same. Everybody's style was different, how you talked about the

Passer, whether you made jokes...(and Tukesley Meredith certainly never had)...even what you wore, and how you wore it.

Old Tarrill had been the best shepherd for miles around, and though he'd ended his days in the Sunset Rest-Home just outside Bartlesham, he'd been Brimwold born and bred. And, up to losing his Gloxinia, he'd never left it, nor ever wanted to.

He hadn't coped on his own, though, and before long, his cottage had started going downhill, and the Guild had sent Tarrill off where he could be properly looked after. There'd been no children, and no chance of Tarrill's nephew uprooting hisself from his posh house in Bassett Bream, so Shepherd's Cott had been sold as it stood. Some brother and sister had bought it, Granny had heard, kept themselves to themselves.

And seemingly they didn't go in for decorating or gardening, because the place looked just as broken-down as it had before.....shame the way things turned.

She pulled on the new Passing-Robes Festa'd made: nice, bright, glittery sort of material that shimmered and changed colour every time she moved. She thought they'd cheer everyone up, unlike them things old Tukesley used to wear...

As a matter of fact, she'd shoved all the Grandmaster's Ceremonials away in a cupboard and forgotten about 'em. Least, she had until Bevis Tate dragged 'em out and made a lot of noise about displaying 'em, even starting a Seers' Museum....well, let him get on with it, if it took his mind off sulking because she'd been made Grandmistress. He wanted watching, that one.

Festa put her head round the door and said: 'Sheep's here Mum.'

Granny straightened her collar. 'Ta, Festa.' She did wish the girl wouldn't call her MUM, and go in for all that bobbing and curtseying, just because she was Grandmistress.

She'd known Festa all her life and always been plain old Granny to her, but Position did funny things to folks, and, being Undermistress, the girl seemed keen to do everything right, which she supposed you couldn't fault. Mebbe she'd settle, once the novelty wore off.

She went out into the Guildyard to greet Tarrill Poskenway's sheep, who'd come to say their goodbyes. There were nine of them, from tegs to old gimmers, all hand-reared in Gloxinia's kitchen, and most of 'em revived in Gloxinia's oven.

Course, Tarrill had long retired when he adopted 'em, but folks would keep bringing him orphaned lambs, which he never could refuse, so that he ended up with nine pets...the children him and Gloxinia never had, she supposed...growing up into nine hefty great sheep that gave his old dog something to practice on, and kept the grass down.

They'd all slept in the kitchen, too, where they'd first come back to life, and every one of them housetrained as any dog. Perilla Pearce took the lot when Tarrill went into the Home, and they lived with her menagerie up at the Sanctuary.

Granny emerged to find them all eating their heads off, as usual, while Perilla sat under the trees, smoking a cheroot. On seeing Granny, see leapt to her feet, choking and showering hot ash down her front.

'Sight save us, Bryony!' she stamped the remains of her cigar into the ground. 'What the blithers have you got on?'

One or two onlookers sniggered, as well they might: Perilla, clad in a striped jumpsuit with matching tennis-shoes and a back-to-front baseball cap, looked remarkably like a large windbreak.

'Me Passing-Robes, if you must know,' Granny retorted with as much dignity as she could muster. She indicated the enthusiastically-munching flock.

'Are them sheep of yours going to leave us *any* grass?'

'Come on, girls!' Perilla gave the nearest ewe a hearty smack on its fat rump. 'Snack's over! Gather round!' Grufty eyed them warily.

The sheep, still chewing, wandered over. *Give her her due* Granny thought, *she's got 'em under control. Like lambs, they are.*

'Right them, line up!' Perilla barked. The sheep, each of which wore a bell round its neck, had all been shorn (by Perilla, naturally) and looked extremely smart. They arranged themselves according to seniority, the old black-faced Marler at the front, followed by the six Durberry Downers, with the twin Stockinby tegs bringing up the rear.

'And quick MARCH!' Perilla ordered, at which the flock tripped smartly into the Guildenhall, jostling together at the back.

'Well!' Granny was proper impressed. They could certainly teach some of the kids a few manners. 'You've trained 'em well, Perilla!'

'Nonsense,' Perilla snorted. 'Intelligent animals, sheep. Specially those Lowland Marlers! Nothing to it!'

Which wasn't quite true. Because, for all her bluff, there wasn't an animal alive Perilla couldn't handle, or didn't care about.

The Guildenhall, Granny thought, looked beautiful: flowers everywhere, and packed with folks....Tarrill had been well-liked. Wasn't just that, though...he'd been the last of a breed, part of a world gone forever.

She kept the Ceremony light, and short as well, bearing in mind the average age of the congregation, and its tendency to seize up once it'd been sat awhile. Joster Posskenway, who was stone-deaf and what you might've called the Black Sheep of the family, got up and bellowed a funny story about his brother's shepherding: how he'd once near broke his arm, delving about inside a ewe, trying to turn twin lambs, and only got it back, all covered in blood and dung and mucuous, once the lambs was born, but it'd been black and blue for weeks....

He cackled at the memory, and then, with an evil smile at the women present, produced a grey, matted relic he swore was the first lamb's tail Tarrill'd ever docked...(even pointing out the scars where he'd pulled the ticks off of it)...and insisted on everyone having a good look, in his brother's memory.

The thing was stiff, musty and greasy. Those that hadn't already gone green listening to Joster's story gagged, passed it on and wiped their hands as best they could....all except Perilla, who sniffed it, studied it, and looked as if she might've been able to taste it as well....at which point Granny, feeling a song might be in order, signaled Highmaster Powell to get the organ going.

After the singing, Joster having got through three verses of 'The biggest ram in Bartlesham' before anyone could intervene, and only stopping because he'd forgotten the words, everyone went up to say their goodbyes.

And Tarrill, laid out near the organ on his Passing-Bed, grinned sociably back with big, borrowed dentures because he'd lost his own, years ago, out on the hills, and never replaced them.

They all filed past, and everyone said how well he looked. Course, it was being so brown did it, from working outdoors. You'd of thought, Pergola Blunt whispered, he'd been off sunning it somewhere exotic.

And last of all came the sheep, bunting at Tarrill's head and hands as if to wake him, blowing soft on his face as he'd once breathed life into them when they'd been but a sneeze away from dying.

They laid him to rest alongside Gloxinia, and Grufty watered the grave as a mark of respect. Then everyone settled themselves in the back room of the Guildenhall to enjoy a good gossip over Tassie Bough's buffet.

Joster refused tea, explaining that he'd brought his own liquid refreshment, and after a few nips from his silver flask, shambled round bawling: 'Who wants a feel of me lamb's tail then?'

When everyone had gone, Granny went into the ante-room and flopped down in the saggy chair she'd never got round to replacing, while Festa banged about sweeping up.

'D'you reckon it went all right, Festa?'

The girl came over and leaned on her broom. 'Oh, yes, Mum,' she said, 'everyone fair enjoyed 'emselves....all except Midmaster Tate.'

Granny sat up, as far as the chair would let her. 'Bevis Tate?' she never saw him. 'What was *he* doing here?'

'I dunno,' Festa said, 'they was hanging around the porch, him and that Ritro Bowers, taking notes. But his Block kept slipping and, well, he weren't thinking happy thoughts.'

Taking notes, eh Granny thought. She'd be having words, but not now. Time for a quick nap before Gorrie came to take her and Festa home....her eyelids were just drooping when she felt the girl behind her, *hovering,* and she couldn't be doing with hoverers. Her Auntie Rhinum used to do it, breathing heavy and coughing so's you couldn't relax.

'Yes Festa, what is it now?'

'Please Mum, there's a man.'

There would be. 'And what you done with him?'

'Made him wait in the Guildenhall, Mum and said I'd see if you was decent.'

Granny raised an eyebrow. 'And d'you reckon I am?' She really didn't ought to tease the girl.

But Festa said, with surprising dignity: 'Yes, Mum, you look a treat in them robes. Shall I show the gentleman in?'

'Er, no, give us a hand up and I'll come.' Granny felt quite ashamed of herself: there was a lot more to Festa than she let on.

But when she recognized her visitor, she wished she *had* been sitting down, because even after all them years she went dizzy and her heart lurched as Tobin Hackett gave his little-boy lost grin and said, as if he popped round every day: 'Now then, Bryony. Any tea going?'

Sitting opposite, teacup in hand, she had chance of a really good look at him, once Festa had done staring and gone back to sweeping.

Wasn't every day you met up, after half a lifetime, with the man who'd jilted you, and the worst of it was, he didn't look no different. Bit greyer and more weathered mebbe, but still nothing on him….she'd bet he could still put his grub away, and reckoned that he probably could. Say what you liked, Tobin had always been a grafter, up and doing, never still.

P'raps that was why he didn't look his age, which was more'n she could say for herself…he laughed and, mortified, Granny realise she'd left her mind wide open: his own was tight as a trap. 'You ain't changed neither, Bryony.'

'Me? Nonsense! Course I have!' It was bad enough that Grufty had gone straight over and laid his head on Tobin's knee…he needn't think he'd get round her as well! 'Don't be wasting your sweet talk on me, Tobin Hackett!'

'Sorry, Bryony. Forgot I was talking to a *Grandmistress* there for a minute.' He set his cup down and glanced hopefully at the teapot, but Granny was having none of it.

'Well, and what you brings you to me door, all these years on?'

'Two things. Heard about old Tarrill, and wanted to pay me respects. He taught me no end when I was a lad. I used to bunk off school and go up Brim Knap and him and a b....'

'You were *here*?' Granny interrupted, 'at the Passing-Ceremony?'

'Sat at the back, didn't I,' Tobin grinned, 'with the sheep. Good touch, having them, give the place some ambience. Mind, they've had a bit of a chew at your florals, and there's a few droppings under the pews that lass of yours hasn't found yet, but then you can't expect sheep to appreciate social niceties, can you?'

Just in time, she saw the mischief in his eyes: same old Tobin. Used to drive her up the wall with his teasing, her...and Mariander. No. She wouldn't think about it.

'Anyway,' he went on, 'me dad passed on.'

'Did he,' Granny said. 'Oh dear.'

'All right, I don't blame you for being bitter, Bryony. Didn't do you any favours, did he? But it's all water under the bridge now. Anyway, it seems I've inherited the house in Lemmingwold....funny that, remember how he used to say he'd leave everything to the Cats' Home rather than give me a penny?....so I've come to sort things out. Couldn't pass up the chance of seeing you, now I could I?'

'Why not? You managed well enough all these years!' Strange how bitterly it came out, when she'd thought herself long over it.

'Wasn't easy for me neither,' he said softly. 'After I...well, a clean break seemed best. I went down Scallyford Way after Mum's Passing...too much bad blood between me and Dad. And that's where I met Dolly, through working for her Dad. After a while, we got wed, and when the old man died, we took the farm on. Raise three fine boys, and they run things now.'

'Are they...?' The question hung in the air.

'Not Seers, no. Dolly was...an Outsider. The line dies out with me.' He sighed. 'And I lost Dolly last year. You'd've liked her, Bryony.'

Granny sniffed. '*I'm* sure.'

'You would, you know. She'd a good heart, and she tried to understand about the Seeing...but it wasn't like with you and me, Bryony, though I never let on. I wouldn't't've hurt Dolly for the world, but I....just couldn't get you off me mind.'

Granny listened in amazement: she'd never considered herself the sort men hankered after.

'And you,' he went on, 'never wed, did you? I kept up with the news, see. You should've found someone, Bryony....'

'Oh, don't flatter yourself, Tobin. I've had me moments, believe me, but what with one thing and another, I never did get chance to take up that Seminary place.'

Tobin sighed. 'Pity. You always did have the Mindpower, gel.'

'Oh, no question,' Granny said, 'couldn't make use of it though. And then when Tolly ran off....s'pose you know about that an' all?....well, it fair broke Mam's heart, and she took ill. Someone had to mind her, so I couldn't go swanning off to get educated, could I?'

Tobin shook his head. 'What a waste. You've made up for it since, though. Grandmistress, eh! Couldn't believe it when I heard!'

'I do all right,' she said, defiantly, 'enough to keep me mind in.'

'Reckon I've got a bit behind.' Tobin had the grace to look abashed. 'Comes of not wedding a Seer. Look, Bryony, I'm going to be around...things to sort....could I pay you a visit out at your place? I take it you are still there?'

'Oh, yes, I'm there all right.' *Me and me black cat. Proper old maid I am.* 'I reckon you can call round if you want...after all, we're both old enough to know our own minds this time, ain't we?'

'Let's make it soon, eh?' He stood up to take his leave, scratching Grufty's head in farewell. 'He's all right. Working dog, is he?'

'Yes, he's a qualified electrician,' Granny said, adding deliberately, 'and he ain't mine, he's Mariander's. She's moving out here soon, so you'll be able to call on both of us.'

A fleeting hurt crossed his face. 'Don't, Bryony. That's all in the past. If you won't have a lift, you coming out to see me off?'

'If I must.' She followed him out of the Guildenhall: Festa had to lean right round the organ and then stand on a pew with one foot on the windowsill to see properly, but she reckoned the Grandmistress looked, as she told her mam later, sort of *radiant*.

He's been a good lad, kept his head down, bided his time. Even let the cats and dogs be, though they'd have done for skinning-practice. Got them all shit-scared, though, knowing he's about.

Can't risk it though, not on new territory. Don't want to go arousing suspicion, does he, can't make a move until he's sure....but it's hard, knowing that it's out there somewhere, his prey. Got the smell of it in his head, hasn't he, and it's getting stronger with every full moon.

Hilary Bottomley blitzed her outside windowsills with spray disinfectant, briskly wiping clusters of twitching, moribund insects into oblivion with a wet cloth. Horrid, unsanitary things....especially butterflies, with their flappy, fluttery wings.

'You'll have to put a fence up, Aubrey.' She wrung the mangled bodies into a bucket. Her husband, dressed for dirty work in one of his collection of clean, pressed boiler-suits, sighed. If his wife insisted on a fence, then a fence she would have, and he'd be the one doing the job, under her supervision. He made one last valiant attempt to get out of it.

'Why,' he said carefully, 'do we need a fence?'

Hilary frowned at a cobweb glistening in the sunshine: it had no business cluttering her frontage. One swipe of the cloth took care of *that*.

'Honestly, Aubrey! Don't you ever *listen*?'

All the time, dear he thought glumly, spreading, as instructed, a clean, ironed sheet beneath the cartwheel he was preparing to rub down, lest any flakes of rust polluted the gravel.

'That old woman I told you about! What if she buys the bungalow? We can't have her *overlooking* us....' She shuddered, recalling that Stare...'Or throwing her empties into our garden. And we certainly don't want that filthy animal of hers getting anywhere near Truffle! Do we, Aubrey?'

'No, dear.' Automatic response. 'Perish the thought.'

'So you'd better leave that little job you're doing and fetch the wood, while you've got your working-clothes on.'

'Oh, but I...' so much for watching the Test Match later on. Aubrey, however, knew better than to argue. '....might be a while, though....' he corrected himself, glancing at his watch and scrambling into the car, 'because they have to re-callibrate the platen-settings on the grimble-jibber to accommodate planks of the appropriate H4 fencing-quality....and we only want the best, don't we, my love?'

He'd taken off in a shower of gravel before she could answer. Hilary opened her mouth, and then closed it. Aubrey was altogether too cheerful, too co-operative: he was definitely Up To Something.

Never having visited the local woodyard, though, she wasn't to know about the fridge with the beer in it, the colour T.V. in the office, or the gathering of regular escapees enjoying the cricket.

Through the dining-room window, lonely as a Princess in a high tower, gazed the sad little face of Truffle, the Bottomleys' Queen Courvalier bitch.

Truffle was not allowed in the bedrooms, or on the furniture (unless Aubrey could smuggle her onto his lap on the rare occasions when Hilary went out without lining a job up for him) because of Hairs and what Hilary termed Secretions, or even into the garden, because 'a bitch's water,' Hilary had read in a magazine, 'will ruin your grass and wither your shrubs.'

Truffle did not have Walks, she had Exercise, meaning her on one end of an extending-lead and Hilary on the other, Super

Doggy-Do Pooper-Scooper at the other. Her whole routine was ordered, hygienic, and boring. Dimly, she recalled her Dam and three litter-sisters...the chasing and the play-fights and the comfort of warm bodies....but that had been long ago, that life was over. Perhaps it would never be as good again.

Or so she'd thought, until she'd spotted that funny little mongrel in next door's garden, strutting about, cocking his leg up on everything. He hadn't been on a lead, and didn't look as if he ever had been.

And all of a sudden, ancient Pack-memories began to surface, and with them longings too powerful to ignore.

Scavenging in ditches. Rolling in fresh manure, or rotted-down bird. Ratting. Chasing cats up alleyways and rabbits across fields. Running free, ears blowing in the wind....

Of course, he was ill-bred, not an ounce of pedigree in him. He wasn't young, or handsome, and he was a funny shape: his legs were too short, and he waddled. But none of that mattered, somehow, because he looked *fun*. And Truffle wasn't going to rest until she got to know him better.

'You ain't *still* driving that thing!'

Tobin smiled fondly upon his van. 'Old Aggie?' he murmured. 'Wouldn't part with her, would I? And besides, it's been a challenge keeping her on the road.'

Granny studied the vehicle she used to think of as Tobin's 'bit on the side', he spent that much time with her. Funny how jealous she'd been, though all in all, she decided that Aggie, with not a patch of rust to be seen, had probably worn better than she had herself, and it was a fair comparison, because she reckoned they were about the same age.

The van was an odd, greeny-brown colour Granny doubted you could get nowadays, with wooden running-boards and two big brass lamps on the bonnet. She suppose that she and Aggie were approximately the same shape, too....sort of short and squat, but for all that, she still hoped she hadn't ever looked quite so much like a Bladderjack toad on wheels.

'Still time to change your mind, Bryony!' Tobin grinned as he climbed in. He patted the seat beside him. 'Best leather, nice and comfy....we could go by way of Fossetby Flood, remember?'

Oh, she remembered, all right. Remembered like a pain through her heart. Remembered like it was yesterday...and vowed she'd never get caught again.

'No, thanks,' she said, stiffly. 'Gorrie's taking us home.'

'Right you are.' He rolled the window down, forcing the heavy brass handle round like a crank.

'When can I come and visit, then? Tomorrow all right?'

Granny considered. Her head said it wasn't wise to encourage him....but when had she ever been wise where Tobin was concerned?

'Not tomorrow. I got....things to do. Best make it the weekend.'

'Lovely.' The engine still purred like a full-bellied tiger. 'Have the kettle on, eh? Be just like old times!'

Now that, she mused, was exactly what she was afraid of.

A full moon hung, like a pound of best butter, over the night-fields.

Up at the Manse, the Animal Sanctuary lay quiet, apart from the steady clopping of Yaw, the insomniac donkey, endlessly pacing the parquet in the Great Hall.

Out in the paddock, the ewes were settling. They'd been down in the Hollow all day, bingeing on clover: now was time to digest and ruminate.

Nine sets of mandibles worked rhythmically on those small, tasty specially-saved squishy bits, and thirty-six stomachs rumbled companionably beneath the hawthorn hedge.

Old Gimmer, the black-faced Marler, was banging on about the size of ticks these days, nivver saw 'em that bog when she was a teg. And then what about them clegs and horseflies down yon Hollow, eh? Twice the sting on 'em they used to have....

The rest of the flock sighed, shifted, and bleated in polite agreement. Gimmer was a nine-shear, many-lamber, and Senior

Sheep. You didn't mess with her, not if you knew what was good for you.

By the time she'd eventually run out of steam, there was nothing left to munch. Quaather, one of the Stockinby tegs, bored with counting stars (mainly because she wasn't sure what came after 'arn, tarn, tethera, fethera') ventured: 'I spy, with my little eye....?' But there were no takers, and one by one, the flock began to nod off.

Only Horna, Quaather's twin, lay awake, racked with guilt. All that *clover!* How *could* she have eaten so much, when it wasn't even winter? She could just *feel* her stomachs expanding. She'd never be slim in a summer's dipping!

Course, it was all right for Quaather, never gained an ounce, did she, even with a full fleece on....well, she'd just have to cut down tomorrow, that or work it off, jogging round the meadow. If she slept now, maybe she'd wake early, and do a few laps of the paddock....except that she wasn't sleepy. She tried imagining an endless queue of shepherds, old hobbly ones, climbing the five-bar gate and limping round Four acre field, but even *that* old favourite didn't work.

Sighing, she got up to stretch her legs, and then....she saw it. A great, grey wolf, lit by the moon, and circling the paddock. It was looking straight at her, with big yellow eyes, and licking its lips.

Granny couldn't sleep, either.

Nothing unusual about that: many a night she stayed huddled by the fire, letting her mind roam the Brim Valley and sometimes, if there weren't too many thoughts circulating as far as the Inchwoods, or even the Weald of Bart.

Only now, she couldn't settle for love nor Hem-flowers. It was Tobin, of course, coming back, stirring things up. She didn't know whether she flattered or sorry, didn't seem to know anything anymore. It was like being seventeen again, without having the looks....and Mariander wasn't going to be overjoyed when she found out, neither.

Course, Tobin hadn't *meant* to string her along, but she'd been young and silly and believed every word of his teasing, and then there'd been his Dad, another Seer-hater. Why hadn't Tobin stood up to him when he'd told all them lies about her. And telling Tobin the upset would kill his Mam....*why hadn't he been strong enough to stand by her and see things through?*

Waiting in the Guildenhall, looking lovelier than she ever would again, with the music and the chattering of relatives and the scent of the Helm-flowers, and knowing that he wasn't coming....how she'd hated him then...

.....but that had all been a long, long time ago: she'd been proud and hot-tempered. She thought mebbe she understood folks a bit better now.

Her and Tobin had been good together: true-matched minds, even better than with Jago, her first love, and most folks never found once that in a lifetime, let alone twice. And she'd opened her mind to him, the closest a pair of courting Seers could ever get, closer than anything physical.

She couldn't help smiling, even now: if her Dad had been alive, he'd've killed the pair of 'em if he'd known what they got up to without ever stripping off.....if only Tobin had let things be. If only....she dozed at last, beside the dying fire.

Horna, quick on the uptake, also had a good pair of lungs on her. Even as the wolf jumped the paddock-fence, she blared a warning to the others.

Old Gimmer, dreaming of a Dappleby tup she'd once known, snorted awake, bleating: 'Hey-up! What's to do?' to be confronted by the sight of the intruder cocking its leg against *her* private fence.

'BY THE CRINGE!' she bellowed, eyes blazing red, 'THAT DOES IT! Right, lasses, GO FOR THE GOOLIES!'

Perilla, who'd ventured outside for a smoke and a brandy, was just in time to witness the commotion as nine ewes saw off what looked remarkably like a marauding wolf.

She heard the sound of splintering wood as the fence went down, and then a lot of aggressive bleating, followed by a long-drawn howl which, for some reason started off *basso profundo* and finished, well, almost *castrato*....Perilla smiled to herself and lit a cheroot. Those ewes could take care of themselves, which was precisely why she'd left them out in the paddock Better than any guard-dogs, or even geese, come to that.

The wolf interested her, though. She'd only caught a glimpse, of course, but she could tell it wasn't one of those Helmwood jobs like Bryony Beamish' brother had…different breeding-line altogether, and most definitely not a hybrid. No, this one was in another league altogether….bigger, coarser, better-muscled. Nice stifles, good thick coat, plenty of feathering. It must've escaped, then, but she couldn't offhand think of anyone who *bred* the things…

Trouble was, if word got round those damned trigger-happy farmers there was a wolf on the loose, it wouldn't last the week. Well, she wouldn't say anything, not yet, anyhow. She'd try and find out where the animal had come from, maybe catch it if she could. Not that she thought it'd dare come back, if it ever intended fathering cubs.

Whistling, she set off to fetch hammer and nails. Better mend that fence and round up those ewes before they chased the unfortunate wolf halfway to Lasterby…

As night deepened, nine self-satisfied sheep settled down in their paddock, bells tinkering gently as they sniggered together.

And somewhere across the quiet fields, a wolf howled his pain and humiliation to the uncaring moon.

The blood-lust roared in his head and his whole body tingled as he heard the old familiar howling that brought out the hunter in him….

Mariander came over next morning, to look at Properties.

Granny and Grufty met her off the bus, and going along High Street (Mariander having insisted they pop into Brimbank Crafts and Tearoom to sample their cinnamon teacake.) Granny couldn't see the point of spending good money when they could've gone home, so Mariander sighed and said, all right, her treat, when they ran into Tassie Bough, who'd been to PENNYPINCHER.

'Tassie!' Mariander beamed, 'ain't seen you in years! We're just off for a cupper tea....come and join us, eh?'

'Don't mind if I do.'

Tassie plonked her tartan shopping-trolley down in the middle of the pavement, and Grufty christened it when she wasn't looking.

'I hear you're moving out this way.'

'News travels,' Mariander said drily. 'Matter of fact, that's what I've come for....look a few places over. Show you some details when we get sat down.'

The Tearoom had a CLOSED sign on the door, and Granny was all for going home, but Tassie, who knew the proprietress, banged on the door.

Eventually, a long freckled nose pushed its way under the net-curtain, and an aggrieved voice snapped: 'Yes?'

'IT'S ME ENID,' Tassie yelled, 'loaded up and gagging for a drink.'

'Oh, Tassie, right.' The nose withdrew. 'Just a sec.'

The woman who opened the door was all red and het-up. She wore a hairnet and an apron with DON'T SHOUT AT ME, I'M ONLY THE COOK! On it, and was waving a sink-plunger.

'Oh, sorry, Tassie,' she bleated, 'only me sink's bunged solid and anyway, we're not officially open for another twenty minutes....would you all like to come in and have a cuppa til we are?'

'Bunged-up sink?' Granny said with interest. 'I can sort that. Dab-hand with sinks, me.' Her Dad'd taught her.

'Would you *really*?' Enid looked as though she might cry. 'Oh, but I'm not sure about....' She'd just spotted Grufty waddling purposefully towards the kitchen.

Granny stopped dead. 'Your choice,' she said. 'Public-health-wise, I mean. Which one you reckons the health-hazard: me dog or your sink?'

'Festa said Tarrill's Passing-Ceremony went off all right,' Tassie remarked as they sat buttering on-the-house scones and teacakes. 'Matter of fact, I've just seen them two bought his cottage.'

'Oh yes?' Granny slipped Grufty a scone under the table. 'Brother and sister, int they? What they like?'

Tassie considered. 'Hard to tell, really. I only saw 'em from the back, cos they were just going in the Surgery, her holding him up. Poor bugger could hardly walk, all bow-legged he was, like he'd got an hernia.'

'Won't be doing no gardening, then,' Granny observed. 'Not that he did a deal before....you seen the *state* of that place? Break Tarrill's heart, it would.' She refilled their cups with on-the-house tea: funny how much better it tasted when it came free.

'How's your Festa these days?' Mariander asked. 'She must be a big girl now.'

'Oh, she'd that, all right,' Tassie said feelingly, 'though I dunno where she gets it from. Fair eats us out of house and home and never ails a thing. Mind you,' she leaned forward and lowered her voice, 'having said that, she's been badly affected by the Rape.'

Mariander went white. 'Rape?' she repeated. 'Rape? But that's terrible! Poor lass, has she had counseling?'

Tassie gave her a funny look. 'Well, I dunno as it'd help much,' she said, 'but we have had her to the doctor.'

Mariander snorted. 'And *he'd* be about as much use as a cardigan on a cod! Men don't understand these things.'

Tassie glanced desperately at Granny, who sat stone-faced, offering no help at all. 'Well, he *seemed* to,' she floundered, 'he said that rapeseed's a common allergy this time of year, and give her some pills to stop her sneezing...reckon you could have sorted her out with one of your remedies, Bryony, only we was that desperate....anyway, just one of them things when you live in the country, ain't it?'

'If you've quite finished, Mari,' Granny said, in a choked sort of voice, 'p'raps we'd best get on and see these Desirable residences of yours.'

Bevis Tate was prowling round Fossetby Mill, taking photographs.

After a while, using the key he'd copied from the Grandmistress' original, he let himself in and began taking notes, which he would type up and relate to the others that very evening.

The place hadn't been touched: it was just as Tukesley Meredith had left it. What an opportunity to poke around! Midmaster Tate had never, for some unfathomable reason, been invited over during the Grandmaster's incumbency, and he was looking forward to investigating the Library, which he understood to be exceptionally fine.

The Grandmaster had bequeathed the Mill to the Bartlesham Guild, and it had not yet been decided who should live there. Grandmistress Beamish was the obvious choice, but she, of course, wouldn't hear of uprooting. No imagination, that woman, no *vision*.....

Bevis Tate thought of the cramped, dark house he'd been unable to sell since his mother's Passing. What wouldn't he give for a house with the potential of this one. So much space for his model-making! And what a Guild-Museum it would make, with himself as Curator!

He was halfway down the basement stairs when the smell hit him. He continued the descent holding his nose. The smell got worse…what *did* it remind him of?....and it was dark, despite the landing-light, gloomy and stifling.

His nerve almost failed him then. But if he were ever to persuade the Guild of his claim to this place, he knew that he would have to explore every corner of it, however unsavoury. Besides which, he was a Tate, and a Tate never turned and ran….well, not unless there was nobody about, they didn't….he'd give it another five minutes before he panicked. He came to a door, and nervously pushed it open.

There was a light-switch on the other side, which he clicked. A dull red glow came into being, but he wouldn't have said it *lit* the room within. Moving gingerly aside, he touched the walls, and shuddered. They were hung, no *nailed* with sheets of plastic, probably cut-up refuse-sacks. Horrible. No wonder the light couldn't penetrate.

There also seemed to be….posters everywhere. He peered, recoiled, peered again. No, no, they couldn't be! Wishing he'd worn gloves, he detached the pictures and rolled them up. He'd look at them later, in a better light, just to confirm he really had seen what he thought he'd seen…

…..and then something, or someone, sighed in a dark corner. It was a regretful, long-drawn-out sigh, like a dying breath, and it frightened the life out of him. He stood absolutely still, listening, for what seemed like a very long time, but the sound was not repeated.

He could creep out quietly, couldn't he? Nobody need know…but then suppose that--whatever it was--came after him, fast and deadly in the darkness and--*got* him on the stairs? What if it was, even now, moving between him and the door, cutting off his exit?

He couldn't stay where he was. He must be decisive! And if he aspired to Higher Office, he must be A Man! A Man such as Tukesley Meredith had been!-he strode towards the unknown horror in the shadows.

Pathetic, really. He held up the deflating remains of what had once, apparently, been some sort of disgusting Blow-Up Sex-Toy--let no-one say that Bevis Tate lived in a vacuum, he knew about such things!--and a warthog, at that! Really, the lives some people led!--he wondered whether the thing was mendable. Perhaps he'd take it home and try superglue, just as an experiment. Anyway, it *was* a *female* warthog, so that was all right--nothing warped about Bevis Tate.

On his way out, he came upon a bed: its smell made him gag. And then he realised--of course. This basement had been Undermaster Coy's domain. And that smell, in concentration, was his.

He wondered whether the Grandmaster had known about this--this *pit*. He wouldn't put up with it, himself. The whole place would need fumigating before *he* moved in. As he had absolutely no doubt that he one day would.

Hilary Bottomley was not in the best of moods. She'd only just got her old toothbrush dunked in lemon-creme cleanser when the doorbell rang *again.*

What an exasperating morning! There'd been a person offering Parish magazines, which were not, as she'd always supposed, free of charge; a perfectly dreadful woman who wanted to talk about Sex in the Afterlife, and then that embarrassing boy who limped and dribbled, collecting for a Handicapped Bus or something equally ridiculous...

And Aubrey was off enjoying himself again...although he of course denied it--instead of being on hand to deal with them all. She would have to speak to him firmly...he must have enough wood for three fences by now and he hadn't even started on the first one!

Did he seriously imagine that tiling-grout cleaned *itself?* Perhaps he still believed the Ironing-Fairy came down and pressed all his shirts while he slept! As if she hadn't enough to do without all these callers!

She wrenched the front door open, and immediately did her best to slam it shut; sadly, she wasn't quick enough. The nightmare old woman jammed her big black boot in the gap, and smiled like a hungry pike.

'Proper Channels this time.' She actually *winked.* 'Got permission off that there Estate-Agent. Come for another look round, haven't we.'

Her horrible dog came and sat down beside her: it was chewing something Hilary didn't even want to think about--and then, providentially, her telephone started ringing. She fled, slamming the door behind her. To her horror, it was Mr. Roach, the Estate-Agent, calling to confirm the viewing. Hilary felt a tension-headache coming on.

'Oh no, please, don't make me!' She could hear herself babbling, 'there must be some mistake! How can I hand the keys over to a person like her? If she moves in, she'll devalue the whole area!'

'Really, Mrs. Bottomley, pull yourself together,' Mr. Roach said, frostily. 'It's hardly up to you to judge our clients...although just for the record, I think she's a very sweet old lady. And anyway, a sale's a sale, she's keen, and...' he paused dramatically, *'she's not involved in a chain*!!....so don't you go putting her off!'

Sweet old lady, indeed! Hilary was blazing, and Aubrey was going to be in trouble for not being there to blaze alongside her! She would do as much as she'd promised Miss Pilbeam before she went into the Retirement Home, but not one whit more. Miss Pilbeam, with her sparkling windows and immaculate skirting-boards had been A Lady, and a credit to the neighbourhood--and she would most certainly never have allowed an animal into her home. Standards had obviously fallen to a new low.

Picking up the keys, she ripped off her rubber-gloves and went to face her prospective neighbours. As an afterthought, she pocketed the disinfectant-spray, because she fancied she could smell them through two double-glazed doors.

But there was no sign of the old woman, or the dog. The permed elderly lady who stood on the doorstep smiled pleasantly and said: 'Morning, I'm Mariander Barnes, come to borrow the keys and have a look round next door, if it's quite convenient?'

Relief flooded Hilary's veins; she only just stopped herself clasping the newcomer to her bosom. Now *here* was someone who looked as if she rinsed her milk-bottles thoroughly! Someone who understood the intricacies of buffing up brass and the importance of removing limescale from around one's bath-taps! A kindred spirit! She beamed like a sun-lamp.

The client eyed her, rather strangely, Hilary thought, and said: 'Well then, could I have the keys, please? Only me sister gets a bit fidgety, what with her legs.'

'Your sist...?' As she said it, the dreadful old woman came stumping out of next door's back garden, the dog behind her, dragging something that seemed to be putting up a fight.

'Here! Catch! Show yourselves round!' Hilary threw the keys wildly up in the air, and ran indoors to have hysterics.

Granny shook her head sadly in the direction of BOTTOM LEA. 'Dint I tell you she was a bit funny? Just imagine living next door to *her*!'

Mariander bent to retrieve the keys, as Granny set off towards the bungalow. 'Come on then, Mari, let's get it over with. Grufty?'

But Grufty wasn't listening. Through Hilary's half-open door, he'd just spotted a vision of canine perfection...the bitch of his dreams.

'It's perfect!' Mariander said, studying the Estate-Agent's particulars. 'Just what I'm looking for. And did you see that avocado bathroom-suite! You what, Bryony?' She could've sworn her sister had muttered something about 'duck-shit'...still, not to worry. She felt too happy to argue. She grinned. 'Not too close to you, neither, Bryony.'

'Well, you're easy pleased,' Granny grunted, secretly glad the house-hunt was over. She didn't mind poking round places folks were living in, but it wasn't half boring when they were empty. Her feet hurt, and she wanted a cup of tea. She nodded towards BOTTOMLEA.

'You don't suppose...?'

Mariander shook her head. 'Not a chance. Ain't been upsetting her, have you, Bryony?'

'Who, *me*? Course not!' Granny said witheringly. 'After all, look what she's done to old Podger's pigsty--must've took some nerve, eh? And then to go and *live* in it--can't help but admire the woman, can you?'

Mariander sighed. 'All right, Bry, it's a monstrosity, and she's a bit houseproud...but if we're going to be next-door neighbours, I don't want any unpleasantness before I've even moved in!'

Granny grunted. 'She don't care for dogs, neither...and she's got one in there somewhere, can't you read it?'

They stood a moment, sending their minds across the intervening distance.

'Poor little bugger,' Granny concluded. 'Ain't happy, is it? Speaking of which, where's Grufty got to?'

He hadn't gone far, you could have heard him in Bartlesham, sitting on Hilary Bottomley's doorstep, howling his love and frustration through the letterbox. He made a surprisingly loud noise for the size of him, and he wasn't budging for anybody.

'Oh, Sight,' Mariander said, 'first impressions stick. Better give her the keys back...SHUT UP A MINUTE, GRUFTY...'

she rang the doorbell and shouted 'Hello? Hellooo?' After a while, she gave up and pushed the keys through the letterbox.

Upstairs, besieged in her bedroom, Hilary Bottomley lay with her fingers in her ears, waiting for that terrible animal noise to stop. When it finally did, quite abruptly, it was a long time before she ventured downstairs and, holding her breath, peeked out beneath the net curtains.

It was all right. She was safe. They'd gone.

They'd finally managed to lure Grufty away with the bar of chocolate Mariander had bought for later. Greed usually overcame his other, even baser, instincts.

He'd every intention of coming back, though, and in the meantime, he'd left a message, an offering, a symbol...the tastiest thing he'd ever got his teeth into. It made his mouth water, just thinking about it, and he knew She would just love it!

Unfortunately, Hilary Bottomley did not appreciate the liquid rat she found on her doorstep. She left it for Aubrey to clear up, and took to her bed for the rest of the day.

Mariander stayed the night, saying she'd go back in the morning and make an offer on the bungalow. Then she went on and on about carpets and curtains and tie-backs and borders until Granny thought her head would fall off with boredom.

Thomas didn't seem to mind, though. He lay quietly on Granny's lap all evening, instead of nattering to be out doing whatever it is cats do in the moonlight.

And that in itself was odd. He did seem a bit twitchy, and Granny wondered if he was sickening for something. Touching his mind, though, what she found there was Fear.

After a bit of a fight, Ricky got Stacey's cardigan unbuttoned. Great woolly thing it was, with big stiff buttons...and under it she was wearing a sweatshirt thing...in Summer! Good job he liked a challenge.

40

'Gerroff,' Stacey giggled, 'with your greasy hands.'

'Chucked it, look!' There was his burger, thrown onto the path with all the other rubbish, and only one bite out of it as well, he'd been so keen to get her round the back. He hoped she'd be worth it.

He pulled her into the shadow of the wall. Sod the moonlight! Nine times out of ten, it'd be pitch-black round here.

He could just hear the disco-noise from the Youth-Centre. Ten minutes, and if he hadn't got anywhere he'd go back and play pool--that couldn't be a *vest,* could it? Unbelievable. He pulled hard, but nothing budged.

'It's a body,' Stacey said helpfully through her bubblegum, 'all in one piece, like a babygro.'

Ricky groaned. It sounded great, really sexy. Why couldn't girls just wear *normal* clothes, with easy access?

Maybe he'd give her a love-bite to get her in the mood, like Steve'd given Kylie. He did his best, but Stacey being three inches taller didn't really help his aim.

'Ugh!' she pushed him away, 'you've slobbered all over me neck!'

P'raps he'd go and play darts til the pool-table was free. One last try then.

'This body-thing,' he hissed, 'how d'you undo it?'

'Oh, it's got poppers,' Stacey said. 'It's a nightmare going to the loo.'

He waited, but she'd gone back to blowing bubbles. Well, if she wasn't going to help, he'd have to suss it out for himself.

Stacey stood passively while he fumbled; chewing gum and blowing the odd bubble. Then all at once she came to life and said: 'Hey, look! There's a dog eating the rubbish.'

He became vaguely aware of snuffling noises behind him. 'So?'

'Aah. It's really cute, Ricky.' She clapped her hands encouragingly. 'Come on, then, poor old thing! Starving aren't you!'

Just when he thought he'd located those sodding poppers, she had to start jumping about...

'It's okay, it's found your burger. Eat it up then!'

41

'Oh, for...' Ricky turned in exasperation, intending to scare the thing off with a stone or two. Starving dog nothing! He was watching a sodding great wolf gagging and spitting his burger out like it was poison. He thought it was going to throw up.

The moon shone full on its face. It had big, yellow eyes, and just for a moment, the look in them reminded him of their Shane when he'd swallowed that wholemeal bread by mistake. P'raps he'd had a lucky escape--he hadn't known the burgers were *that* bad--!

Still shaking its head disgustedly, the wolf bounded over the fence into the playing-fields. Ricky stood gazing after it for a moment, until reality hit him.

Then he ran for the Youth-Centre, abandoning Stacey to the night. Somehow, he'd gone right off finding out how her poppers worked.

And in the shadows, something black oozed out of the darkness and strode off after the wolf.

'When you going to get a proper lav, Bryony?' Mariander, still adjusting her undercarriage, grumbled back from the privy. 'I'm getting too old to have spiders nipping me...'

She stopped dead as Tobin Hackett emerged from the back door with a cup of tea in his hand.

Grufty sat adoringly at Tobin's feet, but he'd have been on his lap if he hadn't been too fat to jump. Up on the mantelpiece, Sham did a very passable imitation of Mariander shrieking when she realised it actually *was* Tobin.

Granny sighed. Why couldn't he have come at the weekend, as agreed? There was an atmosphere even fresh tea and gingerbread couldn't defray.

'You've been *seeing* him, after what he did!' Mariander said accusingly.

'No, she ain't, I just told you.' Tobin scratched Grufty's ear, which infuriated Mariander even more.

'And leave me dog alone!' She would be having words with Grufty about Family Loyalty when she got him on his own. 'Coming back here, upsetting everybody!'

'You can't half keep a grudge going, Mari,' Tobin said admiringly. 'Must be fifty years you've kept it up! Look, what's done is done. We all got our path to tread, our own furrow to plough--!

'Don't you dare go philosophical on me, Tobin Hackett!' Granny didn't think she'd ever seen Mariander so furious. 'You jilted Bryony, and that's that. Once a heart-breaker, always a heart-breaker, so there!' Yah-Boo hung, unspoken, in the air.

'See who I like!' Tobin said defiantly.

'Not my sister, you won't!'

'Try and stop me, sparrow-legs!'

'Pigeon-chest!'

'Poodle-hair!'

They'd ended up nose to nose like battling bulldogs, and all at once, Granny lost her rag.

'FOR SIGHT'S SAKE!' She thundered, 'KEEP OUT OF MY LIFE! I'M A GROWN WOMAN AND I'LL SORT MESELF OUT!

Tobin and Mariander stopped in mid-shout, Grufty jumped up, barking, Thomas hissed from under the sideboard and Sham fell off the mantelpiece before remembering he was a bird and fluttering embarrassedly back up.

Mariander had gone very red in the face. 'Poodle-hair!' she muttered furiously. 'Poodle-hair! Dearest perm I've ever had!'

'You never liked me, did you?' Tobin sniffed.

'Too right, I didn't!' Mariander snapped, ' and still don't, come to that!'

Granny wondered whether to go and sit in the privy and let them fight it out, but then she noticed the time.

'Better get a move on if you're going to see about that bungalow,' she reminded Mariander.

'Ooh, I see!' Tobin said eagerly, 'House-hunting, are we. Mate of mine did that last weekend--'

Granny groaned. 'Yes?' she snapped. 'And?'

'Shot three bungalows and a semi!' Tobin cackled. He turned to Mariander. 'Well, best be off. After all, don't want you missing your bus, do we!'

Mariander folded her arms. 'I see,' she snapped, 'trying to get shot of me so's you can get your feet back under the table! Well, it won't work. If you're staying, then I'm so am I.'

'Suits me.' Tobin sat back and sipped his tea.

On the other hand, Granny thought, the privy could be a very restful place this time of year, specially if you took a bottle of home-made chickweed wine in there and made a morning of it...

'You'll *both* have to go,' she said firmly. 'It's me morning for scrubbing me corsets.'

Quite a lot of glaring went on, specially when Mariander realised she'd missed the bus into Bartlesham and the lift with Tobin that Granny suggested was the only way she'd get there in time to see the Estate-Agent *and* catch her train back to Inchester- -she also laughed incredulously when she saw Aggie, Tobin's old van, and made a number of wounding comments; whereupon he did a fair bit of muttering about ungrateful skinflint hitch-hikers, but in the end they'd no choice about driving off together, because neither of them would make the first move...and both of them swore they'd be back.

Granny sank thankfully into her chair. Sisters, eh! And Men! She was definitely too old for all this Romance and Rivalry stuff.

That full moon brought a flurry of wolf-sightings.

The creature..(reportedly the size of a lion)...ran amok at Shamford, demolishing the Tennis Club's Annual Riverside Bar-B-Q & Disco. And it had, apparently, enjoyed the feast...dips, jacket potatoes, onions, peppers, mixed salad, even dressings and condiments...everything, in fact, except the meat.

Mallory Gembert came upon it, bold as you like, outside the Jessie Lambert Centre, right in the middle of Bartlesham. He said it was gazing into the ornamental lake, for all the world like someone looking in a mirror--and then it sat back and give out the saddest, soulfulest howl he ever did hear. And then Baz Braine, just leaving the 'Rat & Pitchfork' saw the Grange Farm geese...a bloodthirsty gaggle if ever there was one...harrying the wolf the length of Burrows Lane.

Indignant letters arrived at County Hall, and the 'Bartlesham Bugle', demanding that Something Be Done, and one man called Radio Tanglewood to announce sadly that he'd stopped believing in the Bartleshire Dog-Warden, because, unlike Boggarts and Dobbies, nobody had ever actually *seen* him.

An anonymous female caller then suggested darkly that there *had* been a Warden once and he'd disappeared but she'd bet he was still on the County Hall Computer just like the £15 she owed in Back-Rates what they wouldn't let her forget about so's they could draw his salary and then his pension and spend it all on outrageous drunken junketing--finally, the Dog-Warden himself rang in to say that contrary to what uninformed folks thought, he couldn't be everywhere, could he, and anyway he didn't work after 5p.m.

But Granny knew nothing about all that; she never read newspapers, or listened to the radio; after all, she'd got her own mind-receiver, right there in her head. And it was picking up distress-signals.

It wasn't til lunch-time that Granny noticed Grufty was missing.

She'd been busy all morning Concocting; boiling and thickening til her eyes crossed and her glasses steamed up. By the time she'd done, every available surface was cluttered with containers of stuff bubbling, cooling, hardening, gelling.

She'd always been interested in Herbal Remedies...got it from their Mum, her and Mariander, and both done all right out of it. Amazing what you could do with a few weeds and a little know-how, and even more amazing what folk's'd put in their bellies or on their skins if they thought it was doing 'em some good.

She rubbed her eyes. She'd treat 'em to some of that stickwort gel when it'd cooled off. But first, she wanted a cupper tea and a piece of cake...and that was when she missed Grufty, who wasn't where he should've been, sitting beside her with his tongue hanging out. Come to think of it, he'd been acting strange ever since they'd looked round that bungalow. Not ill or anything, more...mopey.

Yesterday, a cat that wasn't Thomas had walked across the path, right under his nose, and he hadn't moved a muscle. And he hadn't touched his dinner, nor even chased Sham, who preferred meat to birdseed every time, away from it.

He'd never gone off before, and she only hoped he wasn't getting into mischief. She should've noticed he'd gone, shouldn't't've left that door open!--but it was hot, inside and out. She thought back over all the dogs the Beamishes'd had; roamers, the lot of 'em, and not one of 'em had ever felt the pull of a lead. But they'd none of 'em had got into trouble, either, because they were country-bred.

Grufty's life, what they'd been able to find out about it before Mariander got him, had been rough. Scrounging and scavenging round the streets, dodging traffic and bad folks. He could look after hisself in the city, all right, but he didn't know country ways--what if he'd tangled with barn-rats, twice the size of any other sort? Or gone down the water-meadows after swans? Could he even *swim,* come to that? And, sight, *did he know about the Grange Farm geese?*

She was just on the point of getting her coat on when he came mooching up the path, drooped into the kitchen, drank almost a full bowl of water, and flopped down on the hearthrug, sighing like the last breeze of Summer.

She offered him some cake: he ignored it. A butterfly drifted past, unchased.

Grufty turned his face to the wall. Well, if he wasn't going to share his worries--she touched his mind. So that was it! She should've realised. Falling in love, at his age! But then she thought of her and Tobin, and relented.

'Come on, then, Grufty. What's she like? Is she pretty?'

His mind carried a fleeting image of silken, feathery softness, a melting dark-brown gaze and a sweet, heady musk. But then came a picture of Grufty himself, barking defiance as he retreated from a fusillade of stones and soil--and she understood.

'Oh, Sight.' She stroked his head. 'You ain't gone and fallen for that Bottomley woman's dog!' Trust Grufty. Mooning over some silly lap-dog with a long pedigree and a hostile owner.

'Well, I only hope she's worth it,' Granny told him. Grufty sighed again. *Oh, you bet your bones she is.*

Hilary Bottomley was fuming. Again.

'Honestly, Aubrey! That horrible little dog was outside all morning! Howling!'

'Really? I didn't hear a thing, dear.' It was quite true. Aubrey had been locked in the garage, listening to the Test-Match commentary on his earphones. He'd only emerged because they'd stopped for Lunch.

'What *have* you been doing in there?'

Aubrey thought quickly. Hilary, he knew, was quite capable of searching the premises for traces of tobacco, alcohol, or girlie magazines. And she had the unerring nose of a Customs & Excise sniffer-dog.

'I was Measuring,' he said grandly,' Calibrating.'

She didn't believe him, but any mention of what she called Men's Things unnerved her. She glared, and went on. 'It was leering, as well.'

'Oh, come on, dear,' Aubrey protested, 'dogs can't...'

Hilary sniffed. '*That* one can. I simply daren't let Truffle out while she's...interesting.' She shuddered. 'Suppose it...got near her? She coughed, delicately. 'Just remember what that stud-fee's costing...and what the puppies will fetch.'

Aubrey remembered, all right. Too much to risk any accidents.

'Of course, he belongs to that awful old woman. *You* know, the witch in the cottage. I do wish you'd go and speak to her.'

It was then that Aubrey, who'd never had the pleasure of meeting Granny, said a remarkably foolish thing.

'Oh, I'm sure she can't be that bad! I'll pop along and see her. On my way down to the woodyard.'

'This alleged wolf,' the Assistant Chief Constable barked, 'absolute load of old bollocks!'

Sergeant Gilmore, the A.C.C.'s Acting-Chauffeur, hid a smile. But Councillor Finch wasn't having that. 'We've got eye-witnesses,' he said firmly.

The A.C.C. snorted. He knew all about so-called witnesses. Forever

seeing whatever they expected to see. And, over the years, they'd seen the lot. U.F.O's, Big Cats, Alligators in the River Bart, Fairies on the allotments; even Unicorns! Swear on their kids' lives...until it came to hard evidence. Then it was a different story, oh yes indeed.

'Remember the Aliens-in-Pennypincher scare?' he said drily. 'Lay you a tenner it's another bloody stray dog.' He smoothed the banknote flat on the tabletop.

'Put that away!' Councillor Finch hissed. 'The Press are here! One whiff of bribery and corruption--'

Sighing, the A.C.C. pocketed the money, wishing he was somewhere else. Like having his teeth pulled. Or his ears syringed. Silly buggers on the County Council had called this Emergency Meeting to discuss the wolf-sightings. They'd requested a police-presence, and he, as usual, was it. Waste of a bloody good gardening afternoon.

Assistant Chief-Constable Herbert 'Daisy' Root was an old-style copper, from his large, polished shoes to his large, polished head. He never travelled when he could *Proceed In A North-Westerley Direction.* He spoke, not as others did, of cars, yobs and pubs, but of Motor-Vehicles, Firearms, Villains and Public-Houses; and always thought of his wife as ALPHA-DELTA-ALPHA.

Old-fashioned he might be, but nothing sexist about *him*! He regarded W.P.C's as a bloody good idea, so long as they stuck to comforting women, runaway kids, and lost dogs. Good for morale having girls on the Force...pretty ones, of course; they smelled nice, curbed the men's swearing, brightened things up with pot-plants and so on.

If only they'd stop bleating on about Girlie Calendars and accept so-called Sexual Harrassment in the spirit in which it was intended--put 'em to work alongside red-blooded men, what did they expect?...

Across the room, he spotted the Bartleshire Dog-Warden...old ECHO-ROMEO-INDIA-CHARLIE. Feller looked uncomfortable, as well he might. He'd be in for some stick if he didn't catch this big dog and make the streets safe for decent citizens.

It was unbearably stuffy; he did believe they'd got the heating on--in summer! No wonder the bloody rates were so bloody high! Unfortunately the coffee, which might've kept him awake, was undrinkable--which was one way, he supposed, of keeping costs down.

He found himself nodding off. Good job that pretty little wench was taking the Minutes. At least he'd have something to show the Chief Constable, because he hadn't taken in a word anyone had said.

As expected, the so-called witnesses were a sorry lot...three silly girls, who sniggered, and an old maid who smiled vacantly when asked to detail what she'd seen; and a disreputable-looking chap who freely admitted sighting the animal after an evening spent imbibing alcohol in the 'Tick and Teazel'.

Then there was a shifty-looking youth who looked in need of a haircut and some good military discipline.

They all seemed convinced they'd seen this alleged lupine, but the A.C.C. didn't believe a word of it. Full Moon, eh? People often went funny round about then...imagination running riot, and all that sort of thing. As for that youth-...touch of the narcotics, if he wasn't mistaken; Brimwold mushrooms, probably--next thing he knew, someone was shaking him. 'Sir!' Sergeant Gilmore hissed, 'Wake up!'

'Wha--?' Everyone in the blasted room seemed to be glaring at him.

'*Thank* you, Sir,' the Chairman said sarcastically, 'and now perhaps we can get on.'

'What's he blathering about?' The A.C.C. snapped.

Sergeant Gilmore grinned. Good old Daisy. 'You was rather drowning out the proceedings, Sir. *Snoring*,' he added maliciously.

'Oh! Ah! Quite.' the A.C.C. blew his nose, 'What's been going on?'

'To summarise,' intoned the Chairman, glaring at the A.C.C.'In view of public concern, it has been decided to appoint another, temporary Dog-Warden, until this--erm wild animal has been caught.'

'Is that it then?' The 'Bartlesham Bugle' reporter wanted to know.

'By no means!' The Chairman looked immensely pleased with himself. 'We shall also...at considerable expense...be erecting Notices.'

'Saying what, exactly?'

'Er...that dogs must be kept on leads. At all times. On pain of a heavy fine. And it has been agreed,' he shouted above a rising tide of derision, 'that the Police should offer 24-hour patrols.'

The A.C.C. paled. *When* had it been agreed? Who'd agreed it? He must've been asleep, the cunning bastards! How would he explain this development to the Chief Constable? Dammit, they *all* believed this wolf-tomfoolery! He was hopelessly outnumbered. What could he say but: 'Certainly! Absolutely! Let you have details afterwards! *Sergeant!*' he hissed. 'Have we got a couple of spare Plods we can shove onto this wolf-patrol thingy?'

Sergeant Gilmore, visualising a pair of reluctant Harry Hedgehogs being beaten up by a class of five-year-olds, smiled happily.

'Oh, yes, sir,' he said. 'Got just the men for the job.'

In the doorway, the recently-appointed caretaker hovers, listens, smiles to himself. Turns the thermostat up a bit so's the buggers'll go home early, and then off to the basement, trying to hold his excitement down.

Safe amongst the central-heating pipes, Gwylym Jenkins pulls the scrap-book from its hiding-place, sinking into the deckchair he nicked years ago from Penaninc Beach.

Studying the newspaper-cuttings, he smiles again, not pleasantly. But then, he's waited a long, long time.

Six, eh, Six witnesses, all prepared to stand up in public and swear blind they'd seen it...-and three good sightings, quite apart from all the others he'd heard about...and every one of 'em at Full Moon. What did that tell you, eh?

Course, old Joe Public, wouldn't connect it, would he? He had, though, straight off, because he'd been there, seen it happen, spent half his bloody life moving around the country chasing bastard misfits just like it...good few weeks now, he's been out after it...

Better lay the clothes out, then, them he's been keeping so long: check the old weapon over, get his fitness levels up.

Hasn't lost the touch, has he, still the best there is, and soon as the Moon's full, he'll be out there proving it. Because all them sightings can't be wrong, can they? No, this confirms what he's suspected. Looks like he's found himself another werewolf.

So *this* was the old woman's place, Aubrey mused. Quite picturesque, really. Better not tell Hilary...she'd only go getting Ideas.

He saw a scruffy little mongrel mooching round the garden and cocking its leg up on the water-butt. He laughed to himself. If that was the potential Stud Hilary had been going on about, he didn't see the problem.

He'd just tell the old woman to keep it fastened up. She'd probably press a cup of tea and some freshly-baked seed-cake on him...they did that in the country...he'd admire her collection of Toby-jug and her display of corn-dollies, they'd shake hands like good neighbours, and he'd be on his way.

She came to the door brandishing a meat-cleaver. She was wearing a blood-soaked apron, and her hands, face and hair were streaked with red. From inside the cottage came a terrible, long-drawn-out shriek.

Aubrey took a step backwards. Perhaps she was in the middle of butchering something before winter, to keep her going through the bad weather...they did *that* in the country, as well. Best keep on the right side of her. Never annoy a woman with a chopper...

'Good aft...' he began.

51

She looked him up and down. '*And* about time!' she snapped. 'Come on, then, this way!'

Before he could argue, she was stumping off down the garden, slashing at nettles as she went, and muttering to herself.

The mutt he'd seen came up behind him and started sniffing his trouser-legs. It seemed fascinated by the smell of them, and glued itself to his heels as he followed the old woman.

She was standing outside a brick-built privy. 'Well, get a move on!' She flung the door open. 'I ain't got all day!'

He peered nervously inside, unsure what he was supposed to be looking for.

'No, not there!' She pointed with her cleaver. '*There!* The seat!' It was quite badly cracked, he could see that now, but this had gone far enough.

'I've come about the dog!' he protested.

'Bog, privy, call it what you like, just fix it, eh? I've had me legs crossed all day, waiting on you!'

He tried again, but her eyes burned into him, sapping his will, and a kind of fog crept over Aubrey's brain. He felt...almost peaceful. After all, what choice did he have? And what did it matter anyway? If he didn't do her bidding, the old woman would hack him to bits and salt him down for the winter, and if he didn't tackle her about the dog, Hilary would get him when he went home. For once in his life, he felt he'd rather face Hilary.

He'd do as he was told, and mend the lavatory-seat, forget about the dog, lie to Hilary. Maybe he'd get away with it this time. Terror plucked at his sleeve. *Oh, God, no he wouldn't. Hilary always knew when he was lying.*

'I'll get my tools from the van,' he muttered.

She'd thought of that one too. He couldn't escape, because she sent the dog to keep an eye on him...and *he* knew that *it* knew and, in some strange way, *she* knew, exactly what was in his mind--the dog seemed obsessed with his trousers. As he worked, it went over them minutely, savouring them as though they'd been sprayed with exotic perfume, finally baptising them with its own pungent fluid. Several times.

And he couldn't do anything about *that*, either, except grit his teeth as it soaked in, because the old woman was standing over him, watching, and running her finger upand down the cleaver-blade --nor did she offer him a cup of tea when he'd finished...not that he could've drunk one. He just wanted to get away. He could still hear those dreadful shrieks...maybe she'd got the last handyman in there? The milkman? The postman? The *policeman*?

She waved the cleaver cheerily as he scrambled into the van. 'How much I owe you?' she called.

Throwing her a terrified glance, he rammed the van into gear. 'Nothing!' he shouted wildly. 'It's free! Have it on the house!' Skidding in the rutted lane, he took off towards the sanity of the wood-yard.

'Ta very much,' Granny grunted, and, smiling to herself, went back in to finish chopping her beetroot. Sham, who didn't like being left on his own, immediately stopped shrieking, and Grufty, savouring the musk he'd found on Aubrey's trousers, plunged into soppy dreams about Truffle.

People shook their heads in disbelief that Bartleshire Council could actually get its finger out when it wanted to. By the weekend, every town, village and hamlet bristled with threatening official notices:

DOGS MUST. DOGS MUST NOT. OFFENDERS WILL BE. DOG-OWNERS WILL NOT BE. KEEP OUT. KEEP OFF. NO THIS. NO THAT. OR ELSE....and each notice carried the logo of a small, black dog bisected with a thick red diagonal line.

Most of the locals had a healthy disregard for official signs, especially forbidding ones. None of their dogs could read, anyway, and as there was no mention of WOLVES MUST NOT, they refused to bow to what they regarded as Dogist Victimisation by Officialdom.

Which was all well and good until the Dog-warden's Reign of Terror began.

Over in Lemmingwold, two sheepdogs were detained going about their lawful business, and then Podge, Mrs. Rowe-Henry's elderly labradale was apprehended as he ambled arthritically down to the baker's for his morning bun.Mrs. Rowe-Henry was furious, because she had to pay a fine, but not half as upset as Podge, who'd been intercepted en route, and therefore missed his elevenses.)

One of Perilla Pearce's flugel-hounds, out tracking in its own time was nabbed crossing the Brockway, and at Fossetby, a venerable gun-dog, peacefully defecating beneath the same hawthorn hedge it had patronised for years was caught in the act and arrested.

If a detainee wore a collar bearing its address, the Warden would shove an earnest note through the owner's letterbox, pointing out the drawbacks of roaming dogs, pleading for greater responsibility in future, and, in very small print at the bottom, detailing the hefty fine required to re-unite pet and owner.

Nowhere was safe. Street or lane, car park or river-bank, night or day, any loose dog was fair game. As the locals could have predicted, there'd been no more wolf-sightings since the last full moon; so the dog-in-the-street was getting the flak instead.

Granny got all this from Tassie Bough, who'd called in for a cuppa on her way back from shopping.

'Honest, Bryony, folks are looking over their shoulders,' she grumbled, helping herself to another rock-bun, 'where's it going to end, I'd like to know?'

'What's this here Warden like?' Granny asked. 'You set eyes on him yet?'

'*I* ain't,' Tassie said, 'but Gorrie has, and he says her name's Samantha.'

'Samantha.' Granny sniffed. 'One of them educated types, is she?'

'Woman with a Mission, by all accounts,' Tassie said. 'And you want to watch Grufty, because, mark my words, she'll be hitting Brimwold next...where is he, by the way?'

'He's here somewhere,' Granny said vaguely, still mentally adjusting to the notion of a female Dog-warden.

'But he ain't hanging round the cake-tin,' Tassie objected.

'When was this female out your way?' Granny asked urgently.

'Well, yesterday,' Tassie said, 'and Deepinwold the day before...oh, Sight...'

They looked at one another. Granny sighed. 'I know where Grufty's gone,' she said. 'Get your coat on, Tassie, and we'll fetch him back...if we ain't too late.'

Bevis Tate studied the photographs. Considering the poor light, and the secrecy required, they'd come out rather well.

Highmistress Beamish cradling Tukesley Meredith's head on her...ah, bosom, and weeping. Most unseemly. Grandmistress Beamish, red and flushed, waving a wine-glass about at the Grandmaster's Wake. And lastly...there were several of these...Grandmistress Beamish on her own porch, menacing a boiler-suited workman with some sort of meat-cleaver--savagely, he thrust the prints back into their envelope.

Excellent photographic evidence of the Grandmistress' moral and mental instability, they might be...but not enough to discredit her, let alone depose her.

He needed more, much more. But he'd get it--you could always find what you wanted....if you looked hard enough.

The Bottomleys cowered in the hall while Granny hammered on their door.

'Don't answer,' Aubrey hissed. 'She'll soon get fed-up and go.'

But Granny wasn't going anywhere. Flipping the letterbox open, she roared, as though reading his mind: 'I know you're in there! And I can wait all day!'

Aubrey gasped and tried to flatten himself against the radiator.

'SET THE WARDEN ON ME DOG, HAVEN'T YOU!' Granny bellowed. *She'd got that much out of their muddled thoughts.* 'WHERE'S SHE TAKEN HIM, EH?' *Why wouldn't their stupid minds tell her?*

Hilary cracked first: it was the idea of the terrible old woman camping on her doorstep in full view of all the neighbours that did it.

'THE WARDEN'S TAKEN YOUR NASTY LITTLE DOG TO THE POUND AT BARTLOCK!' she screamed. 'And because you can't control it, 'she added, daringly, 'you'll have to pay a fine to get it back, so there!'

'AND WHO,' Granny bawled, already knowing the answer, 'SHOPPED HIM?'

'I DID!' Hilary shrieked. '*No*, Aubrey, I won't pretend! That animal's been here all morning, howling so loudly I couldn't concentrate on my stairwell!'

'Is that SO,' Granny said quietly. 'Well, don't let me stop you. Be seeing you. Soon.'

'Oh, God.' Aubrey was rolling on the carpet, arms clasped protectively round his head. 'You've done it now.'

'Nonsense! You have to stand up these people!' So why did Hilary find herself shaking? 'Get up this minute!' She snapped. 'You're flattening the pile!'

'Thought I was plumber,' Aubrey snivelled.

'I haven't the faintest idea what you mean,' Hilary retorted. 'Have you been drinking?'

'But...didn't know who I was!' Aubrey hiccupped. 'Now...she's seen van...knows where I live...come back and get me!'

'What'll we...do now?' Tassie puffed. There was no keeping up with Bryony when she was good and mad. 'Gorrie's..gone fishing. Ain't no...use ringing up.' She still liked saying that, because they'd only just had the phone put in.

Granny stopped dead, glaring up and down the High Street. 'We're going to Bartlock,' she said quietly, 'one way or another.'

'Mebbe we could *commandeer* a car, like in war-time,' Tassie suggested. 'Even a tractor or a milk-float...'

'Good idea.' Granny stepped into the road, and held her hand up just as Tobin Hackett's van came round the corner of Deeping Lane.

'Fancy you *still* driving this old thing!'

Tassie hadn't been at all keen on accepting a lift from The Rat Who'd Jilted Bryony All Them Years Ago, but he'd talked her round, and now she was in the back of Tobin's van, squashed amongst a great pile of Sight-knew-what.

She looked round in amazement; in one small area alone, there was a trombone, a diver's helmet, a baby's highchair, and a cuckoo-clock--'What *is* all this junk?'

She pulled out a mildewed fur hat, and flung it away in disgust. 'Pooh! It don't look like you've had a clear-out in the last fifty years, neither!'

Granny snorted. 'Same ole system. Still bartering, eh? Goods for Services?'

Tobin wagged a finger. 'Never throw out what you might need,' he admonished. 'Everything's got a use, if you wait long enough.'

'Well, it ain't passenger-friendly,' Tassie complained, moving a portable hair-drier, a beach-umbrella and a stuffed pike, 'climbing over this lot. You wanter get one of them hunchback cars like our Dilly's.'

'Never mind all that,' Granny put in impatiently. 'Just put your foot down, and let's get to them kennels before Grufty does!'

'SLOW DOWN!' she snapped, as they came into Brimby.

'I dunno,' Tobin grumbled, 'not five minutes back you was telling me to speed up....'

'No, it's Grufty!' Granny exclaimed. 'He's close...can't you read him?'

Now that she mentioned it, they could. He *was* nearby, and he wasn't happy. As they rounded the next bend, Granny yelled: 'STOP!' and Tobin slammed the brakes on. Tassie fetched up against a cardboard box marked: EDIBLE CONDOMS/GOOSEBERRY FOOL FLAVOUR. Nice to know Tobin was into that Condom-Bleu cookery....

The Warden's yellow van was parked on Main Street, and they didn't need the Sight to hear Grufty howling his head off.

'Right, then,' Tobin said, 'Let's go get him out of the slammer.'

There was no sign of the Warden, but her van was securely locked, not that that presented much of a problem once Granny put her mind to it.

Grufty, mortified, came squirming out on his belly, unable to meet Granny's eye. During all his years on the city streets, loner or pack-leader, he'd never once been caught, by *anyone*. He slunk, tail-down, into the back of Aggie, and sulked on Tassie's lap.

'Here, have a look at this!' Tobin called. He sounded amused.

In the middle of the pavement, beneath one of the Council's DOGS MUST NOT signs, was a pile of dog-mess, ringed in red chalk. And inside the circle, someone had written BAD DOG!

'I see the Warden's been busy,' Tobin said. 'And that ain't the only one, look!'

He was right, too. Every single desecration in the immediate area had a chalk ring round it, and a stern comment beside it.

'Well, that's told 'em!' Granny said, 'Just so long as they can read, eh? What say we push off home now, save Grufty's face a bit?'

'Fine by me.' Tobin eyed the rear door of the Dog-van until he heard the lock engage, and then jam. 'Hang on,' he added, concentrating until all four tyres had deflated. He winked at Granny. 'You're slipping, Bryony. Always attend to your details.'

Granny grunted. 'Reckon I owe you a cuppa at that.'

'Cuppa, nothing!' Tobin rubbed his hands together. 'We're celebrating a victory here! Let's have some of your marrow-wine!'

Rog. and Steve were on Wolf-Patrol; Sergeant Gilmore's words engraved on their memories.

'Don't let me down on this, lads. I'm counting on you. In fact, the whole of Bartleshire's counting on you. As I said to Old Daisy--that's Assistant Chief-Constable Root to you...Sir, if there is a Wild animal out there, roaming the countryside, terrorizing the peasants...then my lads will apprehend it. Sir.'

They should've been ecstatic. They'd served their sentence, paid their debt to Society, done their stint in the Harry Hedgehog suits. They'd got their patrol-car back, and been issued with helmets, shields, infra-red binoculars and, best of all, a tranquilliser-gun, like vets or safari-park game-wardens.

All good stuff, until it came to the pitch-dark creepy reality of midnight down the Brimbank Nature-Trail, when it was all too easy to believe anything. They'd be laughing if they could avoid confronting an actual wolf. And if only they didn't have these nagging doubts....

'Rog?' Steve squinted through the night-glasses: there was no moon. A hare sprang into focus, ears twitching as it listened to the darkness.

'SHOOM! SHOOM!' Rog. was playing at immobilising the sleeping ducks with his stun-gun. 'What?'

'Why do we get all the crap jobs?'

'We don't. PEE-OWW!'

'We *do*. Remember Unicorn-surveillance?'

'Yeah--JUM!JUM!--but we were in the vicinity.'

'And Brim Knap? The wrinklies' drugs-bust?'

'That wasn't official,' Rog. snapped, lowering the gun. 'We were Using Our Initiative. Like in the Harry Hedgehog Road-Safety Campaign?'

'Don't get bitter! Have a toffee. What you've got to remember,' Rog. Said soothingly, 'is we get picked because we're lateral thinkers.'

'Oh yeah?'

'Yeah! This sort of offbeat assignment...the Wolf-Squad...it's our thing, our speciality. And like the man said, if it's out there, we'll bag it! BUDUM! BUDUM! BUDUM!'

Gwylym Jenkins, done with his boiler-suit and his day-job, dangerous in black. Scary in biker-boots, long leather coat, big, threatening hat.

Is he not magnificent? Does the earth not tremble to his walking? Does his shadow not block out the very sun? All right, going a bit far there, does it buggery...but soon, soon, the Bounty

Hunter will take the werewolf, leading it as the moon draws the tides.

Ready and waiting, Blodwyn humming softly in his fist. Ah, Blodwyn, Blodwyn. How long she's waited, lying coiled in that drawer, while he's been searching. He'll never forget the first time he saw her, up the Pen-y-Dreadfyl Sheepdog Trials…(three of the buggers found Guilty and sentenced to collars and leads.)

There she'd been, lurking in the wet grass, eyeing up all them fat collie necks, and, first off, he'd thought her just an old, abandoned choke-chain. But then she'd sensed him, and if his reactions hadn't been so quick, she'd've had him, for sure…wrapped herself around his throat and squeezed the breath right out of him….but he'd met her sort before, something to do with Pen-y-Dreadfyl Castle and its Black Arts, he reckoned…and instinct'd took over. He'd grabbed her then, good and tight, at that special place just behind the third link, so's she couldn't loop herself round his neck.

Oh, she'd tried, mind, every trick in the book, whipping and slashing at him like some maddened serpent, but he'd held firm until she'd tired, and eventually, he'd mastered her. Hadn't been easy, mind, training her, nor holding her back when she got over-keen, but on the whole he reckoned it'd been worth it.

Over the years him and Blod'd seen Life, and, of course, Death, shared some laughs, snapped some necks…so now he stands prepared. As the Wolf within the Man, so the Hunter within the Caretaker...what a Stud. What a Killing-Machine.

And what a long way he's come from the slag-heaps of Pant-y-Gyrdl.

A wind got up in the early hours, roaring through the Beechwood and whipping the treetops. It prowled round the cottage, rattling the windows and trying the latch. But Granny only half-heard it, because she was thinking about Tobin, and listening to the past.

Dry your eyes, Bryony. You're well rid.
Be another one along any day now.
Ain't a man in this world worth a woman's tears…

She wondered about that part of herself she'd left in the Guildenhall, all them years ago, shrivelled up to nothing where the loving in her should've been. Would she have been any different, less selfish, if she'd wed Tobin? Had his kids? Become a *real* Granny?

Or would she have lost more than she gained, stopped being herself? There was plenty did. Maybe she wasn't cut out for all that sharing and giving…but if that was true, why should Tobin still bother her? Why did her heart lurch like a young girl's when she saw him? She supposed there was no fool like an old 'un.

Was that why she hadn't she told him to sling his hook soon as he'd shown his face? Why she kept mindblocking so's he couldn't touch her real feelings?

She knew the answer to that one, anyway. *Real feelings hurt.* And she'd learnt, long ago, that if it hurt, leave it be.

Grufty lay warm beside her, snoring into the eiderdown. Good ole Grufty, always where he should be, never let her down.

The wind tore at the thatch, but it held. Tight as a drum. Gobber'd done a good job then. Least there was still some things you could count on.

Grufty soon got fed-up with lying low; lust overcoming his fear of the Dog-Warden. So when Granny went to the privy, he gave her the slip.

By the time he reached 'Bottom Lea' the sun was well up, and he'd got company. Rivals for Truffle's affections lined the pavement, jostling for position. Three pairs of eyes swivelled to note his arrival before returning to their vigil.

Big Averdale, first-cross Gastonaard, Brimmerhund with muscles. Grufty cocked a scornful leg on the lampost. Call themselves studs?...pack of wimps, the lot of 'em. Short legs or not, he'd have been straight over that gate in his younger days...he swaggered over intending to personalise it, and found himself confronting a sort of miniature gargoyle.

He hadn't seen the minute Torvier defending the gate. It bared needle-teeth and the whole pack backed off, Grufty included. Size of a cat it might be, but he'd once tangled with a dog very like it, and knew from painful experience that they always went for the undercarriage, and hung on.

Wearily, the pack settled down to keep watch, staying well away from the Torvier. A kind of matiness grew out of shared misery.

They'd been there all night, Grufty learned, and got precisely nowhere: that Truffle couldn't move without a Human in tow. They'd learned to be quiet, and to beware of the Bitch-Human, who didn't like howling, which she counteracted with buckets of cold water. Late on, the Gastonaard confided, the front door had opened, but it had only been the Dog-Human eating one of those smelly smoke-sticks. His nose wrinkled at the memory, and it was generally agreed that humans only chose them because they hadn't the teeth to deal with a decent knuckle-end.

Hilary Bottomley came downstairs and, without pausing to take her rollers out, telephoned for the Dog-Warden.

Thuja and Statia turned up early at Granny's. Thuja's car looked nearly as loaded as Tobin's van.

'Can't stay, just come to tell you Mum's moving in at the weekend,' Statia said. 'And this is all the stuff she won't trust to the removal-van.'

'All right, is she?' Granny asked. She hadn't heard from Mariander since her uncomfortable meeting with Tobin.

'Fine.' Thuja looked puzzled. 'Busy packing up, you know how it is. Anyway, we'd best get on, we're going straight back when we've finished. Mum says love to Sham and Grufty.'

'No 'love to Aunt Bryony,' then. Oh, well, let her eat worms. Granny waved them off, and went back to her baking.

Something kept prickling at her memory, but she didn't manage to bring it out and scratch it til she finally sat herself down with a cup of tea.

...*Grufty. Love to Grufty. But where* was *he?* Oh, Sight, no. Not *again*.

She knew before reaching 'Bottom Lea' what she'd find...or, rather, not find. No Grufty, certainly. Only a small, bedraggled Torvier, a ragged strip of ribbon fluttering from the wreck of its topknot, sat triumphantly guarding the front gate.

It curled its lip at Granny, and she knew that somehow it'd managed not to get nobbled...well, you didn't mess with a dog like that if you knew what was good for you....but Grufty had been there, and he wasn't now.

Which meant the Dog-Warden must have got him again.

Aubrey Bottomley chose that moment to back his van out of the garage. As he got out to shut the door, Granny was waiting for him.

Aubrey went white. He'd been sleeping better recently. The nightmares had receded, and he no longer woke screaming his terror of that geriatric axe-woman. He'd even started believing she might leave him alone.

But it was no use. She'd found him. Half in and half out of the van, he looked wildly round for something to defend himself with.

She didn't move, didn't say anything, just stood there in her long black coat, arms folded, with those terrible eyes burning into him. What was he to do? What could he do? Hilary wasn't there to defend him, having gone to a coffee-morning...

'Right.' she said grimly, after a very long time. 'Bartlock Dog- Pound, and be quick about it.'

'Wait here,' Granny snapped. Aubrey switched the ignition off. He daren't do anything else, and anyway, his hands had locked solid from gripping the wheel so tightly.

She held him personally responsible for her dog's disappearance. He knew because she'd told him. All the way to Bartlock.

The Pound was a series of long, depressing brick-built buildings. Granny stomped up to the nearest one. There was a small grilled window set in the wall, with a bell next to it. The only way through was a turnstile, like the ones in public lavatories. Also on the wall was a plaque reading: BARTLESHIRE COUNTY COUNCIL CARES. Granny stared at it grimly, whilst leaning on the bell. And even before the barking and howling started, she picked up on the fear and desperation echoing in her mind. What a place this was.

Aubrey watched her nervously. He couldn't help feeling sorry for whoever was inside.

'I've come for me dog.' It was a statement that brooked no argument. The girl who came to the window wore a badge inscribed: MYNAME IS HELEN AND I LOVE DOGS. She was determinedly cheerful. But, then, she was new.

'Name?' she asked brightly, fingers poised over her keyboard.

'Grufty,' the old woman snapped.

The girl typed obediently. 'And when was your dog brought in, Mrs. Grufty?'

'You being funny, or what?' The old woman Loomed: she did it very well. The long black coat helped no end, but it was mostly the eyes....Helen's day was being spoilt now. Why was everybody who came to claim their dog so *cross*? You'd have thought they'd be glad to get their pets back!

Calm down, Helen, she told herself, *patience is the thing in this job, especially with the elderly,* and poor souls like this Mrs. Grufty trying to integrate back into the community. For all she knew, the dog might be poor old Mrs. Grufty's only friend....

'Let's start again, shall we?' she said, slowly and carefully. 'Can you remember your name?'

'Course I can. Beamish, if it's any business of yours.'

'Well done! How are you spelling that? And is that Mrs. or Miss? Never mind, I'll just put Ms., shall I?...and you say your dog was picked up and brought here?'

'Yes, this morning, by that Warden-woman!' Granny snapped. 'Minding his own business, he was.'

'Really? How awful for him,' the girl murmured absently, tapping away.

She could hear Grufty howling, she'd know his voice anywhere. He was mad as a wet hen, yes, and ashamed of being picked up, but he wasn't in fear of his life yet....not like them others....

'Oh dear, oh dear,' Helen tutted, wagging a finger at Granny. 'Fancy at! Your naughty doggy wasn't wearing a collar with his name and address on it!'

'And a good job, too!' Granny expostulated. 'Else everybody'd know where he belonged!'

'Yes, but it's a legal--' Helen was experiencing a reality-shift. Most people felt the same after a few minutes' conversation with Granny, but she wasn't to know that. She jabbed at the keyboard instead: nice and solid.

'There's just the Reclamation-Fee, then, Ms. Beamish.' She tried another smile, but it fell off.

'You what?'

Funny how cold it had gone all of a sudden. 'You pay us a Fee and we release your dog,' Helen said fearfully, wishing she'd stayed at County Hall, colour coding paper-clips. 'We only keep them seven days, and then if you haven't paid, I'm afraid...'

Aubrey watched open-mouthed as the turnstile sort of buckled and *fell apart* when the old woman strode through it. The young girl she'd evidently been talking to ran after her; reminding him for some reason of a butterfly trying to halt a rhinoceros. Behind her, the office collapsed.

Daringly, he got out of the van and stood basking in the sunshine, chewing a toffee he'd found under the dashboard. He supposed he could have made his escape, but he knew she'd have caught up with him, and anyway a sense of horrid fascination had crept over him. He did rather want to see what was going to happen next, and so long as he wasn't the focus of the old woman's attentions, he thought he might even enjoy it. It was even better than a morning at the Woodyard.

He helped himself to another toffee and stood mesmerised as roofs slid off and buildings disintegrated. It was completely unreal, like watching a film, yet none of it surprised him. One glare from those eyes, he had no doubt, would demolish anything....but he wasn't prepared for the great tide of dogs washing out of the Pound.

*Dogs of every conceivable shape, size, colour and pedigree--
or lack of it. Huge, loping hounds with enormous paws, lean,
ribby runners and small, sturdy torviers. Black ones, white ones,
sandy and tan and spotty and blue-roan and merles and
harlequins--*

Aubrey leapt back into the van, and sat cowering as they
surged past: most of them paused to water his wheels. He chewed
frantically, watching a brick wall wobble and fall like a stack of
dominoes.

*Hairy, smooth, wire and flat-coated dogs; lop-eared dogs
and drop-eared dogs and prick-eared dogs, some with plumed
tails, or whippy, pipe-cleaner tails, and one with no tail at
all...and all of them going like the clappers, and barking their
heads off.*

And then the old woman appeared amidst the devastation,
arms raised like some ancient prophet.

'Don't forget!' She was shouting, and somehow, her voice
carried above the uproar. He could've sworn he heard her say:
'Those of you with homes to go to, straight there! The rest of you,
make for The Manse! AND DON'T GET CAUGHT AGAIN!!'

She watched as they disappeared across the fields, and then
marched across to the van, her small, smelly dog bounding
joyfully beside her.

A pall of dust hung over what was left of the Dog-Pound.
And even as Aubrey watched, another wall collapsed. He couldn't
help wondering about the young girl. Probably lying dead
amongst the rubble, along with anybody else who'd got in the
way. The first Bartleshire County Council employees to die in the
course of duty--perhaps someone would erect a plaque in their
honour-....

His former bravado seemed to have popped out. He shivered,
all the old fears returning. It was too late for him...she was already
opening the door. She climbed in, accompanied by the dog, which
shook   itself   vigorously,   showering   hairs   and   mud
everywhere...*mud?*--part of Aubrey's brain registered the fact that
there'd been no rain for several weeks.

Rubbing her hands, she settled herself, and squinted out at the ruined Pound.'Ta for waiting,' she said drily. 'That's that, then. All done.'

Aubrey was reaching to switch the ignition on, when she suddenly roared, 'STOP!' and scrambled out again.

What now? Aubrey wondered. What further horrors was she planning before he could get back to the safety of his garage?

A big, sandy-coloured mongrel came hobbling through the ruined turnstile, and stood trembling irresolute in the road. It was lumpy and misshapen as a badly-stuffed chair, eyes cloudy, muzzle white-frosted.

The old woman was stroking it, talking gently to it, and her dog seemed to be whispering in its ears. After a while, she came back with the two of them in tow. Aubrey groaned.

'*This* poor old gel,' she announced, 'was on her last day. Couldn't run, could she. So she's coming home with Grufty and me. You better move all that junk, so I can get her in the back.'

Aubrey braved the watchful torvier, suffering only minor injuries getting through his own front gate, and collapsed onto the settee without removing his boiler-suit.

When Hilary swept in, full of plans for him to re-decorate the kitchen in the Oriental Peasant style of the one she'd spent the coffee-morning envying, he was still there.

He didn't even flinch when she told him off for sitting about staining the settee, which was odd. As a matter of fact, he didn't even *speak.* She wondered what he'd been up to all morning, because he certainly hadn't been getting on with the fence. It didn't do to give men too much freedom. Come to think of it, he *did* look a bit odd. Perhaps he was sickening for something...

'Aubrey dear, is anything wrong?' She ventured after another half-hour's immobility. 'What's happened while I've been away?'

Aubrey stirred. He couldn't believe any of it himself--so how could he expect anyone else to listen? But then, he was an accomplice, wasn't he? A Getaway Driver. No, he'd keep quiet, lie low, ask the lads at the Woodyard to provide an alibi...

'Nothing, dear,' he said, 'absolutely nothing's happened all morning.'

Helen coughed up a lungful of brick-dust and considered her career- options.

That had certainly been *some* tremor: the whole place was flattened. What a lot of bricks, though!....she pitied whoever would be doing the eventual Inventory and individual numbering!

Oddly enough, she didn't seem to be hurt. Mucky and more than a bit wobbly, but nothing worse, although her tights had seen better days, but then she could always put in a WF/555 indent for them.

Something glinted amidst the rubble: she picked it up. It was her MY NAME IS HELEN AND I LOVE DOGS badge, badly buckled. She pinned it on anyway, so as to have an official identity if anyone enquired.

And then she remembered--dogs! Had she really seen that ghastly old woman, buildings collapsing around her, letting them all out? She wondered where they'd gone, whether they'd ever be re-captured. And if not, how was she going to account for them all?

She'd need a T98 *for each one*--not to mention a signed and witnessed Unauthorised-Release chit...and where *were* the chits and the T98's? Come to that, where was the office?

And what about the Canine Hygiene & Re-settlement Personnel? If they were buried beneath the rubble, *she'd* be the one to dig them out, and *then* fill in the H777/100's (Accidental Demise in the Workplace forms)--in triplicate and probably by hand, because she was pretty sure the photocopier wouldn't have survived.

And, oh dear, *then* she'd have to send copies to all the relatives! It really was going to make the most enormous workload...!

She'd just started digging with her nail-file when the kennel-maids appeared through the dustclouds; Darren, the Work-Experience lad slouching along behind with his headphones on.

They looked dazed, apart from Darren, who, jigging to an inaudible rhythm, probably hadn't noticed a thing.

What a relief! There'd be someone else to help fill in the T98's after all!...assuming they could find any biros to fill them in with, that was...'Earthquake,' Helen said firmly, before they could speak. If she said it often enough, she might even convince herself.

Over in Deepinwold, the liberated Pack ambushed the Meals-on-Wheels delivery-van outside Lemming Court.

It was a long time since yesterday's dinner, and the day's offering of liver and onions with treacle pudding and custard to follow was making the saliva flow. They moved in, noses twitching. The biggest, a muscular Tor-Valley cross, parked himself by the rear doors, and the others followed, just as the two volunteers emerged from No. 3.

There'd been a bit of a crisis over Mr. Williams' dentures, which he'd insisted the Home-Help had stolen to sell in the Third World. It had taken twenty minutes to locate the teeth in Mr. Williams' shopping-bag, by which time the dinner had set so hard he couldn't chew it anyway-

The driver and her helper, women of courage and character had, over the years, braved many perils to ensure that The Meals Got Through. Ill-health had not deterred them, (although Irene was a martyr to her Heads, and Marjorie to the haemorrhoids which necessitated a foam-cushion on the driver's seat)...neither had bad weather, fallen trees, burst water-mains or roadworks obstructed them.

Over the years, they'd weathered the unscheduled daytime appearance of Snitty Bedford, posing in Deeping Dell wearing only a long khaki mac and a leer...and they'd jolly well seen *him* off...imaginative propositions from some of their elderly gentlemen and, once, a confrontation with a gang of rough, hairy chappies on motorcycles who'd tried to hijack the toad-in-the-hole, and lived to regret it.

As though a piffling pack of dogs was going to worry a couple of ex-Girl Guides with six brothers between them!

Irene clapped her hands bossily and shouted: 'SHOO! Bugger orf, the lot of you!'

The Pack eyed her, but didn't shift. Odd. It always worked with the Labs. But then, these weren't labs--more like a circle of wolves waiting for the campfire to go out.

'I'll see to it, Irene.' Marjorie strode determinedly down the drive. 'Authority's the thing. You have to show 'em who's Boss.'

The pack surged forward, delighted to see some action. At last somebody was going to feed them.

Marjorie, to her credit, still had but one thought on her mind.

The Meals must, at all costs, Get Through. Marching round to the back of the van, she opened the door and grabbed an armful of dinners destined for Nos. 4, 5, and 6a. Optimistically, the Pack closed in, and Marjorie hesitated. They *did* look awfully hungry.

Then remembering Father's advice, she looked them commandingly in the eye. 'Come on, chaps,' she pleaded, 'play the white man.'

They slavered, all over her shoes. One of them actually started chewing her skirt. And for perhaps the first time in her life, Marjorie froze.

'Marjorie! Get a grip! Diversion!' Irene sounded like a visiting General. Marjorie needed no urging. Tightening her headscarf, she shut her eyes, hurled the dinners to the waiting Pack, bunched up her skirts, and ran.

Gravy and custard oozed and pooled in the roadway. It didn't take the dogs long to ransack the open van and wolf down the rest, containers and all. Good feed, and then they'd be off to see what Perilla Pearce had to offer.

The residents of Lemmingwold Villas watched with interest from the Recreation Room.

'Never knew yon Marjorie could run like that!' Mr. Keable observed admiringly. 'Good pair of legs on her an' all!'

'Well,' commented Miss Hillyard, 'blessing in disguise if you ask me. Liver and sausage day, weren't it?' She suppressed a shudder.

The others brightened. 'Now you come to mention it, it were.'

'There you are, then!Every cloud has a silver lining, eh!' Mr. Keable rubbed his hands together. 'Reckon we've had a lucky escape. Let's get some junk-food down us! I'm for pizza. With the lot on it. Anyone else?'

The elderly bitch settled comfortably by Granny's fire, grateful for any kindness, and Boggy curled himself protectively beside her.

'Well,' Granny said, stroking the matted fur, 'I bet you're a lovely colour when you've had a wash and brush-up--reckon I'll call you Toffee.' And humming contentedly, she went off to put the kettle on.

She wasn't really tuning in, so the wave of subversive muttering that flooded her mind took her by surprise.

Toffee. Toffee. How can I tell her? She's been so kind.

Mine was too. But she called me Grufty! Got no dignity, has it?

Mine came up with Sandy. So unoriginal.

She meant well, but I--sort of fancied meself a bit of a Gloria. I haven't always been this shape, you know.

I bet you were a right cracker in your day--it was always Clint for me. Or Chad. Even Rocky, at a pinch. Tough and streetwise, you know? But did I get a choice?

I know what you mean. I'd've liked Marilyn. Scarlett. Or Talullah. And Clint's a lovely name--studdish.

You reckon? Well Grufty isn't, that's for sure. Doesn't half put the bitches off...I'm a laughing-stock back home. Soon will be here, as well. What chance have I got, eh?

They never think, do they? Saved from the jaws of death, and now I'm going to be turned into Toffee.

Granny couldn't believe what she was hearing. Teatowel in hand, she stormed through the doorway, roaring: 'I've never heard nothing like it! Names are only labels, when all's said and done! You're Grufty, and that's how you're staying! 'As for you--'

her voice softened, 'you're a guest. What d'you <u>wanter</u> be called?'
Pore old thing, she was thinking, she's been through such a lot.

The big bitch looked almost coy. *Well* she replied *if it's all
the same to you, could I be Krystle?*

They both saw it. It was real, it was huge, and it was too good
to be true.

A shadow passing into moonlight, it crossed right in front of
the Panda. Steve raised the stun-gun, and took aim at the wolf
through the open window. Couldn't miss! Had it in his sights,
ready to drop it, when a voice straight out of the graveyard said:
'Drop the goddamn gun, and no sudden moves. Now out of the
car, nice and easy, and getcha goddamn hands up, the both of you,
else you'll be heading for Boot Hill. Look you.'

Bevis Tate hung the prints up to dry. They *looked* superb; he
could only hope the detail was there, because he'd been using a
telephoto-lens for the first time.

Of course, when he moved into Fossetby Mill, he wouldn't
have to do his developing in a *box-room*; he'd have the whole
basement as a Hobbies Area. Once he'd purged all trace of
Undermaster Coy, of course.

The inflatable warthog that he'd requisitioned, however,
currently occupying a corner of his bedroom, had patched up
quite satisfactorily. He'd called her Edna, because she reminded
him of an Aunt who'd always insisted on kissing him--same
complexion, probably.

He went into the poky dining-room; really, a man of his
abilities shouldn't have to live like this. He'd spend a few minutes
on his New Project, until he could inspect the photographs
properly.

His Matchbox model stood half-finished on the table. Its
construction was now at a critical stage, and he wouldn't be able
to continue with it until he'd gained access to Bartlesham
Cathedral, and abstracted a piece of the South Transept. It would
have to be a very early visit, he decided, because there was
always some busybody threatening to report you for wielding a
pickaxe in a public building...

Squinting through a Jeweller's eye-glass, he studied the model galleon from every angle. The exquisite mermaid figurehead, the mahogany deck-planking and the intricate cobweb-fine rigging.

Then he picked up the champagne-magnum and set it down again, frowning. Try as he might, he could not see how it was possible.

It was proving a rare challenge indeed, trying to get a bottle inside a ship...

Story of his life, Steve thought bitterly, throwing the stun-gun down onto the road, and wincing as something snapped off it. First halfway cool piece of equipment Bartleshire Constabulary put his way, and some bastard nicked it. He wondered how he'd explain *this* one away.

He and Rog., hands up, turned slowly to find themselves facing a black-clad apparition--long coat, big boots, hat the size of an umbrella hiding its face--that struggled out of the bushes going: 'Ffaffyn thorns!' and snatched up the gun.

What with the shock and the darkness and the voice echoing eerily round the oversized hat, the whole thing should've been quite scary, except that, from boot-tips to hat-crown the character confronting them wasn't any taller than your average ten-year-old.

And yet, somehow, neither of them felt reassured. They eyed one another uneasily: that'd never been a *kid's* voice, had it? So what were they dealing with here? Some psycho-midget with wild-west delusions, by the look of it.

Rog. went for the placatory, talk-the-loony-down-off-the-window-ledge-before-he-stains the-pavement approach.

'All right, come on, pal, let's talk about it! Whatever you want--cash, helicopter, amnesty for your mates, we can work it out! Give us the gun back!' He was uncomfortably aware of the thing, broken or not, pointing steadily at his midriff--'and we'll go easy on you. It'll be okay, honest!'

The man in black studied them impassively, as far as they could tell, what with the shadows and the ten-gallon headgear. For all they knew, there might've been eyes glittering under that

hat, a scarred face, a flamboyant moustache, a sardonic smile playing around the corners of the cruel mouth....after a while, he struck a match on his boot and applied it to something they couldn't see. Smoke billowed out beneath the hat.

Finally, after a particularly nasty bout of coughing, he replied: 'No dice. Nothing I want from you guys. And keep off the wolf--it's mine. You got that? I see you within a mile of it, I'll blow yer goldarn heads off. So keep them hands up, and git walkin' 'fore I start shooting, isn't it?'

'You what?' Steve said faintly, eyeing the Panda. It'd be a bloody long walk back to Bartlesham.

'Yeah!' Rog. snarled. 'Who you ordering around, shortarse? You haven't even got a proper gun!'

'ROG.' Steve dug him urgently in the ribs. 'Shut up.'

'You what?'

'He mightn't have a gun, but he's certainly got a weapon!'

Rog. shut up. 'Oh, right.' He could see that the guy was twirling, in his free hand, something that he couldn't quite...something thin and whippy that hummed unpleasantly, glinting faint and menacing in the darkness. And for some reason just looking at it tied his bowels in knots.

'I dunno what that is,' Steve hissed, 'but nice it's not, and I think we ought to do as he says.'

'Okay, you win!' Rog. said. 'We're out of here.'

Fifty yards away, he paused, turned, and, not really expecting an answer, shouted: 'Who the hell are you, anyway?'

Laughter grated like a knife scraping bone. 'Well now, there's some calls me Stalker and there's some calls me Skinner. Name I go by's Killer Calhoun, Bounty Hunter. Remember that and tremble. In your nightmares, Boyo.'

Next morning, Granny went down to PENNYPINCHER for extra dog-food. That Krystle couldn't half eat: not that she begrudged it, because it meant she was picking up at last. The dogs seemed to be getting on like holly and ivy anyway: she'd left them curled up together.

Down the street, she saw someone come out of "Shepherd's Cott", but couldn't quite make out who it was--then all at once, her head was filled with someone else's shame and worry, and she quickened her pace, because if she'd got to be lumbered with all that mind-clutter, she wanted to know a bit more about it.

Tiny little body she was, not young, but, it was a fair bet, not so old as she seemed.

She looked worn out, though, like she'd been up all night, and she was lugging one of them tartan shopping-trolleys like Mariander'd got, the sort took all the skin off your shins when you got behind 'em--so it was a fair bet she was on her way to PENNYPINCHER too.

Granny fell in beside her and glued a smile on her face. Chitchat, especially with Outsiders, never had come easy.

'Morning!' She said, in her best welcome-to-Brimwold voice. 'Moved into Old Tarrill's place, haven't you?'

The woman just kept going, head down, walking and worrying.

'Off down the shop, eh?' got nowhere, so Granny tried another tack.

'See you got one of them trolleys then saves your arms does it my niece keeps saying she'll get me one and anybody tries anything you can bash 'em with it can I have a go then?'

She came out of her trance then, rearing like a threatened earwig.

'No you can*not*!' She had quite a loud voice for such a small person. 'I've all our Kenneth's old medicine-bottles in here, and I don't want them smashing to bits before I get 'em filled!'

'Who's Kenneth then?' Granny asked with interest. 'Is he ill a lot?'

The cloud of worry quickened when she said the name.

'What's it to you, eh?' she snapped. 'He *might* be a neighbour...or me lad, me Dad or me uncle. For all anybody knows, he could be me secret fantasy man, him cuts the grass on the Village-Green, the firm globes of his youthful bum filling out his jeans as he moves--' she leant on the trolley to get her breath back.

'Only he ain't, is he,' Granny said gently.

'No, course he ain't.' She laughed, bitterly. 'But you can dream, can't you. Even at my age. Kenneth's me younger brother.'

'Ah.' Granny nodded understandingly. 'I got one of them.'

The woman looked up then, and she'd got a face full of trouble. 'I doubt you got one like mine,' she said.

'Tell me more.' Granny hefted her moleskin shopping-bag, and got ready to solve a few mysteries.

When she got home, there was a horse tied to the fence, eating the heads off her sunflowers. After a few Strong Words, Granny moved it up a bit.

She wasn't ready for visitors. She'd wanted time on her own to think about that Kenneth...but it seemed she wasn't going to get it yet awhile. Resignedly, she pushed the door open, choking on the reek of cigar-smoke, and said: 'Hello, Perilla.'

Perilla Pearce sat contentedly in Granny's chair, smoking and scattering ash liberally over the two dogs sitting at her feet. She smelt, as usual, of horse-sweat and damp dogs, and was wearing one of her Working Outfits--army boots, combat trousers and a red sweatshirt proclaiming: DOWNTOWN BADBOYS.

Her iron-grey hair was hacked off short, like a lad's; you'd never guess, Granny reflected, that she'd enough money to buy every hairdresser's shop in Bartleshire--nor that she spent every penny of it on animals in trouble.

'Bryony!' Perilla boomed. '*And* about time! Been here hours! That horse of mine behaving itself, is it?'

'It is now,' Granny said shortly, going to put the kettle on.

'So this one's a refugee, is she?' Perilla stroked Krystle's head. 'Poor old thing's been through it, hasn't she? And me and Grufty have got re-acquainted...been a bit of a bad lad, hasn't he, huhhuhhuh!'

She clicked her fingers and Grufty rolled over to have his tummy tickled.

'Getting caught by the *Warden*,' she reproved him, '*I* don't know. Got a collar and lead, has he, Bryony?

Eager to please, Grufty waddled over to Granny's hatstand and fetched them.

'What the blithers d'you call *these*?' Perilla said witheringly.'Waste of time and money!' Grufty shot Granny a look of undisguised triumph. 'Never train him with these! No, a good strong check-chain, that's what's wanted!'

Grufty disappeared under the dresser. 'With BIG LINKS!' Perilla added. 'Sent that pack of brutes from the Pound over to me, did you?' she snapped. 'Thought so.' And, unexpectedly she grinned: like sunshine illuminating a grim old building.

'Good show, setting 'em free. Wish I'd done it meself. Got 'em all bedded down with my lot--soon have 'em re-homed, though there's a rather nice Lansterhound I just might hang on to.'

'Ta, Perilla, knew I could rely on you,' Granny said. 'Cupper tea?'

'Got anything stronger?'

'Well...' she'd been saving the Sorrell Gin, but now seemed as good a time as any...'reckon I might find a bottle of something.'

When they'd got settled, the bottle between them, Granny said: 'And to what do I owe this honour, then?'

'Thing is...' Perilla slugged back half her drink and topped it up from the bottle, before spitting her cigar-butt into the fire...'all these Dog-Laws. Dratted nuisance, I grant you, but *most* people...' looking hard at Granny...'can't control their animals at all. Haven't a clue. So I reckon it's a good time to get some Obedience Training classes going round the villages. Been round putting notices up. Hope I can count on you...' she nodded towards Grufty, who hadn't even ventured out for fresh gingerbread...'*and* him, of course.'

'Good idea!' Granny said, knowing there wasn't a dog Perilla couldn't master. Apart from running the Animal Sanctuary and the Boarding-Kennels, she was also a top breeder and Flugel-Hound judge...which meant she stood no nonsense.

Granny smiled at Grufty. Smugly. *You wait* she told him. *Just you wait.*

When Perilla eventually heaved herself up, there wasn't much left of the morning, and nothing at all of the gin.

There wasn't much left of Granny's nasturtiums, either, she noticed, when Perilla climbed aboard the horse, which had a guilty expression on its face and a strand of greenery dangling from its mouth.

'By the way!' Perilla rammed a hard hat onto her head. 'Meant to ask…what actually *happened* up at the Dog-Pound?'

Granny tapped the side of her nose, and grinned.

Perilla roared with laughter, lit another cheroot, and took up the reins. 'Up to your neck in it, eh! Thought so. Well, my lips are sealed...can't have our Grandmistress getting Struck Orf, can we!'

Somewhat unsteadily, she rode into the Beech Wood, almost falling off as she turned to shout: 'Village Hall! Tuesday Week, Seven sharp and don't be late!'

It was a good job, Granny observed, that the horse knew its way home.

Trust the Old Man's hernia to play up at the first hint of trouble.

A.C.C. Root had not had a good week. What with bus-loads of silly buggers turning up to gawp at the Ambarrow corn-circles, and the associated Hot-Dog stalls, tea-bars, journalists and T.V. crews clogging up those narrow lanes, the whole of Bartleshire Constabulary was united in praying for an early harvest.

After which the report from the so-called Wolf Patrol had landed on his desk, and had him reaching for the indigestion tablets by the middle of page one.

It really was the most incredible load of old donkey-droppings it'd ever been his misfortune to stand in. He wondered why he'd ever approved the Patrol in the first place?

Wolves and cowboys and Bounty-Hunters roaming the countryside indeed--on his patch! Even more ridiculous than those unicorn stories awhile back.

And worse, it appeared that some undersized felon had, singlehandedly, managed to deprive the two aforementioned officers of valuable Police property, to wit: one specially-equipped night-patrol car--(eventually recovered minus wheels, lights, engine and radio)--and one excruciatingly expensive Stun-gun!

They were all On Something, these young coppers, had to be. Probably kept a stash of drugs and bottles in the Panda to while away the hours of darkness--someone ought to have breathalysed the pair of 'em, soon as they started coming out with all this twaddle.

But none of this had compared with the Bartlock Bombing. Terrorists at large, by God! Bloody typical, that was. Animal Liberationists, he'd have bet his pension on it, otherwise why pick on the Dog-Pound?

But the Bomb-Squad had drawn a blank, and those boys missed nothing. They'd found absolutely no trace of explosives; so now, based on the statement of the Ingress and Egress Administration Officer...(Office girl she'd have been called in his day)...they were back to the Earthquake Theory.

The girl had already given several radio and T.V. interviews to that effect, and nobody had come up with anything better.

Then how to explain the photographs he'd just received through the post? An extra complication he could have done without. There was no note with them, no explanation. Just six glossy black-and-white enlargements, some of the sharpest he'd ever seen.

Who was the old woman with the black coat and the white hair? Even without his glasses on, he knew he wouldn't like to cross *her*. She had her arms raised like an Old-World Prophet...or a Saint giving a Blessing.

And behind her...he *did* put his glasses on to make sure...piles of rubble, recent rubble, with clouds of dust still rising from it.

Suddenly, the scene clicked into focus in his brain. And all at once, he knew what he was looking at. The ruined Dog-Pound, no less. And he'd eat his truncheon if that wasn't the perpetrator, right there in the frame...whoever she was.

Somehow, he wasn't too keen on finding out. Couldn't he just lose the photographs and say nothing?...but no, he was a copper, and it had to be done. He'd supposed he'd better start circulating the pictures...but how much simpler if it *had* been a bomb. Or even an earthquake.

Some instinct told him that either would have proved a lot less trouble than this old woman was going to be.

Nightfall, moonlight, concealment, and the Bounty-Hunter gloats. *His* den, his memories, *his* trophies.

Vampire-skin hangs leathery on the wall, claws clenched as though to gouge out the very plaster. And the Face on it...took its time dying, that one, and it showed.

A wraith-skin, barely there, flimsy and insubstantial in its polythene-bag. Daren't handle the thing, in case it falls to bits. He's labelled it, though, RATHE, and the date of its Execution. Not that there'd been much to its body...he'd sent *that* off in an envelope, first-class mail.

Lot cheaper'n most of 'em, mind. He grimaces, remembering the postage & packing on that banshee...and postage, of course, isn't refundable 'cause he's freelance. Has to send the dead ones Special Delivery, doesn't he, particularly in warm weather....

There's an ogreskin, a charred phoenix, couple of fairy-derms, soft as soft--bloody girly fairies, poncing about with flowers in their hair: he grins at the memory. Pull them gauzy little wings off and where are they, eh?

And, course, the werewolf-pelt, head still attached. He fingers the rough, matted coat. Werewolves make good hunting, because they're elusive and part human-cunning, but most of all because they got no choice about being that way.

The eyes regard him glassily...still, he fancies, with a touch of the moon in them. He took that one alive, the way the Lab. prefers 'em, better experimenting that way, so they say, and it pays more, too...

So long as they send him the skins when they're done...and they always do, his little bonus along with his fee, what does he care? He runs his thumb along the blade of the skinning-knife. Sometimes he can't resist using it, just for fun, and sod the profit. Bastard supernaturals, eh! He hates 'em...and always has ever since that poltergeist ran amok in Mam's lavvy. They want wasting, the lot of 'em, and he's the boy to do it, all right.

And if he can't have 'em, well...there's always plenty other creatures roaming the night that the Lab, can use.

Cats, dogs and suchlike. They won't starve, him and Blod., oh no...new area, he'll have them before they know it, just like he always has.

Tobin turned up the next evening, dressed to kill and carrying a bunch of flowers that he obviously hadn't pinched from anybody's garden...as if she hadn't got plenty in her own! Now she'd have to find a milk-bottle to put 'em in. He'd even had a shave.

'Get your coat on, Bryony.' He grinned. 'Not that you'll need it, it's warm out.'

'Why,' Granny grunted, 'would I want me coat on? I'm all right here, ta very much.'

'No you ain't.' She did wish he'd stop grinning like that. ''Cos I'm taking you out fer dinner.'

'You what?' Granny couldn't remember her last meal out.

'I've booked us a table at Bartlesham Grange. If we get off now, we can
have a drink in the Orangery.'

What could she say? In a daze, she found herself getting into Tobin's van. How did he always manage to get round her, despite herself?

She just wasn't the *sort* went in restaurants, except on Guild-business. Couldn't stand all that dressing up and being waited on, apart from working out how much it was costing for half the amount she could've had at home...

Still, it *was* Tobin's money, and if he wanted to throw it about, well...And he'd been right: it was a lovely evening. And she supposed it was nice being chauffeured, instead of catching buses.

Tobin drove slowly, weaving about as he pointed out things of interest along the way. Fortunately, the lanes were quiet, else they'd've had a rare queue behind, because he certainly couldn't see out of the rear window, what with all that stuff piled up in the back.

They stopped on Bartlesham Bridge to watch the swans. Granny was just wishing she'd got something to give them when Tobin said: 'There's a sliced loaf in the back. That'll do 'em.'

Sight wouldn't she ever learn? Letting her mind slip like that. He was having a bad effect on her, was Tobin.

When they'd fed the swans, they stood awhile watching folks coming and going--walking dogs, fishing, even paddling. And the young 'uns, couples, glued together, nobody else in the world but them--she'd forgotten what *that* felt like.

And then Tobin whispered: 'Nice spot for a bit of togetherness, ain't it. Stop off on the way home, if you like...there's some lovely willows down by that towpath, and I've got an hammock in the back of the van.'

'Yes, you would have,' Granny snorted. 'Well, there'll be none of that hanky-panky with *me*, Tobin Hackett. Let's get off and have some dinner before I lose me appetite.'

'You're the Boss.' With exaggerated courtesy, he opened the door and settled her into her seat.

Bartlesham Grange hadn't changed one bit in the fifty-odd years since she'd last been there...and that'd been strictly in at the Tradesman's Entrance, because that Veronica Stebbings from Guildschool had had an holiday job in the kitchens...except maybe there were more posh cars in the drive.

What would her Mum and Dad have made of it? They'd always considered it out of their class. For a moment, she wondered what she was doing there herself...and with Tobin, too. But that was Outsider Thinking. She'd as much right to be there as anyone else, and enjoy it. And she'd better do it before Mariander moved in and started interfering...

Aggie wasn't at all out of place amongst the other cars...in fact, Granny thought her a deal better-looking than most of 'em, and more dignified as well. Maybe Old Age *did* have its compensations, after all...

They made their way up the wide, stone steps to the swing-doors. The uniformed commissionaire stood aside to let them through, and then frowned at Tobin. A hefty arm barred their way.

'I'm sorry, Sir.' Don't *look* very sorry, Granny thought. 'You can't come in here without a tie on.'

'What?' Tobin fingered his tweed jacket. 'Get on with you, decently dressed, ain't I?'

'Hotel Policy, I'm afraid,' the doorman said. 'Don't matter what else you're wearing...no tie, no admission. Let your standards drop and where are you, eh?'

'Nowhere, I s'pose.'

Tobin seemed quite calm all of a sudden: he winked at Granny and said: 'Just wait here a minute, Bryony, and I'll have a look in the van.'

He knew full well she was getting her mad up, and all for having a go at that doorman...she wondered if he'd got a box of ties in the van. Wouldn't surprise her one bit if he reappeared in a dinner-suit...

But he was wearing the same clothes, except for the two long, springy plastic things, a black one and a red one, knotted together round his neck. He strolled up as if he wore them every day, grinned at the doorman and said: 'Respectable enough for you? Can we come in now?'

The doorman looked Tobin up and down, from the polished brogues to the pair of jump-leads dangling over his shirt.

'Okay, I s'pose so,' he said. 'Just don't start anything, that's all.'

To her own surprise, she'd had a lovely time.

The meal had been all right, once she'd been in the kitchen and given the Chef a few tips on beef; after all, hers had arrived nearly raw instead of cooked proper...*and* with sauce all over it, instead of gravy.

Tobin had enjoyed hisself as well, even allowing for them jump-leads dipping into his soup. He'd've taken them off, but the doorman kept popping in and daring him to do it, so's he could throw him out.

They'd stopped by the river on the way home, but the hammock hadn't been mentioned. Instead, Tobin had pulled two deck-chairs out of the van.

And there they'd sat, listening to the water, and the birds, just like in the old days...

He'd been inclined to linger, but she'd packed him off after a last cupper tea, so's she could put her mind to that woman's brother, Kenneth.

Betty, her name was, Betty Potter. And it wasn't so much what she had said as what she hadn't.

Seemed she was worrying herself into the ground over something Kenneth had done, and looked like doing again. Wasn't something he could help, neither. Some sort of a *urge*. Mebbe he was another flasher, like Snitty Bedford. No, couldn't be, she'd've heard...well, mebbe he was ill, then, and having some sort of treatment wasn't working right...

If only she'd been able to penetrate that great cloud of worry: like trying to see through river-fog, it was. That Betty might be an Outsider, but she'd a strong mind on her. Mebbe she'd had to have to survive....

Krystle was flat out on the hearthrug, but Grufty was restless, and, what was more, hadn't eaten his dinner. He laid a pleading head on Granny's knee, and sighed like the West wind.

'Oh, all right, then,' she grumbled, lifting the latch. 'Off you go, and don't worry. I'll sort things out that end.'

Grufty ran as he hadn't for years, driven by something older and stronger than leg-power.

Yet a small part of him wanted to turn tail and run. Back to warmth and light and the safety of home...away from the new Terror that stalked the night--the one that definitely wasn't the Dog-Warden.

The torvier, looking more sewer-rat than pedigree, was still defending the gate.

Outside BOTTOM LEA, the Averdale, Brimmerhund and Gastonaard sat on hopefully; cold and bored but more determined, after their brief imprisonment, than ever.

Hilary Bottomley had gone to bed and left them to it: after all, tomorrow would be Truffle's Wedding-Day...and nothing was going to prevent it.

The others acknowledged Grufty's arrival by shuffling up a bit...*and Granny did the same by sending each mind an irresistible food-image.*

Huge, steaming meaty platefuls of dinner. With gravy. And biscuits. And left-overs. They could see it, smell it, all but taste it. It called them home, and they drooled, torn between greed and lust.

The Averdale cracked first. He was a big lad, and he liked his grub. With hardly a backward glance, he betrayed his Loved One for a dish of mince, and loped off towards the home where his long-suffering owner was, even now, imagining him squashed on some dark road.

The Gastonaard and Brimmerhund weren't far behind. The torvier, however, was made of stronger stuff. In an optimistic moment, his owner's husband, who'd wanted a Giant Brushund, had named him Fang, and ever afterwards he'd lived up to his name, being possibly the most stubborn, cantankerous little dog in the whole neighbourhood.

He was here for a purpose, and he wasn't giving up for any smelly no-hope mongrel. Granny's food-images didn't touch him: he'd always been a fussy eater. In fact, Fang didn't *like* food very much--not dinners, anyway. He much preferred titbits.

His ribbon, a green one this time, positioned only that morning by his doting owner, hung drunkenly over one eye, along with his topknot. The rest of his hair stood up in aggressive spikes around the small, ferocious face. He curled his lip, and uttered a tiny but nevertheless warlike growl.

Granny sighed. There was always one. Still, she had to admire his nerve.

With a soft click! her mind unlocked the front door, and gently pushed its way into Truffle's kitchen-prison.

The Courvalier twitched back her long, silken ears, but, cowed by a lifetime's acquaintance with Hilary Bottomley, she hesitated.

Bet I can guess your name, beautiful said a lusty voice in her mind. *It's Princess Truffle, ain't it. And you'll never guess mine. But I'm the one that's set you free, so I win your paw. Come out here and we'll be off to the woods...*

With a small joyful bark, ears and tail streaming, Truffle launched herself into the night, and she and Grufty ran free, deep into the Beech Wood. Fang made a valiant effort to keep up, but his short legs tired long before theirs, *and, let's face it,* Granny told him, *three's a crowd.*

Still, she couldn't help feeling a bit sorry for him, and it was pure chance that she hit upon a chocolate-egg image--enough to send Fang sulkily home, though, because they were his favourites.

And the mood he was in, there'd better *be* some chocolate eggs, or someone would be getting nipped. Round the undercarriage.

Soon after dawn, Granny drew them homewards, ushered Truffle inside, and, using the last surge of energy from her tired mind, shut and locked the doors behind her.

Aubrey and Hilary snored on, oblivious. And Truffle, sighing dreamily, settled down on her bean-cushion. *That Grufty had been every bit as much fun as she'd known he'd be.*

Next morning, Hilary armed herself with the hosepipe, and prepared to stand guard as Aubrey smuggled the Bride out to the car.

There was no need, though, because there wasn't another dog in sight.

The Mating went ahead as planned, although Truffle did seem rather underwhelmed by the whole thing. Only to be expected, said the groom's owner briskly, even the snapping and snarling--maiden-bitch and all that.

Hilary, finding the whole thing utterly distasteful, made Aubrey take her to a nearby coffee-shop, where she spent the time totting up her future profits on a pocket-calculator.

The puppies, she estimated, would bring in a small fortune, and Truffle could produce at least one litter a year, until she got too old.

Tomorrow, she'd order the peasant-style kitchen she yearned for, and possibly, if Aubrey behaved himself, she might treat him to a motorised grass-cutter--

It's nearly that time again that irresistible moon-pulling time like he's the tide can't stop it can't help it just gotta get out there and do it...

Moonlight flooded the bedroom, and Hilary Bottomley woke to the sound of Truffle howling. But there was something else, too...something deeper and darker that made her rollers prickle...

'Aubrey, Aubrey, get up and see what's making that terrible noise!'

Aubrey, who'd had an exhausting day carpeting the garage, toolshed and greenhouse (under Hilary's supervision), groaned, turned over, and plunged straight into a blissful dream about Hilary's incurable laryngitis.

Crossly, Hilary shoved her feet into fluffy mules, knowing Aubrey only slept deeply to annoy her. Well, if he wouldn't defend his wife and property, she'd have to investigate--although if she *was* murdered by a burglar, she'd be sure to come back and haunt him.

She slipped a matching jacket over her baby-doll nightie, pausing to admire herself in the mirror, and glare at Aubrey, snoring rapturously. A brief squirt of perfume, and she'd be ready for anything. Especially an intruder.

Years ago, someone had remarked that moonlight flattered her...(or had it been shadows?)...anyway, *she* still believed it, even if Aubrey was blind to her beauty.

She could hear Truffle carrying on in the kitchen; she would sort *that* little madam out later.

But the other, louder noise, she now realised, came from *outside*...tiptoeing downstairs, she peeked through the lounge window.

Whatever was out there would be getting the sharp end of her tongue. These Country Noises really were too much; not at all peaceful. Owls and bats and cattle and...and...

Sitting on next door's drive was an enormous grey dog, for goodness' sake, howling its head off. The *nerve* of it, especially when she'd just got rid of all those others.

To her disgust, she saw it bite a big lump out of Aubrey's new fence that he hadn't even creosoted yet, and then cock his leg up on it! Well that was it! She'd go out there and take a broom to it! Waking decent people like that, and fouling their property!

And where was that Dog-Warden, she'd like to know? She'd be phoning the Council first thing in the morning. Of course, by the time she'd fumbled about in the utility room, found the broom, unlocked the front door and stormed outside, the animal was nowhere to be seen.

As she glared up and down the street, it came prowling round from next door's back garden, spitting out bits of Aubrey's fence. It peered through the dark windows as though inspecting itself in a mirror, and then, apparently not liking what it saw, it then sat back on its haunches and howled at the moon.

As Hilary rushed forward, broom raised, something tiny scuttled out of the shadows, and the howling stopped abruptly. She saw the dog's hackles rise, and its whole body tremble as it faced something on the path--

Hilary's vision was excellent: (it had to be, for fear of missing anything)...so that she registered every small detail as the fieldmouse, *snarling*, ran between the dog's hind legs and bit it somewhere very painful.

Blaring like a foghorn, the dog ran for its life, and she saw its huge, yellow eyes and its great, plumed tail, exactly like a...

Hilary hadn't run anywhere in the last forty years, not since netball lessons, but she gave chase anyway, waving the broom and screaming abuse. It was quite fun really.

The Wolf-Patrol had cruised the High Street: dead boring. Nothing moved.

Happily, they turned onto Brimbleby Way just in time to witness An Incident.

'Is that what I *think* it is?' Rog. gasped as a zonking great wolf limped bow-leggedly past, sobbing like a baby...

'Not sure.' Steve was staring transfixed at a broom-waving middle-aged woman in rollers and an unbecomingly short nightie. 'Whatever it is, though, it wants a bloody good ironing.'

'Quick!' Rog. wrenched at the steering-wheel. 'The stun-gun!'

Tyres screeched as the car shot forward: they lowered their visors, and Steve took aim.

The woman, wobbling along on her mules, had just caught up with the wolf as they drew level: she started banging it enthusiastically with the broom.

Rog. rolled his window down. 'Here, stop that, Madam! That's Evidence!' She carried on bashing.

'Go on, Steve!' Rog. hissed. 'Zap it one before she kills it!'

Steve raised the stun-gun to shoulder-level and steadied it. 'It's bloody heavy, Rog.' And then Rog, was yelling: 'Look where you're point-...'

It was very quiet with the engine off, once the wolf's howls had faded into the night.

'Whoops,' Steve sighed. 'Missed again.'

On the back doorstep of Mariander's bungalow-to-be, a she-mouse sits smugly grooming her whiskers. Small she might be, bit exposed and vulnerable out there in the moonlight, but she's having a quality moment, because she's seen that wolf off, all by herself...prowling and howling and scaring the kids. They'd moved here to get away from all that...

Who needed a he-mouse anyway, cluttering up the nest, fathering litter after litter and gnawing all the best bits off next door's goodies?

Clean and presentable again, she slips back through the gap beside the air-brick. And just let that smelly dog came back, the one carried her about like a piece of cheese. And as for that really big dog, well, *he* won't be fathering any more litters for sure.

Her mind and his mind connected. Glancingly, but it was enough. So that was the way of it. Well, first thing in the morning,

Granny vowed, she'd be round that Kenneth's place, and sort him out.

'Great stuff, Steve. Did I mention it's fifty points and a sodding Commendation for one in a nightie? Oh, and you get to stick the head on your wall?'

'Well *you* couldn't have hit the bloody thing, smart-arse. Not with *her* jumping all over it, you couldn't...so what we going to do with her?'

Hilary lay in the road, snoring loudly. Her mules had come off when she fell, but luckily her rollers had held. It would have cheered her up considerably, had she been conscious, to know that, whatever happened, her hair would have a bit of a wave in it next day.

'Well, we can't leave her here,' Steve said. 'She's a traffic-hazard.'

'But we don't know where she came from,' Rog. objected.

Can't be far, can it? We'll just look for the house with the light on, and--drop her off there.'

'What, just dump her, you mean?'

'Why not? It's a warm night. Anyhow, you got any better ideas? Like telling Old Daisy about The One That Got Away?'

'Okay, you win. I'll take the head-end. One, two thr--'

'God, she's a dead weight,' Steve puffed as they heaved the still-snoring Hilary into the patrol-car.

'A sturdy, well-nourished mature female in her middle years,' Rog. said.

Steve looked at him. 'Come again?'

'That's what they'd say about her if she was on the slab. Saw it on 'Pathology Today.' Right, let's try round this corner--'

'Bingo!' Steve pointed. 'Light on over there--oh, yeah, that's her sort of house, all right.'

Nothing stirred in "BOTTOM LEA". 'Doesn't look like there's anyone around,' Rog. said. 'Let's unload her. *Quietly.*'

'You got any booze?' Steve said as they tried to extract Hilary from the back seat without her nightie riding up any further.

'*Booze*? Now? You want to see a counsellor, mate.'

'You what? No, not to *drink*, dumbo. I've had an idea, that's all.'

'Well...I think there's some lager in the boot, that we took off those kids outside the Youth Club, but I...'

'Right. Great. I'll have a look.' Steve dropped Hilary's curlered head onto the pavement. It bounced.

'...was saving them for later,' Rog. said, forlornly.

Steve came back with an armful of lager. 'Got 'em!'

'Oh, great. What now?'

'Now,' Steve said, 'we lay her on the lawn...yeah, between the gnomes--and stand clear.'

Opening the first can, he sprayed the contents liberally over the recumbent Hilary. The second, he placed in her unresisting hand, closing the fingers round it, the third he hooked onto the nearest garden-gnome's fishing-line, and the rest, he piled beside her.

They stood back to admire the effect. Hilary, flat out and lager-soaked on the gnome-infested lawn, was smiling like someone having a *very* private dream. Froth glistened round her mouth and chin.

'Cool!' Rog. said admiringly.

'Look at her arms and legs going!' Steve said. 'Just like our Rex chasing rabbits in his sleep!'

'Somehow I don't think it's rabbits she's after,' Rog. said doubtfully.

Steve pulled the tell-tale dart from Hilary's neck and hid it in his pocket.

'Let's get the hell out,' he said, 'and hope she thinks it's all been a dream.'

Granny went round the back, pausing to gawp at the garden...or, rather, where the garden had been when Tarrill lived there.

Poor old bugger'd been so proud of his fruit and veg., and his roses won prizes every year...he'd throw hisself in the Brim if he could see it now. All them great big holes, like a bomb-site, stumps for apple-trees, and nothing left of the hedge...even Tarrill's sheep had never made *that* much mess. She knocked at the back door...no answer.

She'd try the front again, then. They were in, all right. She'd seen that Betty, not five minutes earlier, hanging out her thermals. *She'd* not feel the benefit come winter, if she was finding it cold already. Wait til she'd weathered a real Brimwold winter...

She could *feel* the pair of 'em, pretending they wasn't there. And she knew they weren't answering 'cos they were just plain scared. But she wasn't giving up, even if she had to take her mind to that door, because she was coming to realise how much Betty and Kenneth needed help. She banged loudly, shouting: 'Come on! I know yer in there!'

The whole place was falling to bits...all the windows boarded-up; paint peeling and woodwork splintered. And there were some *very* nasty scratch-marks all the way down the door-frame....

The door inched open, and Betty's voice snapped: 'Bugger off! We ain't even got round to *single*-glazing yet!'

Granny couldn't see a thing. She wondered how Betty'd found her way to the door. P'raps she ate a lot of carrots.

'It's me, Bryony Beamish.' She wedged her foot in the door, just in case. 'You nearly give us a go of your shopping-trolley the other day...that brother of yours in, is he?'

'No!' Panic filled the voice and mind.

'I think he is,' Granny insisted. 'Morning after the night before, I expect. Come on, Betty, stop playing games and let me help.'

'You can't,' Betty said brokenly. 'No-one can.' But she offered no resistance as Granny pushed past.

'Where is he then?' She groped her way inside, blinking like an owl, because it was pitch-dark.

'Watch your step!' Betty warned. 'Let me go first--and keep to the walls, else you'll break your neck.'

She produced a torch and, like a cinema-usherette, led the way towards the light--or, at least the dim glow of a single naked bulb swinging forlornly from the ceiling.

And Granny blinked again, in amazement this time, because she found herself standing in Betty's sitting-room--or what'd *been* Betty's sitting-room before it got demolished.

It was dark because of the boarded-up windows, although a few tattered bits of curtain clung grimly to the ruined pelmets. And Betty'd been right about the floor: it was a death-trap. There wasn't so much as a scrap of lino, and the floorboards were splintered, with nails sticking out at all angles.

There were a few gnawed bits of skirting-board left, and in the middle of what passed for the floor was the remains of a tufted rug--or, more like, Granny realised, all that was left of the carpet.

There'd been wallpaper once...big cabbage-rose pattern, judging by what was left, and huge lumps of plaster were missing from the walls. And something had been having a go at the furniture as well...

'I know, I know,' Betty followed Granny's gaze. 'He's a bugger for chewing, is our Kenneth.'

There was an angry thumping from the shadows, and then something launched itself at the nearest chair-leg and splintered it, all the time snarling what sounded like 'WARG! WARG!'

'Oh, ignore him,' Betty snapped. 'Won't answer to Kenneth. He's always like this when he's having his monthlies. Would you like a cup of tea?'

'Do you know,' Granny said, faintly. 'I believe I would.'

Bevis Tate lurked outside the garage, trying to look like a petrol-pump.

Slipping the camera inside his jacket, he hid behind the morning paper. He'd photographed the Grandmistress going in, and, by the Sight, he intended to snap her coming out as well.

Whatever she was doing in that Outsiders' hovel, she was certainly taking her time about it. Not that he minded. His evidence, when he presented it, must be comprehensive.

A more technologically-minded person might have invested in a camcorder, but Midmaster Tate relished the disciplines of composition, focussing and lighting; the darkroom rituals of developing, printing and displaying.

And most rewardingly, the Final Exposure.

They sat on chewed-up furniture in the ruined lounge, drinking tea out of best china cups...at least, Granny and Betty did.

The wolf drank from an enormous bowl with DOG'S DINNER written on it, wagging its tail furiously when the biscuits came out.

'If you behave,' Betty said, 'you can have a *plain* one. He's not allowed in the kitchen,' she told Granny.

It was, without doubt, one of the biggest wolves Granny had ever set eyes on--big and gaunt and grizzled. It'd make two of Lukor.

'And how long has he been like this?' she asked.

Betty considered. 'I lose track. Since about Tuesday, I think.'

'No,' Granny said, 'I meant, how long has he been a werewolf?'

'Here, lads, take these and pass 'em round, will you?'

Rog. and Steve, booking off-duty, took the bundle of posters without looking at them. They intended splitting before that woman woke up and lodged a formal complaint.

Granny's photo glared down from the wall in the front office.

SUSPECTED ANIMAL-RIGHTS ACTIVIST/TERRORIST read the caption. HAVE YOU SEEN THIS WOMAN?

Rog. saw it, and went pale. Out in the yard, he unrolled one of the posters Sergeant Gilmore had given them. That face again...

'It's *her* isn't it, Rog? Think we should tell the Sarge we know where..'

'You out of your mind?' Rog. hissed. 'Just get rid of the pictures, and play dumb. We're in enough trouble as it is!'

'Hey, lads!' Sergeant Gilmore yelled from the front desk, 'Hurry up and bring her in, will you? She's putting me off my tea!'

'It all started with that coach-trip last year,' Betty said. 'Experience The Wonders Of Kravenia In 10 Days With Fully-Reclining Seats...and guess who wouldn't have his jabs? Or take his course of Lupizol before we went?'

The wolf, glaring, slurped up the last of its tea.

'Couldn't happen to you, could it, eh? Not our Kenneth!'

In a fury, the wolf overturned its tea-bowl, howling: 'WARG! WARG!'

'Well, go on, then,' Betty said, coldly. 'Do your worst! But I ain't calling you *that*, however much you show off!' She turned to Granny.

'Thinks he's Warg, the Night-Stalker. I ask you! Is that any name for a grown man?'

'This Kravenia,' Granny said, to dilute the atmosphere. 'That'd be Abroad, would it?'

'It would.' Betty sighed. 'Mysterious Land-Locked Realm Of The Werewolf, according to the brochure. Oh, and Beer-Toffee. Chief export, I believe. And it *would've* been a nice little break. Only that day up in the mountains, Kennikins here had to go and get himself bitten, didn't he?'

The wolf hurled itself at the shredded curtains. Granny was surprised there was anything left to swing on.

'Give this dog one of his beetroot sandwiches...and then we found out it wasn't a dog at all,' Betty concluded. 'Well, I tell you, it ruined the holiday. Can't claim on the insurance if you haven't had your jabs or taken your medication.'

'No,' Granny said slowly, 'don't s'pose you can, really.'

'One week's incubation,' Betty said, sadly, 'and then it was full moon. Missed the Beer-Toffee Fest, the Goat-and Beetroot-Roast *and* the Ethnic Gipsy Dancers, didn't he?...I'd to go to 'em all on me own.'

'Not a lot of fun, then,' Granny observed.

'Well,' Betty said thoughtfully, 'the swimming-pool was out--unless someone threw him a stick, that is...and he shed hair everywhere. But he *did* get to that Fancy-Dress party...and won first prize. Nobody could work out how he got his head off.'

'You *have* had a time,' Granny said.

Betty nodded. 'Don't I know it...I won't forget that journey home in a hurry. It was a nightmare. How our Kennneth avoided quarantine, I'll never know. Even in sunglasses and a baseball-cap, you couldn't do anything with them ears...'

Granny tensed herself for a anti-Kenneth reaction, but luckily the wolf, busily shredding a newspaper, wasn't listening.

'Once we got home and it wore off,' Betty said, 'we thought that was it...hah! Little did we know it was only the beginning. Next few times, I tried keeping him in...off his head with moon-madness, he was. Straight through the door and I mean *through* it...and off round residential Ampleshott...can you imagine?'

'So you moved somewhere quieter,' Granny said.

'We had to.' Betty said. The wolf had stopped shredding and was listening intently, head on one side. Silent tears flowed from the great yellow eyes as Betty said: 'Because that's when we realised--being a werewolf's not a one-off. It's forever.'

Aubrey snoozed blissfully on. Without Hilary to dig him in the ribs and remind him of his duties, he was free to dream--

When he surfaced, she wasn't beside him, which was odd, because she always expected a cup of tea and a compliment first thing in the morning.

He wandered downstairs, unable to enjoy himself because of a nagging feeling fate would catch up with him sooner or later. The house was unnaturally silent. Truffle greeted him cautiously, and Aubrey slipped her a surreptitious biscuit.

There was no sign of Hilary, and nothing out of place: as usual, he could have delivered a baby on that gleaming, sterile work-top.

He knew he'd pay for it later, but, for now, Aubrey intended taking full advantage of the situation. *He'd have a bacon sandwich. In the lounge. With his feet up on the coffee-table.*

He and Truffle were just settling themselves in front of the Test-Match, when Aubrey happened to glance outside. And what he saw put him right off his bacon buttie.

There she lay, his yoke-mate, in her nightie and curlers, flat out on the front lawn amongst the garden-gnomes. And a cluster of interested neighbours had gathered round to watch Mr. Johnson from across the road apparently giving her the Kiss of Life. And then the door-bell rang.

Hilary awoke with a monumental headache...and then realised that that perverted Mr. Johnson was *assaulting* her!

A good, hard kick in the rude bits soon *sorted* him out-- Aubrey, summoned by another neighbour, was just in time to help him, gasping and wheezing, to his feet.

'Well, really!' Mrs. Johnson snapped. 'Of all the ungrateful...! Percy's got a First-Aid certificate, you know! But then, what can you expect? 9a.m., and the woman's absolutely sozzled!'

And Aubrey realised with horror that she was probably right.

Hilary reeked of booze. Her...extremely short...nightie, now that he came to notice, was lager-stained. And she was surrounded by cans of the stuff. In fact, it looked as though she and the gnomes had had a heavy night of it...

'Well, now you've seen him,' Betty said. 'You still reckon you can help?'

'Not me, maybe,' Granny said, feeling her way to the door. 'But I think I know a woman who can.'

Sight, how could she have forgot about Mariander moving in?

All that Warg/Kenneth stuff had driven it out of her mind...well, she'd best get down there with some fish and chips, save her cooking.

Be funny having kin around after all them years. Somewhere along the line, she'd got out of the Family habit...came of not having kids, she supposed. Just so long as Mari left her some space, they'd get on fine. Because kin or not, she liked her own company best.

'Oh, it's you, is it,' Mariander said. 'Brought any old boyfriends with you?'

'If you mean Tobin,' Granny snapped, 'then no. I came to lend a hand...and brought us a bite of dinner. But if you're that way out, I'll go home and share it with Grufty.'

'No, hang on, Bryony...don't go.' Something caught in her voice. 'Let's find a place to sit down.'

It was difficult, but in the end Granny spotted two garden-chairs and pulled them out of the removal-van.

Three men were clomping in and out with boxes and tea-chests; Granny had never seen so much stuff in her life. She wondered if her sister'd chucked anything out, or just brought the lot.

Mariander sat picking miserably at her fish and chips, but it wasn't til she let her mind slip that Granny suddenly realised what an upheaval it must've been for her.

After all, she'd lived in that other house ever since she got married. And places, good or bad, were always a part of you, same as memories. How would she feel herself if she had to uproot after a lifetime? She cursed herself for not being a bit more welcoming.

'Eat up,' she said, 'and then I'm taking you down the caff for a nice pot of tea.'

Hilary Bottomley peered through a gap in the curtains.

Fish and chips on the front lawn, indeed! Her home was being de-valued before her very eyes! Not that she felt inclined to go and remonstrate, because she was still having the headaches.

And she hadn't ventured out since her public humiliation. She knew the neighbours were still sniggering, and as for Aubrey--! That faint, pitying smile every time she asked him to do the shopping or go to the Post Office--and the cruel comments. He really was getting almost rebellious.

'You're *sure* you wouldn't like anything from the Off-Licence, dear? Beer, lager? A bottle of sherry? Or how about a drop of *Gnome-Brew*--?'

He simply would not believe that she didn't drink. And neither, now, would anyone else.

If only she could remember what had led up to that dreadful scene on the front lawn. There were only fragments...she knew policemen were involved, and, she rather thought, a mouse chasing a wolf...?

But who in their right mind was going to believe any of that, when she didn't believe it herself?

'I'll be all right once I've settled in,' Mariander sniffled. 'It's just that everything seems a bit strange at the moment.'

'Well, it *is* a change from Inchester.' Granny re-filled their cups.

'At least it's more peaceful in the country,' Mariander said.

Granny thought back over the past few weeks, remembering all that business with the Warden and the Dog-Pound, and her re-kindled romance, if you could call it that, with Tobin, not to mention the werewolf roaming Bartleshire every full moon....'Oh yes, it's that, all right,' she said.

'About Tobin,' Mariander said. 'I'd no call to say what I did.'

'No, you hadn't.' Granny folded her arms. 'Reckon I'm old enough to make up me own mind.'

'Course you are. It's just that I ...dint want you getting hurt like last time.'

'Don't you worry about me.' Granny said it gruffly, hiding her feelings. Beamishes never had gone in for showing their soft side.

'So long as you know what you're doing,' Mariander said. 'I shan't say another word. Anyway--thanks for coming, Bryony.' She blew her nose, noisily. 'And now we'd best be getting back and see what them removal-men's broke. Thuja and Sepia's coming later, so you will bring Sham and Grufty over, won't you? I haven't half missed 'em.'

'Got a lodger as well,' Granny said. 'Quite a story *that* was...'

'Oh?'

'No, don't matter.' She somehow didn't think Thuja would approve of what had happened at the Pound. Very hot on Proper Guild Procedures, was Thuja. 'It'll keep. Plenty to tell you, once you're settled.'

She stayed until everything was unloaded and all the boxes in the right rooms. Mariander looked a bit happier once she'd found the kettle.

'Sign here, missus, just to confirm everything's intact.' The foreman handed Mariander a pen. 'And if you don't mind me saying, that's a lovely Treadwell vase you got there. I know a bit about these things. If you ever find a matching one, you'll be a rich woman.'

But Mariander, tired out, wasn't listening. She'd had enough for one day. She rested the invoice on a packing-crate.

'Sight, this pen won't write...'she looked as if she was going to cry. High time Granny was off home to feed the animals.

'Course it will, Mari,' she said impatiently. 'Just put your weight on it.'

Mariander stared at her, open-mouthed, and then wrote: M. BARNES. 10 stone 8lbs--

The village hall was crowded for the first Dog-Training session. Mrs. Clarkson, from the Haven Boarding-Kennels & Cattery was taking registration, and Perilla's elder son was sulkily setting out chairs.

John Hardy was telling everyone who'd listen what a waste of time it was him coming: no problem with *his* dog...Got him Right There...whereupon his short-haired Enska lunged at Mrs. Darnley's lap-dog, detaching enough fluff to fill a duvet.

Beatty Moore, towed helplessly into the hall by a muscular mobile hairball, threw her money down in despair. 'Never train him! Never in a million years!' she wailed, before taking off again like a novice water-skier.

All round the room, hackles were rising, tails swishing, growls swelling: harrassed owners were prising their dogs apart.

And in the middle of it all stood Granny, sweltering in her black coat, and worn-out before she started, and Grufty, intent on protecting her, whether she needed it or not. Mariander, busy unpacking, hadn't come, but Granny, unfortunately, had promised Perilla, and there was no getting out of it.

She was worn-out because of Grufty's new check-chain with the Big Links, as prescribed by Perilla. Grufty, unused to restraint of any kind, had bucked and bounded like an unbroken colt.Then he'd yawed from side to side of the lane, nearly yanking Granny's arms off. And she hadn't been able to get near his mind, because it had taken all her concentration to hold him as he'd skittered about in the mud.

Then just when he got going, he'd put all four brakes on.

But all that aside, she had to see Perilla, and tell her about Warg/Kenneth..well, more Warg than Kenneth, really...because, from what she'd seen, that werewolf was getting more out of control with every full moon. Apart from which, there'd soon be nothing left of SHEPHERD'S COTT...

Then Perilla herself, menacing in a black shell-suit and basketball-boots, and accompanied by her younger son...(the one she borrowed her clothes off? Granny wondered)...strode into the hall, and clapped her hands.

'QUIET!' she bellowed.

And every dog in the room fell silent.

'THAT'S BETTER!' Perilla roared. 'Now. We are here to train dogs in Basic Obedience, and that process starts as soon AS SOON AS WE ENTER THIS HALL.'

Fang, the Torvier, who aspired to territorial rights over the whole building, if not the whole village, cocked a defiant leg on Mrs. Clarkson's table. There was a momentary shocked silence, and then Perilla, snapping her fingers, bawled: 'MOP!'

Everyone looked at everyone else: eventually, someone handed their dog to a friend, and scuttled off to do Perilla's bidding. She was that kind of woman.

'RIGHT!' Perilla folded her arms. 'We will now learn to walk our dogs with DECORUM! And remember...you're the boss! Whatever emotions you're feeling WILL TRAVEL STRAIGHT DOWN THAT LEAD! Ready...dog at your left-hand side...handlers and dogs...forward!'

They must have circled that blasted hall forty times: it had been hot and tiring work. But funnily enough, there'd been no more growling or skirmishing, and after the first few minutes, every dog in the place had been walking sedately. Except Grufty.

But even he'd settled once Perilla had shown him up. He'd made a few optimistic lunges at the pretty, long-legged Salamar tripping along in front, and she'd rounded on him, teeth bared.

Perilla wasn't having that. Not in her class. Marching over, she'd seized Grufty's lead; whereupon he'd stuck his chest out and treated the Salamar to a she-knows-me-I'm-teacher's-pet grin, before being almost yanked off his feet.

'NO!' Perilla had bawled. 'LEAVE IT!'

Fang, though, had no intention of being forgiving and forgetting. He'd kept taking sneaky little nips at Grufty's dangly bits when he thought Perilla wasn't looking...though Perilla missed nothing...and when she'd moved him to the other side of the room, he'd whirled frenziedly round and round on the end of his lead, like a conker on a string.

But his small size had been against him, and once he'd exhausted his considerable store of energy, he'd had to content himself with pulling faces and growling under his breath.

And after a while, even he and Grufty had walked sedately, sat when told to and--the ultimate submission--laid down on command.

'HMM,' Perilla had said, eventually, glaring critically round the room,

'It's a start, I suppose. Bags of practise everyone, same time next week.'

As subdued dogs and owners filed out of the hall, a lot more slowly than they'd gone in...Granny managed to corner Perilla, who'd just lit a cigar, and explain about Kenneth's little problem.

'Wolf?' Perilla's eyes lit up. 'Big grey job, strong hocks, bit of a wimp?' She drew thoughtfully on the cheroot. 'Sounds like the one my ewes saw off a while back. Been wondering what'd become of it. 'Hey, Jeg!'

Perilla's younger son, wearing the back-to-front baseball cap that went with his mother's outfit, slouched over, swinging a check-chain.

'Yeah?'

'Bryony here's found us a real live WEREWOLF! What about that for a challenge, eh?'

'Cool,' the youth said. 'Train that, train anything. When do we start?'

'Well, I call that totally indefensible.' Chervil, Perilla's older son, brushed dog-fluff off his smart/casual jeans. 'What about Conservation, for a start? I mean, werewolves are an endangered species, aren't they?'

'Sight's sake, you two, keep your voices down!' Granny hissed. 'Poor thing ain't even come out of the wardrobe yet!'

'Oh, Tosh,' Perilla said, 'everyone's gone. Nobody here but us chickens! Got the jeep outside. Lead me to this creature of the night, Bryony...I shan't sleep til I've seen it!'

Crouched in the shadows with his tape-recorder, Bevis Tate cursed as the lights went out.

Never mind, he'd a good idea where the Grandmistress might be off to. And just as soon as he'd got that moped going, he'd be right behind her.

Granny turned to watch the single following headlight.

That man was starting to get on her wick. Fussy and flabby-minded--it was a mystery how he'd ever got as high as Mid-Master. Following her round, taking notes and pictures, didn't signify if it kept him out of mischief, because she could look after herself.

But getting close to that poor ole werewolf, who couldn't fight back, well...she really was going to have to do something about Bevis Tate.

'Well, well, well.' Perilla squinted into the rear-view mirror. 'I do believe we've got company...and it's that fussy old Midmaster Tate, if I'm not mistaken.'

'You ain't,' Granny said. 'He's after the werewolf.'

'Soon lose *him*.' Perilla put her foot down. 'Soft old bugger.'

'Speeding's dangerous,'Chervil sighed.'And swearing solves nothing.'

'Oh yes it does,' Perilla muttered, 'makes me feel a whole lot better.'

'Go on, Mum, give it some welly!' Jeg encouraged from the back seat.

They soon out-distanced the moped, but Perilla drove almost into Bartlesham before doubling back. She wasn't taking any chances because, as she said, Bevis Tate was the last person you'd let in on a secret.

They passed him, on the other side of the Brockway, pedalling frantically to get his machine going. Perilla, with a blast on the horn, shot through a nearby puddle at high speed.

'YES! Got him!' Jeg chortled. 'He's well wet!'

'I thought that was pretty anti-social, actually,' Chervil sniffed.

'Just whose side are you on?' Granny snapped.

'It's not a question of *sides*,' Chervil said. 'It's all about tact and negotiation and considering the other person's point of view...'

Perilla regarded her elder son thoughtfully. 'Ignore the little bugger, Bryony,' she remarked. 'He's Rebelling. Developing a Social Conscience, gets it from that College of his...anyway, we might've put old Tate out of action for tonight...but if I know him, he won't give up easily.'

'Bring a torch,' Granny warned, as they reached "Shepherd's Cott.. 'You'll need it.'

She noticed that Perilla had also armed herself with a rolled-up newspaper, which, for anyone else about to face a werewolf, might've seemed a touch inadequate. But then, Perilla wasn't anyone else...

They reached the back door just as Warg smashed through it at high speed. From inside, Betty could be heard screaming: 'Just you come back here, our Kenneth!'

Whereupon Perilla brought the werewolf down with a flying tackle, got him in a headlock, and marched him back through the splintered door.

She still played occasional prop-forward for Bartlesham Wenches, the team she'd founded, and it was obvious she'd lost neither speed nor weight.

Granny followed, Jeg, behind her, going 'Good one, Mum!' and Chervil muttering darkly about 'using violence to impose one's will on dumb animals.'

They didn't need the torch after all, because the kitchen was unexpectedly neat and well-lit. Betty, looking petrified, was cowering beside the freezer as Perilla scolded the wolf.

'Now *that*,' she was saying, brandishing the newspaper, 'was BAD.'

Warg, pressing himself into the wall, rolled piteous eyes at Granny.

'Well, come on, then, Big Boy!' Perilla barked. 'Let's have a good look at you! STAND! Show us your hocks!'

He glowered while she strode round him like a show-judge, lifting his tail, feeling his back, and studying his coat.

'Hmm,' she said, at length. 'Well-muscled, good stifles--bit over-sized for the Show-Ring, though.'

Granny blinked. Was she missing something? Did someone, somewhere, really show...? No, no, course they didn't.

'Now then.' Perilla tapped the wolf's snout. 'Open up and show us your choppers.'

Warg, backing away, gave a half-hearted 'Grr.'

'Who's afraid of the Big Bad Wolf, eh?' Perilla laughed heartily. 'Let's see if your teeth match your temper!'

Sulkily, Warg parted his lips. Perilla peered, blanched, and went 'Oosh!' in a shocked sort of way. 'Here, Bryony,' she said quietly, 'have a look at this.'

It was no wonder, Granny thought afterwards, that Warg's mouth was such a mess, what with eating houses--and you had to remember he *was* on his second...but it still came as a shock. Fair made you wince, in fact. He hadn't many teeth left, but what there were, and the state of his gums with all them splinters...!

Jeg was entranced by the werewolf. 'What's his name?' he asked.

In perfect unison, Betty said 'Kenneth' and Granny said 'Warg.'

'*Kenneth*!'The youth snorted derisively. 'What a dorky name! Warg, though, that's really cool...'Betty glared, and the wolf wagged furiously.

'Course, there's no excuse for Bad Habits,' Perilla was saying. 'And most of this is Pure Boredom. Training's the thing...not easy, but it can be done. Jeg, bring me some of those newspapers from the Jeep, there's a good lad.'

'And fetch Grufty while you're at it,' Granny said. 'Can't leave him out there all night.'

As Jeg came back in with his bundle, Warg suddenly released an almighty howl before sinking his teeth into the nearest wall. Wood splintered and plaster crumbled, releasing clouds of fine white dust.

Grufty, who'd gone swaggering in to see what was what, hid behind Granny as Perilla swooped on the wolf.

'NO, NO, NO! BAD!'And she whacked him across the nose with a rolled-up newspaper. Then she tossed him the bundle Jeg had brought, which he immediately attacked.

'Displacement, see,' she informed Betty, who was staring, open-mouthed, at the remains of her pine-panelling. 'Handy stuff, newspaper...distracts from the fixtures and fittings. Always keep some in! And remember, when you're breaking bad habits, Think Puppy! Or, in his case, ' she amended, 'Cub.'

Betty gazed helplessly round her former kitchen, the one room in the place she had, until now, managed to keep werewolf-free. She studied the fine coating of dust, the shredded newspaper-and-plaster-strewn floor, and then watched her lupine brother, busy worrying, with evident enjoyment, last week's headlines. He was not an inspiring sight.

'Thanks,' she said weakly, 'for the tip.'

'Told you I knew a woman who'd sort him out,' Granny said brightly.

'Well, now that he's occupied, how about putting the kettle on?'

Bevis Tate limped home, pushing the unco-operative moped. His shoes squelched with every step, as his anger grew.

Ostracize him, would they, humiliate and soak him through and ruin his tape-recording! And they were all in on it, whatever *it* was.

The Grandmistress and the Pearce woman *and* her brats...well he'd get at the truth, see if he didn't, and then have them all Struck Off--for Outsider Dealing.

Tobin shifted uncomfortably in Granny's easy chair, and woke with a start.

Sight, but his back ached! He'd never straighten up again. Hadn't meant to drop off, had he, but he must have been there hours, waiting. Never locked her door, Bryony didn't...he'd let himself in, thinking she'd gone down the garden.

He shivered: the fire had died down almost to nothing...best mend it, he might be there awhile yet. He could hear Sham whistling softly through his beak, and Krystle lay comfortably curled at his feet...which meant she'd taken Grufty with her. The thought reassured him.

He consulted his watch...where in the name of the Quests had Bryony got to til this time? Could she be...out with somebody else? A pang of jealousy shot through his vitals with a force that startled him, knowing he'd long ago forfeited any rights to jealousy...

No. He laughed at his own imaginings...she wasn't the sort, never had been. Wouldn't even go out with *him*, back in the old days, if she could have a night in by the fire, mind-wandering...Mariander, now, she'd been *quite* a different proposition...he'd go and check she hadn't died in the privy, then settle himself down to wait on her, however long it took. Because he'd something to ask her, and he wasn't taking no for an answer.

'...so you can see why we had to move,' Betty was saying. 'Can't hide a werewolf in the suburbs, can you?'

And you can in the country? Granny wondered.

'Just fell right, really. Patched the place up and sold it to one of them Housing Associations. Told 'em we'd been the victims of a prolonged and vicious hate-campaign...very sympathetic, they were.'

'And all he does is bite *things*?' Granny said. 'No maiming or killing?'

Betty snorted. 'Well what do *you* think?' The floor was knee-deep in shredded newspaper, and Warg, play-fighting with Jeg, was having the time of his life. Grufty, who never *played*, sat at Betty's feet, looking supercilious, and being fed biscuits.

'Him? Kill anything? With *them* teeth? Anyway,' she added, virtuously, 'he's vegetarian. We both are.'

'Ah.' That explained quite a lot.

They'd sat there a long time, drinking tea and talking over Warg's prospects. Perilla had only needed to rattle her newspaper once, when he'd seemed about to cock to his leg on the fridge, and after that he'd settled happily to his shredding activities.

'I must say, it's nice having five minutes without him biting lumps out of the walls,' Betty said. 'Mind, our Kenneth always has liked a newspaper.'

Jeg found a sponge ball in his pocket, and threw it at the wall. Warg fetched it back and, tail thrashing, dropped it expectantly at his feet.

'Well, I never!' Betty cooed, 'he's enjoying that, bless him!'

'Ace reactions,' Jeg said, 'for an old guy. Go on then, boy, fetch!'

'Oh, well, he played a lot of football in his younger days,' Betty said. 'Our Kenneth, that is, not Warg. Don't lose them skills, do you?'

Chervil, sitting primly on the least-battered chair, snorted as Warg caught the next one on the bounce.

'Come on, Jeg,' he snapped, 'he's not your pet, he's his own person!'

Jeg paused in the act of throwing. 'Oh, lighten up, Cherv.'

'But you're teaching him tricks that don't use a fraction of his intelligence!'

'You don't say.' Perilla watched the wolf galumph excitedly up and down the room, fetching and dropping the ball, and occasionally colliding with what remained of the walls and furniture.

'All right then, smartarse. Let's have *your* solution. Release him into the Wild so some busybody can shoot him for savaging litter?'

'*That'd* hardly be responsible, would it?' Chervil produced a card from his jeans pocket, and handed it to Betty. 'But you could at least get him some *expert* help.'

SHAPE-SHIFTERS' HELPLINE,

SUFFERING SHAPEISM IN THE WORKPLACE? DUAL-BIOLOGY AFFECTING YOUR SOCIAL LIFE? TROUBLE INTEGRATING YOUR ALTER-EGO? ONE-TO-ONE COUNSELLING, OR CALL NOW FOR DISCREET, SYMPATHETIC ADVICE.

ALL CALLS CHARGED AT LOCAL RATE.

'They're really good,' Chervil said. 'very hands-on, you know? They must be, because they've got an actual vampire on the team!'

'Give me that!' Perilla snapped. Fearfully, Betty handed the card over. 'Not you, Betty, *him!* Where did you get this garbage?'

'Off one of the guys at College,' Chervil said. 'His Dad's a Wraith.'

'And is he still one?'

'Well, yeah, only he's not so *isolated.*'

'Lot of good they did *him* then,' Perilla snorted. 'You've certainly got some funny friends, Chervil. You ought to stay in more...cowboy do-gooders!' She tossed the SHAPE-SHIFTERS card to Warg, who swallowed it in one gulp.

'I'm sure the lad meant well,' Betty said, anxious to make the peace.

'Some of us,' Chervil said, sulkily, 'care. And *some* of us,' glaring balefully at his mother, 'don't.'

'Yes, but you see,' Betty went on, 'this Helpline thingy wouldn't be a lot of use because our Kenneth chewed through the telephone-wire six weeks back. And it's not exactly the kind of thing you want to discuss in a call-box, is it dear?'

'Anyway,' Perilla said briskly, 'I think we'll stick with the Training. Betty, when he's Kenneth, what sort of person is he? Got to tailor the Programme to his personality, see.'

'Our Kenneth? Wouldn't hurt a fly,' Betty said. 'And once he's back to normal, he's nothing like Warg....runs around painting and plastering and patching up the damage--until next time...'

'So his wolf-week's the only problem then,' Perilla said. 'Hmm. That should make things a bit easier. Before we start, though...I'll have him round to the vet and get those teeth seen to.'

Warg, pricking up his ears at the word 'VET', rolled terrified eyes in Perilla's direction.

'Oh, yes, but...' Betty protested.

'And you mustn't worry about paying!' Perilla said, 'I'll take care of all that. I know things must be hard.'

'They are,' Betty said, 'and it's very kind of you, but it's...'

'What *are* you living on?' Granny interrupted.

'Well, the bit we've got left from the bungalow-sale,' Betty said. 'Course, our Kenneth had to give up his job...after all, who'd employ somebody who's off sick two weeks in four?'

'*Two* weeks?' Granny said, 'but I thought...'

'You know how it is,' Betty sighed. 'One week P.L.T., one week being Warg..'

'He could do a paper-round,' Jeg said mischievously.

'This vet's appointment,' Betty said, 'won't be necessary.'

'Eh? Why's that?' Then Perilla understood. 'Oh, I see. Last night of the full moon, isn't it?'

'Exactly,' Betty said. 'Tomorrow he'll be Kenneth again. And he can go to the dentist same as the rest of us.'

At the word 'DENTIST', Warg raised his muzzle and let out the most blood-curdling, heart-rending howl of his life. Granny paused outside what remained of the door, where Betty was busy sweeping up.

'How can you live like this?' she asked her.

'Couldn't do anything else, could I?' Betty said, indignantly.' Kenneth's me little brother, isn't he? And always will be.'

When she'd waved them off, she went back in to flop onto the one armchair with any springs left in it. It was a good job, for her own peace of mind, that she didn't see the black figure lurking in the shadows.

'Oh, not you again,' Granny said wearily. 'What you doing here, anyway?'

'Well that's a nice greeting, I *am* sure.' Tobin scratched Grufty's ears. 'And there's me been sitting here half the night fretting--where you been til this time, anyway?'

'Out on a wild wolf-chase,' Granny said.

Tobin blinked. 'Expect you'll explain that when you're good and ready. Meantime, there's something I wanted to ask you.'

'Not now, Tobin.' Granny helped herself from the teapot. 'It's been a long, hard day, and all I want is me bed. Whatever it is'll keep.'

'Fine, fine.' Tobin fingered the small velvet box in his pocket. 'Come back when you're feeling more receptive then, shall I?

'If you'd be so kind,' Granny said. 'Oh, and by the by, Mariander's moved into her new place...so if you come calling, you'll as likely find me up her place as here.'

'Oh, wonderful,' Tobin said gloomily. 'That'll be two of you bending my ear then, won't it?'

After her broken night, Granny slept late next morning, only to be woken by Perilla bawling up the stairs: 'Come ON, Bryony! Got to get that werewolf feller's teeth seen to! Need you to make sure he doesn't bolt!'

Course, Grufty hadn't barked. Perilla, Granny reflected sourly, would've made a very successful burglar because there wasn't a dog wouldn't welcome her in with its tail wagging...

Blearily, she struggled into clothes, and fumbled her way downstairs. 'I ain't moving til I've had me tea,' she said warningly.

Perilla, who was wearing skintight ice-blue jeans and a vast tee-shirt with JING VALLEY HUNT SABOTEURS RULE on the front, knew better than to argue.

'Tea's made,' she said. 'But we can't be long...got Kenneth a private appointment with my man in Bartlesham.'

'Well, he'll have a job on,' Granny said. 'Whatever's he going to think when he sees them teeth of Kenneth's?'

Perilla shrugged. 'He won't ask too many questions, so long as he gets paid. Anyway, from what I've seen, it'll be a matter of taking 'em all out and starting again...Improving on Nature, you might say.'

'Didn't young Jeg want to come then?' Granny asked as they climbed into the jeep.

Perilla accelerated up the lane. 'Nope. He's only interested in Warg, not Kenneth--and he hates dentists. Besides, somebody's got to man the Sanctuary phone, while Chervil's out on his protest marches...'

'Does he, er, protest a lot, then?'

'You name it. Against everything, Chervil is.' Perilla grinned.' Just like me at his age, so I suppose I can't complain. Totally opposed to this werewolf-training idea, of course...thinks it's cruel.'

'Well I don't go along with *that*,' Granny said, 'but how much use *will* it be? Can't cure him, can it?'

Perilla negotiated a particularly nasty series of potholes, before turning onto the Brockway. 'No,' she replied, her face unusually serious. 'Only wish it could. Unfortunately, once a werewolf, always a werewolf. But you've got to keep trying, haven't you?'

"Shepherds Cott." looked a different place. Not at all like the home of a werewolf. The splintered door had been boarded up, and someone had set out flowers-tubs and hanging baskets.

Pushing her way in to the kitchen, Perilla bellowed: 'MORNING! Anybody in?'

'In here, dear,' Betty called. They found her in the so-called lounge, sweeping up the previous night's debris.

'Where's the patient, then?' There was no sign of either man or wolf.

'Hiding,' Betty said tiredly. 'Petrified of dentists, is our Kenneth, under the bed. Second door on the right--and get ready for a struggle.'

'SILLY BOY!' Perilla was already on her way.

There came the sounds of a scuffle, followed by a series of loud thumps. Granny and Betty looked at one another.

'My money's on Perilla,' Granny said.

Betty shook her head in grudging admiration. 'Well, he's a big lad, and nobody's ever got him to the dentist yet...but I'm inclined to agree with you.

Moments later, Kenneth shambled into the room. He was a greying, big-boned man, wearing a rumpled cardigan, slacks, and tartan slippers, and he was sulking.

'Hate bloody dentists,' he moaned.

'Well, I'm sorry, but you're going.' Perilla, looking flushed, came up behind him and smacked his bottom. Kenneth winced. 'Fine Big Boy like you, scared to get his teethies done! Want to look handsome, don't we?'

'Don't care.' Kenneth collapsed onto the nearest reasonably intact chair. 'It'll *hurt*.'

'Not as much as this broom will if I get near you!' Betty shouted, startling everyone, herself included. 'For once in your life, Kenneth, be a man, not a...well! These people are here to help...and, God knows, we need all the help we can get! Besides which, if you *don't* go, I *will*! And for good!'

Kenneth looked stunned. 'You don't mean it, sis.'

'Oh, yes I do.' Betty folded her arms. 'I've Had Enough.'

The dentist's Surgery, in an area of Bartlesham Granny remembered from before it became fashionable, was extremely posh. Luxurious, even. There was a pot of coffee bubbling away, comfy chairs, and low tables with lots of glossy magazines on them.

Granny had just got stuck into an article about Rural Inbreeding, which turned out to be about turkeys, when Mr. Nash, the dentist, swept in. He bared exquisite teeth at Perilla, who crushed him to her chest, and they kissed, noisily.

'Peregrine! Mwahhh!'

'Perilla, my dear!' You're looking so....' he wrenched reluctant eyes away from her tee-shirted bosom, 'well. And where is this new patient you've brought me?'

Perilla turned to make introductions: Kenneth was nowhere to be seen. It was fortunate that she always carried an Army knife with a screwdriver-attachment on it, because it made dismantling the lock on the lavatory-door a whole lot quicker than it might have been if they'd had to send for a locksmith.

'Well, don't blame me!' Granny snapped. 'He doesn't half move quietly! Comes of all that creeping around at night, I expect.'

Mr. Nash was happy as an astronomer charting an undiscovered planet.

He called in his two colleagues, their assistants, and both receptionists to witness the devastation that was Kenneth's mouth. He was only sorry there wasn't room to include the waiting patients, especially the sweet-eating ones, and give them the fright of their lives. After a while, one of the nurses was despatched to fetch a Polaroid camera.

Kenneth lay, whimpering quietly as the dentist, humming to himself, probed and tinkered, giving his audience a running-commentary.

'Looks exactly like wood-splinters in the gum here, I'll just-- however did you manage that, Mr. er--?'

'Coccer. I kekt agging a go ag de cugoards,' Kenneth mumbled.

'Did you, indeed. And what about all these...er, plaster-fragments, are they?'

'Oh, yeah, weg, I gust ike ge taste og id.'

'Fascinating, fascinating.' Mr. Nash withdrew his implements. 'And the lumps of concrete?'

'I chew a lot of hard things,' Kenneth muttered.

'What? WHAT? Can't understand a word...open wide again, please...'

'I ched, I choo a lodda harg thigs.'

'Ah!' Mr. Nash beamed. 'I *see*! Ladies and gentlemen,' he intoned, 'what we have here is obviously a bizarre eating-disorder...'*Nash's Syndrome*. Perfect. He could visualise it in all the textbooks.'--and just *look* at the wear on these canines...'

And then Perilla burst into the surgery. 'Peregrine, there's nobody on the desk...' she began, then stopped dead.

'...*what* are all these people doing here? And why the camera?'

'I'm taking BEFORE pictures, of course.' Mr. Nash seemed surprised. 'After all, this mouth is the Dental Experience of a Lifetime-

'Never mind all that technical crap!' Perilla barked. 'Get them out of here! Can't you see he's terrified? My poor, brave boy,' she crooned, mashing Kenneth's head into her bosom, 'Perilla shan't leave him again!' The spectators melted under Perilla's glare. Mr. Nash eyed her uncertainly. But no, he couldn't pass up an opportunity like this. Not when he'd got the patient's mouth clamped open.

Sidling out of the door, he muttered: 'Excuse me a moment. I'm just off to fetch my camcorder.'

'Oh, gee gy guest,' retorted Kenneth, bitterly.

Kenneth, Perilla close behind, eventually staggered back into the waiting-room, a large hankie clamped to his mouth.

Granny, on her third copy of 'Yachting World'--nothing but boring boats, and not a laugh in it-...looked up. 'All right?' she asked.

To her surprise, there were tears in Kenneth's eyes. Through the handkerchief, he mumbled: 'Gey've all gog to cug oud! Whoever hearg og a werewulb wid no teese?'

'Not to worry,' Granny said, 'they do really good dentures these days.' He still had a long face, though, so just to cheer him up, she took her dentures out and held them up for his delectation. The waiting patients watched, enthralled.

'Go on, she urged,' pressing them moistly into his hand, 'Have a feel. That's craftsmanship, that is. Bet you never guessed these weren't me own, did you?'

Mr. Nash studied the Polaroid prints of Kenneth's mouth. *Nash's Syndrome.* It had a nice ring about it. With the right approach, he could do very nicely out of this patient.

There'd be lectures to the Royal National Dental-Guild, to which he'd immediately be elected a Fellow...the illustrated book, the video and the television series...and of course, there wouldn't be any nonsense about Patient Permission. The issue simply wouldn't arise because the subject, this whatsisname chappie, would be so flattered by all the attention, he'd co-operate in any way he could...he could hardly wait for the next appointment.

Summer disappeared in the course of a few days. Mist hung over a once-sunlit river, chilling the water and killing off the dragonflies.

Flowers stayed tight shut, damp, sheltering butterflies turned up in the strangest places, and the swallows, who couldn't be doing with the cold, took off in search of better weather.

It was, in fact, distinctly back-endish. Not that Granny minded, because she and her sister were planning to get busy Concocting. And there was so much more room in Mariander's kitchen.

Mariander, having run the herbalist's shop, had decided that a touch of commercialism wouldn't go amiss...nor would the extra cash.

'*Natural*'s the thing these days,' she informed Granny. 'Folks love it. Don't matter what's in your remedies, you can't fail so long as it's all *natural*. And the first thing we need is a Product-Name. Something snappy.'

'What, like Earwigs?' Granny suggested.

'If you ain't going to take this seriously...' Mariander said warningly.

'Well, pardon me for joking!' Granny snapped. 'Right, then. We'd best call it MARIANDER'S, same as the shop. Even if there *is* two of us...'

'No, I've got it!' Mariander cried. 'GRANNY'S! It's perfect! Honest and trustworthy, sort of thing. I'll do the Homoeopathics, and you do the Beauty...' grabbing a note-pad and pen, she started scribbling.

'We'll need proper printed labels--bound to be a local supplier...and nice little pots and bottles...'

'And lots of saucepans,' Granny said helpfully, 'big 'uns.'

'Oh, we won't need *saucepans*' Mariander said. 'That's old-fashioned.'

'Is it? What'll we use then?'

'We'll do it all in the microwave.'

'In the *microwave*?' Granny was outraged. 'Whatever happened to *natural*?'

'Oh, well,' Mariander said, airily, 'natural don't have to mean doing it the hard way, does it? Anyway, I'm off into Bartlesham, see what I can sort out. You coming?'

'No, ta,' Granny said, 'You're the businesswoman. Reckon I'll stay here and boil a few things up the *hard* way...anyhow, it's raining again.'

'So it is,' Mariander said in exasperation, 'and there's me not unpacked me winter things yet. Give us a lend of your coat then, seeing as you're staying here.'

'Keeps everything out, this does,' Granny said proprietorially, buttoning her sister into the old black coat.

'Yes, and everything in, too,' Mariander wrinkled her nose.

'You can always take it off again, you know.'

'No, sorry, I'm grateful, honest...it's just a bit...have you had *ferrets* in these pockets at all?'

'Only the once,' Granny said huffily. 'Doing someone a favour, wasn't I?'

Over the years, Mariander had found it best not to ask too many questions. And, in this case, to keep her hands out of her pockets.

The bus was late. After popping into 'Pennypincher', Mariander stood staring at the puddles and the grey sky, and wondering where Summer had gone.

But at least Bryony's coat was doing its job. The rank smell was strangely warming, a bit like packing your boots with manure. She looked up to see the bus approaching along high Street. At the same moment, a police patrol-car came out of Ridley's Lane and crawled past.

'Just a minute, Bob!' Even through the curtain of rain, the young W.P.C.'s eyesight was keen. Reaching into the glove-compartment, she pulled out a folder.

'Wasn't that...?' she studied the photograph intently. 'Yes, it was! Same coat, same hair...it *is* her! Don't lose her, Bob, she's A Wanted Woman! Just follow that bus!'

Bevis Tate, having, as he thought, followed Granny to the bus-stop, got it all on film. Even allowing for driving rain, bad light and the dripping hedge he was peering through at the time.

The Interception of the Bartlesham bus, the Boarding and the Arrest. Most gratifying, and he trusted that Grandmistress Beamish would now be incarcerated for a very long time.

He would follow the patrol-car, into Bartlesham, however, in order to confirm such a satisfactory conclusion. Stowing the camera away, he zipped up his anorak, pulled down his goggles, and began pedalling the moped into action.

Twenty minutes later, hopelessly thumbing a lift in the downpour, he gave the crippled moped a good kicking while it was down.

When he became Grandmaster, there'd be no more of this exposure to the elements, oh, no. He'd splash out on a vehicle befitting his status...a brand-new, state-of-the-art three-wheeler, no less.

'Gerroff!' Mariander shrieked. 'That's private!'

'Oh, yes, Madam?' Sergeant Gilmore said, with elaborate politeness, 'and what exactly have we got in there, eh? Gelignite? Fuse-wire? Bag of Semtex, perhaps?'

Mariander stared at him in amazement. 'Women's Things,' she mumbled, clutching her shopping-bag defensively.

The Desk-Sergeant sighed. 'W.P.C. Coles and W.P.C. Gray!' he shouted.

'Yes, Sarge?' The room was crowded with police, all staring at Mariander. She distinctly heard one of them whisper: '*Her*? You're *kidding*!'

'Take this...lady's Possessions next door and check 'em over. They're not, apparently, intended for my eyes.

'Right, Sarge.' They picked up Mariander's bag and backed out, still staring.

'Now then, Madam,' Sergeant Gilmore said,' let's get the rest of the formalities out of the way, shall we? Name?'

'That's for me to know and you to guess,' Mariander snapped. 'I'm sayin' nothing.' And sitting down, she folded her arms.

She couldn't fathom any of this. Why she'd been hauled off that bus and read her rights, what she was doing at Bartlesham Police- Station, why folks kept coming in and pointing at her...why them girls had looked at her like that--half-scared, half-respectful.

Why everyone had their minds on bombs, and, most of all, what they were all celebrating, because by the sound of it, there was quite a party going on...after another five minutes of people...waving streamers or blowing party-poppers...peering round doors and whispering, the two W.P.C.'s brought her bag back, and deposited it on the desk.

'Well, ladies.' Sergeant Gilmore rubbed his hands together. 'Checked the contents, have you?'

'Yes, Sarge.' They looked puzzled.

'Yes, and? Are we talking Incriminating Substances here?'

'Er, not exactly, Sarge.' W.P.C. Coles took the initiative.

'Well, secret compartments, then? Come on, woman! What *did* you find?'

They exchanged looks, and then W.P.C. Gray flipped open her notebook and read: 'In zipped side-pocket, purse, green leather, one. Mirror-compact, one. Lipstick, red, one. In main body of bag: Scouring-pads, packet of. Dishcloths: 3 knitted. Washing-up liquid: 1 bottle of. Pink rubber gloves--'

'Aha! I knew it!'

'...one pack of. Toilet-cleaner, one bottle. And potato-peeler, stainless-steel, one. That's it, Sarge.'

Into the ensuing silence, Mariander said: 'I *told* you. Women's Things.'

Rog. and Steve, on their way in with some paperwork, were agreeably surprised to find themselves grabbed and snogged by two young W.P.C.'s, wearing paper-hats.

It wasn't, as far as they knew, anyone's birthday, but there was music, and, even better, paper cupsful of alcohol going the rounds.

'Celebration!' giggled the policewoman who'd arrested Mariander. 'Haven't you heard? We've nicked the Bartlock Bomber!'

Steve spluttered. 'You what?'

'Yeah, she's at the front desk now! Never guess to look at her--'

But Rog. and Steve had gone pale and dashed off. The W.P.C. Looked suspiciously at the wine she'd just poured. Couldn't be *that* bad, could it?

'Psst! Sarge!' Rog. and Steve were hovering round Sergeant Gilmore's desk like flies over dung, and he couldn't be doing with them, especially as the Suspect seemed to be giving him the evil eye.

'Not now, lads, eh?' He swivelled his chair round and hissed: 'Go and have a *drink*! Big day for Bartlesham nick! Haven't you *heard*?'

'Yeah, but Sarge...'

'Bugger off!' He could feel a headache coming on.

'But Sarge, it's not *her*!'

'Don't be absurd!' The Sarge hissed back. 'How d'you know it isn't?'

'Er...smaller,' Rog. said.

'Yeah, and different hair,' Steve chipped in. 'Tidier. Y'know, permed. Anybody can *see* it's not her,' Rog. persisted.

'Not who, eh?' Mariander asked sweetly. 'Just who'd you think I am, eh?'...and then she caught sight of Granny's WANTED poster glaring down at her from the wall, and suddenly she understood.

So *that* was what Bryony had been getting up to, was it, alongside taking up with old flames--a wonder she hadn't got Struck Off years back. She'd be having a few choice words with her sister--if she ever got out of there, that was.

It took a while to get hold of Mr. Roach, the Estate Agent, but eventually he came and identified Mariander...a client was, after all, a client. He also confirmed that she'd spent the day of the Alleged Bombing in his office, tying up details of her recent house-purchase.

He scrutinised the WANTED poster. 'I can see why you thought...there is a *slight* resemblance...' he glanced at Mariander, and added, hastily, 'but, no, Mrs. Barnes looks *years* younger.' Mariander beamed.

'Of course!' It was Sergeant Gilmore's turn to beam. 'It's the coat!' He frowned at Granny's picture. 'Desperate-looking character, isn't she? Looks like some sort of bag-lady.'

'She does, don't she?' Mariander said, maliciously.

'Mrs. Barnes.' Sergeant Gilmore went into Acceptable Face of Policing mode. 'You are, of course, free to go, with our profoundest apologies...'

Mariander gave him A Look. He sighed. 'With a lift to wherever you were going?' Another Look. 'A cup of tea? Cakes?' She went on Looking. And, somehow, she was in his mind, giving it the mental equivalent of a Chinese burn.

'*Lunch*! Allow me to give you lunch! A car home! Compensation for Wrongful Arrest!' What was he saying? Mariander smiled. Smugly.

'And I don't suppose...and please remember, you *are* looking at the face of the Bartlock Bomber...you have any idea who this woman might be?'

Mariander studied the familiar features, the independent hair, and what could be seen of the old black coat. And she was tempted, oh yes. But then--she'd get her own back, however long it took. Just see if she didn't. Family was Family, after all.

'Sorry.' She shook her head. 'Never seen her before in me life.'

'--so I'll see you tonight, at dog-training,' Mariander said.

Bang went Granny's nice, quiet night in...but then, she could hardly refuse, because she'd been under an Obligation, ever since Mariander'd arrived home in that police-car, and she'd had to tell her all about the Dog-Pound and everything.

Not that Mariander had disagreed with the principle of flattening the place. It was being arrested and having her shopping-trip interrupted that'd got up her nose, although she'd a feeling there was more to *that* than Mariander was letting on, if only she'd been able to get past the smug smile and the mindblock...

And she could guess who'd taken them photos. There'd have to be a Reckoning with Bevis Tate before she was very much older.

Hilary Bottomley sat amongst the empty pizza-boxes, trying to remember.

The pizza-boxes were Aubrey's, as were the beer-cans, the fish-and-chip wrappers and the video-cassettes scattered round the room. Unwashed pots threatened to take over the kitchen; six pints of curdling milk stood on the doorstep, and dust sat, triumphant, on every surface.

Not that Hilary cared. She hadn't washed, dressed, combed her hair, because nothing mattered except remembering...

Dully, she'd seen Mariander being brought home in a police-car; it had somehow reminded her of...That Night. She couldn't help thinking there'd been a police-car in there somewhere...if only she could remember how she'd ended up on the lawn, amongst the beer-cans and the garden-gnomes. Where had that missing night gone to, and why?

Well, if it took forever, she'd remember, and then she'd be able to clear her name and hold her head up in the neighbourhood again...

Aubrey and Truffle had been making the most of things. Life, in fact, had been one long holiday. They'd spent quite a lot of time down at the woodyard, where Truffle had become something of a mascot, keeping up with the Test-Match. There'd been lots of walks, and Pub-lunches, and a shared takeaway every evening, after which Aubrey would make for the 'Rat & Pitchfork', leaving Truffle with a selection of chocolate biscuits and the run of the house.

Upstairs, happily releasing chicken-tikka scented burps, Truffle stretched luxuriously across Hilary's silk bedspread.

She could feel the first small movements inside her expanding tummy. And Hilary's bed, she reckoned, would be just the place to have her puppies.

Bevis Tate and two colleagues sat in the 'Rat & Pitchfork' lounge, sipping 'Tigerade' and plotting against Granny.

A public-house was not, Midmaster Tate felt, a morally or aesthetically ideal venue for the exchange of intelligences. However, on an evening which had declined into inclemency, it did boast lavatories...undeniably welcome after several hours crouching in wet shrubbery with a tape-recorder...and tables, which furnished reasonable, if somewhat restricted writing and chart-filling surfaces.

Acacia Barnsdown, who should have joined them, had been unavoidably delayed at the monthly meeting of the Chronic Ear-Wax Sufferers Group (CHEWSOC), which, on reflection was probably just as well, since she invariably misconstrued what little she did manage to hear, and went off in a huff. Easier by far to record the proceedings, and present her with two good copies.

'Your turn, I think,' said Ritro Bowers, indicating his empty glass.

'What?' Midmaster Tate paled. 'Already?' How could they drink so *fast?* Had he brought insufficient funds? And what if they demanded crisps?

'The, ah, correct terminology is, I believe, 'Your Round',' said Basil Worthenshawe, who'd once, long ago, been in a pub.

'Yes, and what's that other expression?' Ritro Bowers couldn't actually boast any public-house experience, but he had, many years ago, stood forgotten outside a beer-tent, whilst his father had socialised within.

'Oh, I know!' he said daringly, 'Get-'em-in, that's it!'

Bevis Tate sighed: there was obviously no avoiding the matter. Conspiracy was, apparently, thirsty work, and they'd each already indulged in half-a-pint of Dandelion and Burdock, plus a glass of Tigerade. Well, if it *was* his turn, it would also be his choice.

Slipping the leatherette purse from his pocket, he approached the bar.

'Yes, pal, what'll it be?' Barney Swallow wasn't holding his breath over three pop-drinkers clogging up two tables with their folders, charts and clipboards. He couldn't decide whether they were Trading Standards, Neighbourhood Watch, or just three sad old gits who'd come in out of the rain.

Bevis Tate considered. What was likely to be inexpensive? 'Three raspberry Teddy-Pops, my man. With straws.'

Barney Swallow opened the little bottles and stuck the straws in them.

'Anything else?' he enquired, with a sarcasm that was completely wasted on Bevis Tate. 'Umbrellas? Cherries? Pickled eggs? Change for the condom-machine?'

Bevis Tate flushed. 'No, thank you,' he said stiffly, handing over the correct money and snapping his purse shut.

Barney Swallow winked, horribly. 'Can't fool me! You lot's Out On The Pull, right?' He leered. 'Only you'd do better in the

Bar...it's Ladies' Darts night. Get lucky, and they'll have a whip-round for some *proper* drinks!'

Bevis Tate snatched up the Teddy-Pops, and bore them away. The arrant rudeness of the man, as though everyone on the planet craved alcohol! Indeed, he'd never even tasted the stuff, having promised Mother all those years ago that he never would, on account of Father's Little Difficulty--all right, Father's Rather Large Difficulty--the one nobody mentioned, but everyone knew about.

Oh, he'd heard the sniggers and the unseemly comments about Po-faced buggers who didn't know how to enjoy themselves, but he did not intend to react. Sobriety was honourable, and, besides, he'd got to ride the mo-ped home in a considerate and law-abiding manner.

Drainmaster Bowers was, he noticed, regarding his drink in a highly critical manner. 'I see you got the large ones, then,' he remarked.

Sniggering, Dancemaster Worthenshawe blew childishly down his straw until Midmaster Tate thought his head would explode with irritation. He'd had quite enough for one evening. Was not a public-house sufficiently mortifying without his Team displaying rebellious tendencies? A good thing indeed that they had *not* imbibed any alcohol!

'*If* we revert to the Agenda!' he snapped. 'Now, has anyone brought the highlighter-pen?'

They could hear the dog-fight right down Gallows' Drive.

Not that it lasted long. By the time they got there, Perilla had broken it up with her bare hands. She'd got two gargling bull-torviers suspended by their collars...no mean feat, considering their bulk.

'Stroppy little buggers!' Chuckling fondly, she dropped both from a great height before wiping blood and saliva onto her pink velour jodhpurs. The torviers slunk away to lick their wounds, and Grufty hid under the nearest chair.

'Don't change, does she!' Mariander hissed. 'Comes of playing all that rugby, I expect.'

Granny was surprised to see Kenneth and Betty sitting by the door: time for introductions.

The Hall was rapidly filling up with dogs and people. They bagged a couple of chairs, and sat down. Granny didn't think Kenneth looked very well...sort of sunken...until she realised that he'd had all his teeth out.

'Our Kenneth's waiting for his gums to heal,' Betty whispered. 'Perilla thought it'd cheer him up to sit in, see how it's done. You know, for when she's training him.'

Kenneth, however, sat hunched inside his cardigan, glaring into the middle distance, and, in fact, looking much more Warg than Kenneth.

'How's it going, then?' Granny asked matily.

A rumble rose from deep in his throat. Clenching his fists, he growled. 'Bastards!'

'Who are?'

'Them buggers down the Benefits Office. Waste of time!'

'Oh, shut up, Kenny,' Betty said. 'Give you another form to fill in, didn't they?'

'And what use is that, eh? Can't eat a form, can you?'

'Why not? You did the last one! That's why you needed another!'

''Scuse me,' Granny interrupted, 'but what's he on about?'

'Oh, didn't you know?' Betty said, scathingly. 'Mr. Big Bad Werewolf here has only applied for Disability Living Allowance!'

'You what?' Granny couldn't believe her ears. 'Not disabled, are you?'

'I am on wolf-weeks.' Kenneth lowered his voice. 'Can't work, can I?'

'Not even as a guard-dog,' Betty muttered.

'And me social life's down the pan. I ain't *fiddling*...only claiming one week in four.!

Granny felt reality slipping away. 'And what did they say, when you applied?'

'Oh, they reckon Lycanthropy's not a disability--how would they know, eh? But you can't reason with them people, so I'm re-applying. And once I've had me medical, they'll see I'm entitled!'

'Medical?' Betty said, faintly. 'You never mentioned that, our Kenneth! You can't just--oh, I give up!'

'And then,' Kenneth lowered his voice again, 'there's the P.L.T.'

'P.L.T.?' Granny said blankly.

'Pre-lunar tension. Over 90% of werewolves suffer, you know. Got a book about it from the library...dead interesting.'

'Yes, I bet it was,' Betty said. 'Pity you chewed it up before I got a look-in! I had to pay for that...on top of everything else!' Her voice had an edge to it, and her mind told Granny she'd had enough.

'HANDLERS AND DOGS!' Perilla roared, 'Heelwork!' And flashing Kenneth a saucy grin, added: 'WATCH and OBSERVE, Big Boy!'

Granny studied her thoughtfully, and as Grufty and Mariander stood up, shifted herself over to sit beside Betty.

'Don't you fret about things,' she whispered. 'Reckon I might have a good idea how to sort 'em out.'

'SEVEN TIMES, with two different men!' Bevis Tate thundered. 'And both of them Outsiders!'

He had an extremely carrying voice. Conversation ceased abruptly. In the bar, Kylie Rivers dart-throwing arm wavered. Even Mallory Gembert paused, glass halfway to his lips, and nothing had ever been known to come between him and his pint.

'AND there's ANOTHER ONE, as well!' Basil Worthenshawe could hardly contain himself. 'I've seen him round at her cottage! He's got a van with a hammock in the back of it!'

A fascinated hush hung over the bar, until someone sniggered: 'Bloody acrobat, eh!'

Bevis Tate glared: Barney Swallow gave him a thumbs-up, and went back to polishing glasses. After a while, interest lapsed and normal conversation resumed.

'So that's THREE of them!' Basil Worthenshawe whispered.

Bevis Tate tutted: he did it extremely well. 'Shameful! Shocking! Flagrant disregard for the Guild!'

Ritro Bowers tutted, too, and Bevis Tate beamed: solidarity at last!

'All accurately documented.' He shook his head sadly. 'Conversations, five. Clandestine meetings in, erm--Brimwold Crafts & Tearoom, one, and Rendezvous and motorised outing, destination, Bartlock Dog-Pound, one.'

'Is it possible that the Grandmistress is conducting--ah--relationships?' Basil Worthenshawe quavered. 'Because, under such circumstances, she could be Struck Off.'

'Indeed she could.' Visions of Grandmastership fuelled Bevis Tate's imagination. 'Oh, indeed she could.'

'What hard evidence have we actually got?' Ritro Bowers frowned at his notes, which, to him, looked rather sparse.

'Photographs,' said Bevis Tate, smugly. 'Tape-recordings. And witness-statements.'

'My word!' said Basil Worthenshawe, 'you *have* been busy! Witness statements, eh! From whom?'

'Well, er--' Bevis Tate consulted his notes. 'Number one, to wit, Enid Montgomery, Proprietress Brimwold Crafts & Tearoom, I quote: 'Yes that's Miss Beamish her what unblocked me sink...'further evidence of fraternisation there, I think you'll agree...'and that's that Bottomley chap him what lives in that funny pink cottage...'most definitely an Outsider, and, interestingly, her companion on that romantic little trip to Bartlock. And we all know what happened *there*!'

He still found it hard to understand why Grandmistress Beamish had not been arrested on the strength of those excellent photographs he'd sent to the Chief Constable. Still, one did what one could. And when one door closed...

'What have you managed to establish, Drainmaster?' he enquired.

'There is a Woman,' Ritro Bowers announced, '*another* Outsider, whom the Grandmistress seems to have been intensively counselling...'

'Ah!' Bevis Tate leaned forward. 'Further malpractice! Details, Drainmaster, and quickly...'

At which point Brassica Bray, crammed into a jungle-print dress and clutching a pint glass, erupted from Ladies' Darts night in the Bar.

'Well, if it ain't OLD TIDDLER TATE!' she roared, wobbling to a halt and treating him to a faceful of stale lager-fumes.

Bevis Tate reddened, Ritro Bowers baulked like a nervous horse, and Basil Worthenshawe's writing went all funny, as well it might, because a great deal of Brassica was, as usual, overflowing her nether garments.

Tiddler Tate, indeed! That insulting and totally undeserved nickname he'd never managed to outgrow....he opened his mouth to protest, and then thought better of it.

In her red plastic stilettoes, Brassica towered over him, her knotty, varicosed legs quite putting him off what was left of his Teddy-Pop. And, besides, she was still holding a dart.

Hitching up her bosom, she took a swig from her glass. Then, her eye falling upon the clutter of charts, graphs, notes and stationery, she winked lewdly at Ritro Bowers and chortled: 'That a stapler in your pocket, or are you just pleased to see me?'

Disregarding his blushes, she pulled up a stool, plonked her drink down and, with a cry of: 'Lesh have a look, then!' snatched at the pile of photographs.

After a few moments shuffling through them she let out a screech that silenced both bars for the second time that evening, and shattered three empty sherry glasses.

'HERE! These are all of BRYONY BEAMISH! What's going ON, eh? You some sort of PERVERTS?'

'Well, really!' Bevis Tate tried in vain to gather up the prints. 'There's no need whatsoever for...'

'GERROFF!' Brassica stabbed at his outstretched hand with the dart: she only just missed. 'I ain't finished looking yet! What's THIS ONE?--her SNOGGING OLE TUKESLEY?...her with SOME OLE GIT in a van...her EATING OUT with another one?...here, you buggers, you're SPYING ON HER, ain't you!'

'No, no, I assure you...' this time the dart thudded into the table-top, right between his fingers, as the pub held its collective breath.

'We're, er, compiling a book,' Ritro Bowers gulped. 'Life and Works of the first-ever Grandmistress...'

Brassica held his gaze for a long, cold moment: there wasn't a trace of inebriation in her eyes, and all at once, mindblock notwithstanding, he felt very worried indeed.

'Cut the CRAP,' she hissed. 'Think I fell out of the nearest TREE? It's sodding BLACKMAIL with you lot, ain't it! Can't handle us girls HAVING IT OFF with anyone, can you!'

The pub exhaled: this was good stuff, better than Ladies' Darts and the Match on satellite put together.

Bevis Tate cracked first. He'd always hated Scenes, ever since Father's Little Difficulty had arisen, and Brassica had always terrified him. But a getaway via her side of the table just wasn't on.

'HO, making a RUN FOR IT, are you, TIDDLER!' she roared, raking her stiletto across his shin. As he fell, he clutched desperately at his two colleagues, taking them along with three half-pint glasses and everything on the table, down with him.

Hitching up a skirt which had anyway only ever been a theoretical concept, Brassica leapt astride Bevis Tate and began beating him about the head with his own clipboard. After a decent interval, she started on the other two.

Spontaneous applause erupted along the bar.

'She's hard woman, is Brassica,' someone whispered.

'She is that,' someone else agreed, 'but she's fair.'

'Right, that's it!' Barney Swallow could move surprisingly fast when the need arose. 'You three, OUT! Take your rubbish with you, and don't come back! Bloody hooligans! You're banned!'

Trade was brisk after they'd left: quite a lot of it revolved around people buying drinks for Brassica.

Barney Swallow was just glad to get his tables back. He'd known them silly old sods'd be trouble, soon as they'd asked for straws.

'So I wondered,' Granny said carefully, 'if Kenneth wouldn't be better off up the Manse, even between moons? It *is* an animal refuge, after all.'

Perilla drew thoughtfully on her cigar. 'Sort of in-house training, you mean? Yes, could be something in that. I've a griffon and a couple of basilisks want sorting out, so he'd fit in. How about it, Kennykins?'

'Suits me.' He ran his tongue round his gums, and winced. 'If you can stand the damage when I get me new teeth.'

'Well,' Perilla snorted, 'we're certainly not house-proud! Can't be, with my lot around! What d'you think, Betty?'

'Mmmm?' Betty was stroking Krystle, who was gazing back in cloudy-eyed adoration. 'D'you know, you're just like my old Myrtle, you're a lovely old girl...what did you say Perilla?'

'Bryony's just suggested your brother shacks up with me,' Perilla said, shooting a look at Kenneth, 'and we'd like your blessing.'

Jeg sniggered. 'Really, Mother!' Chervil expostulated.

Betty carried on stroking Krystle. 'He's happy, I'm happy,' she said, 'and it certainly would save on repairs.'

'I'll drink to that!' Mariander opened a bottle of sherry. 'Anyone else?'

Perilla licked her lips. 'Better not,' she said. 'I'm driving. We'd better get Kenny's jim-jams and toothbrush--whoops, sorry! Lift home, Bryony?'

'No, you're all right,' Granny said. 'We're stopping here the night. Be good for Perilla, eh, Kenneth?'

He paused in the doorway. 'She's some woman, eh?' His eyes were alight, and he seemed to have forgotten the pain in his gums.

'Certainly is,' Granny agreed.

'Well, don't keep her waiting, then! 'Bye Bryony, Mariander, Grufty...Krystle.' Only Granny heard the longing in Betty's voice.

'D'you reckon he'll cope?' Mariander said when the jeep had roared off down Brimbleby Way.

'Cope!' Granny snorted. 'Course he will! Perilla's got him eating out of her hand! It'll give Betty a break, too...speaking of which…' Krystle lay snoozing at her feet. Gently, she probed the drowsy mind.

She's just like the one I had that went away, before I was…caught. She smells the same, and she's kind.

And you're sure it's what you want?

Oh, yes. You don't need me, not really. But she will, when she hasn't got the wolf.

'All right, then.' Granny patted the oversized stomach. 'We'll sort it out in the morning, eh?'

'What you muttering about, Bryony?' Mariander came in with a fresh pot of tea.

'Just thinking aloud,' Granny said. 'Got a low-cut dress, Mari?'

'You remember Bevis Tate?'

'What, him had a train-set in his front room?'

'Still has, so I hear. And never wed. Well, it's getting so I can't move without tripping over him. Got delusions of grandeur, that one, wants to wear the Grandmaster's robes…and he's getting a bit too close to Kenneth.'

Mariander shook her head. 'You've lost me. Where's this low-cut dress come into it?'

Granny looked her straight in the eye. 'I want you to distract him. You know, put him off the scent a bit. Go round his place and seduce him.'

'Go in and open a bottle of something, Jeg, while I show Kenneth round a bit.'

Perilla took Kenneth's arm and led him towards the paddock. Everything was bright in the glare of security-lights.

'Had to get the blithering things put in,' Perilla said. 'You never know who's about these days.' She patted his hand. 'Not very romantic, is it?'

'I…s'pose not,' Kenneth mumbled. They climbed over the fence, at least Perilla did. Kenneth went headlong, and she grabbed his hand, whispering: 'Steady on, Big Boy! Don't want to damage the goods, do we!'

In the paddock, there were...things...shifting and grunting and coughing, stirring uncomfortable memories at the back of his mind.

Down in the hollow, Horna and Quaather were trying to stay awake while Gimmer reminisced about sheep-dips of her youth.

'...shoved you *right under*, them up Bracknell's Farm! Fair took the itch off your hide, though, not like these here namby-pambies nowadays...' ...she broke off, scenting the air suspiciously.

Her sight might be going, but by crikey, there was nowt wrong with her sense of smell!...'Hecky thump!' she bawled. 'It's 'IM!'

Sleepy bleating erupted all around her: she sniffed again. She could *hear* the bugger now, an' all! Well, he wouldn't get away with it a second time! Her eyes glowed as red as in her youth...by heck, she'd got her mad up now!

'Wek up lasses! It's yon bastard tried to fleece us in us own paddock! Go for his dangly bits! CHARGE!'

Perilla sighed as Kenneth went down beneath a sea of mutton. He really was going to have to learn how to stick up for himself.

'How d'you mean, *seduce* him?' Mariander shrieked. 'I ain't that desperate, you know!'

'Take everything literal, you do,' Granny grumbled. 'Calm down and have a cupper tea. When I say seduce him, I mean more...flirt. Turn him in.'

'It's turn him *on*, I think you'll find,' Mariander said icily. 'Anyway, why should I? What's in it for me?'

'Self, self, self, I dunno,' Granny muttered. 'Can't you see what's going on? Wants me out, don't he? And there's plenty more ain't taken kindly to having a Grandmistress 'stead of a Grandmaster!'

'He can't do nothing,' Mariander objected.

'Oh, can't he? And who's going to stop him, I'd like to know? Hom's got his lovesick head on, and Texacum Powell don't want to know, what with his liver and all.

You've seen them WANTED posters with me on 'em--and now he's onto Kenneth. Word gets out that I been abusing me powers helping Outsiders, I'll be struck off quicker than wink!'

'Oh, Bryony!' Mariander said in a small voice, 'I hadn't thought!'

'Never do, do you,' Granny sniffed. 'Well, now's your chance to help sort things out before it's too late.'

'Oh, all right.' Mariander swigged down the rest of her tea, rather feverishly, Granny thought. 'See what I can do. That nice Sergeant Gilmore's taking me out to lunch tomorrow--save your breath, Bryony, 'cos I'm going...and I'm sure he'd take them posters down if I told him they're a constant source of embarrassment to me personally...but as for Bevis Tate, you can forget the low-cut dress, because I'll be wearing me cardigan. And me vest.'

Granny took Krystle round to Betty's place next morning, because a promise was a promise. Besides, Mariander was busy tarting herself up to go out with that policeman, and Granny never could be doing with all that titivating on account of a man.

The Dog-Warden's van was lurking at the end of Ridley's walk, with a female, presumably that Samantha, sat in it. So, they was starting all that again, were they!

The girl gave Grufty, who wasn't on a lead, a severe look...not that he cared. One of the wheels got his sprinkler-treatment, and then Granny, staring hard at the tyres, punctured all four, just because she felt like it.

'You'll be doing us a real favour,' Granny said, lying through her teeth, 'and she's really taken to you.'

Betty looked at Krystle and said: 'Oh, but I couldn't. She's yours.'

Krystle wagged her tail, and Granny wondered why it was some couldn't recognise devotion when they saw it...but then, that was Outsiders for you. Not the first idea what went on in folks' minds.

'No, she ain't mine,' Granny said, 'she's rescued. But she used to belong to someone just like you.'

'Oh, did she?' Betty brightened, and Granny felt the loneliness fall away from her. 'Well, if you think she'd be happy with me--here, I am awful, keeping you on the doorstep. Come in and have a cupper tea. And some cake, eh, Krystle?'

Krystle turned rheumy eyes upon Granny. *I'll never forget what you did for me, but…I think I'm going to like it here.*

When she took Grufty back round to Mariander's she'd already gone out, leaving a strong smell of scent behind her.

But blessed if there weren't a bunch of flowers in the hall, with a note attached. So when she'd put the kettle on, she polished her glasses and sat down to have a read. And blowed if they weren't for her!

The message, scribbled on a piece of torn-off card, was typical.

BRYONY/MARI SAYS YOU'D BE BACK SO THESE IS FOR YOU GET YOUR GLADRAGS ON I'M TAKING YOU OUT TO DINNER SEVEN O'CLOCK YOUR PLACE LOVE TOBIN.

Didn't give up, did he! You had to laugh really. She screwed up the note, and unwrapped the bouquet.

Oh, Sight. This was serious. Yellow Bracksweet, with deep red Angel Blossom! And every Seer knew what *that* signified!

They went to a new place out Shamford way. 'The Garden of Eden', it was called, all done out with proper trees and vines and great big flowering shrubs.

There seemed to be a lot of screeching and squawking going on up in the treetops, like in the jungle. It was hot as a jungle, too, and Granny was soon wishing she'd left her vest off. Sunlight came through a domed glass ceiling, and real butterflies flittered about. One of them rested for a moment on Tobin's head.

'Symbol of love, that is!' He squeezed her hand.

Oh, dear. She did hope he weren't going to get all soppy and spoil things. Course, his mindblock was on, strong as ever, so she couldn't tell if he was kidding or not. But then, you never could with Tobin.

The food was all right, but the crockery and cutlery weren't up to much. The place didn't seem to have any plates, which surprised Granny because it looked busy enough to have afforded them.

They got their main course served in sort of clay bowls, the pudding came in hollowed-out coconuts, there were bones to eat with--although Granny made a fuss and got a proper knife and fork--and they had to drink out of sort of scallop-shells.

What was worse, they couldn't've paid the staff much, because none of the waitresses had proper uniforms--some of 'em wore a few rags and a lot of beads, and the rest of 'em had to make do with skirts made out of straw! And not one of 'em had a pair of shoes to her name!

Tobin was good company, though, and he had her in stitches with some of his Outsiders' tales. When they'd done eating, they went through into the 'Castaways' Bar', and sat in deep wicker chairs that made Granny's hips ache.

Tobin lit his pipe, and Granny filled her pockets with monkey-nuts from the bowl on the table: wasn't often she got chance of any.

All at once, Tobin sat upright, straightened his tie and coughed. He'd got a sort of pained expression on his face, as if he had indigestion. Oh, Sight. Any minute now, he'd ask her to Be His Girl.

'You enjoyed yourself, Bryony?'

'Yesh, ta,' Granny said through a mouthful of monkey-nuts.

'Good, I'm glad. Because so have I--more than you'll ever know. And I got something to ask you. I got money, Bryony, I'm comfortable. But money ain't everything, and...I'm lonely. I was a fool letting you go the first time, and I ain't about to let it happen again.'

He took a small velvet box from his pocket, and opened it. The tiny, perfect shimmerstone glowed pink with its own inner fire.

'The flowers said it. Marry me, Bryony. What'd you say?'

She put the kettle on, emptied the monkey-nuts into a saucer, and sat down to think.

The place seemed empty without Krystle, and even Thomas was out somewhere...just when she could've done with someone to talk to. Well, that'd been her evening upset, and she hadn't had an inkling, not even when she'd seen them flowers. Why hadn't she?

Sight knew, she hadn't wanted this. She should never have let things get this far...and yet. Part of her couldn't help thinking how nice a bit of company would be of an evening. And she wasn't getting no younger...but was that a good enough reason for taking on a husband?

Why was it all or nothing with men? Leastways she'd managed to put him off, for the time being.

Summer's End, I'll give you your answer, she'd told him. And til then--just friends, eh? How did it go?

Your blood and mine mingle as wine
Corn on the stalk and fruit on the vine...at Summer's End.

She'd learnt that at Guildschool: funny how some things you never forgot. And so, she'd got a few weeks' breathing-space...and a whole lot of thinking to do.

Bevis Tate straightened his blotter and surveyed the fruits of his organisational capacity.

Six chairs. Six pen-and-pencil sets. Six rulers. Six rubbers. Six neatly-typed agendae sheets...and six empty chairs.

Still, they'd be here soon, his fellow-conspirators, not at all deterred by that unfortunate fiasco in the public-house. And he'd maintain overall control of the proceedings, because this time he'd got the correcting-fluid. And the highlighter pen.

When he thought of what he'd endured for The Cause! All that lurking in the village-hall, amongst the play-group equipment! He could still feel the hobby-horse in his groin, the pile of easels threatening his ankles and the wendy-house pressing into the small of his back.

All that precarious balancing with one foot on top of the brick-box in order to position the tape-recorder! How they would marvel when he played back the Grandmistress' conversation with the Potter woman and her werewolf brother!

And how long had it taken him to escape from the cupboard after the Grandmistress had mindlocked it! He had suffered poster-paint all over his trousers and what must surely have been the contents of the sand-pit inside his shoes! He was indeed a martyr to the cause.

So, she had discerned his presence and mangled his tape. Fortunate, then, that he'd had the presence of mind to substitute another, secreting the original in his deepest pocket!

Evidence. It was evidence of the most damning kind...enough to convince his colleagues and, thereafter, The Guild.

The doorbell rang. At last! Stepping carefully over the double width railway-track that looped around the carpet, he went to open the door.

And then froze upon hearing the female voice calling: 'Coo-ee! Anybody at home? Let us in, Bevis, there's a good lad! I'm freezing in this dress!'

It was a few years since Granny had been up to the Manse, but it still calmed her like nowhere else she'd ever been, except mebbe the Guildenhall.

It had something to do with the sun on the brickwork, with them old trees and hedges and paths, but more than anything, because this was a place for animals. They were everywhere. Even as she stood, a pair of flamingoes stalked past, apparently on their way down to the lake, followed hungrily by something hairy, with tusks.

'I'm watching you, Roger!' Perilla barked. 'Get back in your bed and leave 'em alone!' To no-one's surprise, Roger did.

'Well!' Betty breathed, 'our Kenneth's certainly fallen on his feet here! Is he behaving himself, then?'

Perilla hesitated, which wasn't like her. 'Matter of fact, Kenny's not having too good a time of it,' she said. 'First night here, the ewes sat on him.'

'What?' Granny gasped, 'when he weren't even Warg?'

'Fraid so. They can smell the wimp in him. They pick on him.'

'Always been the same,' Betty sniffed, 'specially at school. I was the one had to wade in and sort him out.'

'Well, he won't get that here,' Perilla said, 'nobody's got the time. He'll just have to toughen up. Anyway, let's go and find him. Bit early in the day for the hard, I suppose...drop of home-made lemonade go down all right?'

The great entrance-hall was gloomy after the brilliant sunshine. There was some sort of vulture perched on top of a suit of armour, a family of ferrets sunbathing on the window-seat, and a colony of bats hanging, fast asleep, from one of the pelmets.

'So how's the training going on?' Granny asked.

Perilla, surprisingly, pulled a face. She wasn't normally the type to admit defeat.

'Thing is,' she said, 'getting 'em all together. Warg's nocturnal, of course, and so are the griffons, as I'm sure you know.'

'Well, no, I didn't,' Granny admitted. 'Where did you find?'

'Well, dumped, of course! Unwanted Christmas pets. It's the old story, people just don't *think.* Buy 'em as eggs, hatch 'em out in the airing-cupboard, and there you are, cute as can be. But then before you know where you are, they've sprouted teeth and claws and started roosting on the furniture. Not to mention the damage they do with their beaks...and then there's the broken nights. Ever heard a griffon's call, Bryony?'

Dumbly, Granny shook her head.

'My two are litter-brothers,' Perilla went on, 'poor little buggers. Take a lot of time getting 'em right after what they've been through.'

'And how about the other one,' Granny said, 'the whatsit, basil-thing?'

'Ah, the basilisk! Now he's a different proposition.'

'Was he dumped as well?'

'Oh, yes. People think they'll make good guards, and then get upset because they're silent, and they stare. But that's what basilisks do! It has to be said, they're not the most responsive of creatures, but they're cheap to feed. Fortunately, this one's open to bribery--pocketful of gravel and he'll walk to heel beautifully.'

Granny's head was spinning. Five minutes in Perilla's company always left her feeling as if she'd been at the parsley-wine.

'Gravel,' she said. 'I see.'

'Well, of course, gravel!' Perilla said scornfully. 'After all, he's only a pup! Can't expect him to chew boulders, can you?'

'Ah, so that's what that video was about, then,' Betty said absently.

Perilla turned. 'You what?'

'The one our Kenneth borrowed. Said I wouldn't enjoy it because it was a Man's Thing, whatsit, Hardcore Movie. All lorries and diggers and that, I expect. Very boring. I'm glad I gave it a miss.'

'Quite,' Perilla said briskly. 'Well, let's go and see what your Kenneth's been getting up to today, shall we?'

Mariander wasn't getting fobbed off again. She'd barely got over Bevis Tate's doorstep before he'd shoved her back out again.

All red and flustered he'd been, and muttering something about expecting friends...as though he'd got any!...unless they were coming round to play trains--but the sitting-room door'd been open, and she'd seen enough to confirm Mariander's suspicions.

Mariander could recognise a good plotting-and-planning set-up when she saw one. And what had really done it was them big, blow-up photos of her sister...same as the ones at the police-station.

She'd forgotten it was market-day. No wonder 'Susan's Pantry' was so busy. Not that it mattered, because she needed a bit of time on her own.

She was lucky enough to get a window-seat and, having placed her order, sat watching the bustle and thinking things through.

It wouldn't pay, she decided, to underestimate Midmaster Tate, who was a lot more dangerous than he looked. In which case, a lot more subtle approach would be called for if she and Bryony were going to sort him out once and for all…she was startled out of her reverie by someone banging hard on the window. A hideous vision stood on the pavement, grinning horribly and waving its arms about.

Oh, no, it couldn't be…she closed her eyes.

'MARI, you TIGHT-ARSED ole SOW! Buy's a CUPPER TEA, eh?'

Warm, gin-soaked breath blasted her face. She could hear the clashing of large, vulgar items of jewellery and smell that cheap, sickly scent. But it was no good--you couldn't get rid of Brassica Bray that easy, because she had a way of filling a room all by herself.

She opened her eyes, reluctantly, to see her standing there, wearing a short leatherette dress, fishnets, and a ton of make-up.

'Hello, Brassica,' Mariander said weakly. 'I'd ask you to join me, only there's no room.'

'Course there is! She'll SHOVE UP, won't you MISSUS?' The woman seated opposite Mariander sprang to her feet, recoiling from Brassica's overpowering presence, grabbed her handbag and threw some money on the table.

'It's all right!' she burbled. 'I was just going!'

'Well, if you insist, ta very much!'

Brassica crammed herself into the vacant seat, rested her ample bosom on the table-cloth, and lit a cigarette.

'SLUMMING IT THEN, are we?' she snapped her fingers at the waitress. 'SAUSAGE BUTTIE WITH A EGG IN, when you're READY!'

'Sight's sake, Brassica, put that cigarette out!' Mariander hissed. 'And keep your voice down! Folks are looking!'

Brassica glanced around. 'You're RIGHT!' she chortled happily. 'THEY ARE!' But she stubbed the cigarette out (in Mariander's saucer), produced a small mirror-compact and began re-applying blood-red lipstick.

Mariander felt her cheeks burning. It'd always been the same, and even knowing that Brassica had a heart as big as Bartleshire didn't make you want to be seen with her.

'I've moved back to Brimwold,' she said, hoping it would be enough.

'You WHAT? After all that TIME AWAY?' Brassica bawled. 'You must be POTTY!'

'Bernard died,' Mariander said simply.

'Oh YEAH, I'd heard you was a WIDDER.' Brassica wasn't the least bit abashed. 'Still don't know why you want to bury yourself in that dead-and-alive hole though--NO NIGHT-LIFE, is there? And no men with LEAD IN THEIR PENCILS, know what I mean?'

'I'm afraid I shall have to ask you to leave, madam,' said a polite voice at Brassica's elbow. 'You're upsetting my customers.'

Mariander glanced round: a haughty-looking woman stood there, quivering with indignation.

'Oh, YEAH? And WHO are YOU?'

The woman's bosom quivered. 'I, madam, am Susan. The Management.'

'HO, REALLY. Well, I ain't leaving til I've ET ME BUTTIE.'

'That is unfortunate, Madam.' Susan leaned forward and hissed: 'And tough. Get back among your own kind, you raddled old scrubber!'

Mariander's stomach lurched as it regretted the lunch it wouldn't be getting. But sharing a table with Brassica tarred her with the same brush, and she'd no option now but to leave as well.

'Come on, Brassica.' She stood up and gathered her things together. 'Best go somewhere you can shout to your heart's content and nobody'll notice--how about the 'Wormwood Arms?'

'Dint wanter eat in your poxy cafe, anyhow.' Brassica shouldered her plastic handbag, and waddled out with all the raddled dignity of a mature woman wearing spike-heeled shoes and clothes forty years too tight for her--and only Mariander saw the tears in her eyes.

The Public Bar of the 'Wormwood Arms' was packed. Unfortunately for Mariander, they didn't do food, unless you counted pickled eggs, because food interfered with serious drinking.

Brassica slapped two pints of sweet cider down on the table.

'So what brings you to town, then?' Oddly enough, and despite the noise, she didn't shout on her own territory.

Mariander sighed. 'I'm...calling on somebody. Guild-business.'

Brassica eyed her keenly. 'It's on account of your Bryony, ain't it?...your block's slipping. Don't worry,' she added kindly. 'Bound to happen at your age. So who's this person you ain't so keen on?'

Mariander took an experimental sip. The cider wasn't actually too bad if you drank it quick. 'Remember Bevis Tate?'

'Old Tiddler! Do I ever! Used to be one of them Environmental Health Buggers when I worked behind the bar here. Bloody pain in the backside, he was--still is, come to that.'

Mariander's hackles went up. 'You've seen him recently?'

'Had a run-in up the 'Rat' with him and his playmates the other night. You know they've been spying on your Bryony? Meant to tell her, only I've been a bit busy...what they after her for?'

Mariander sighed. 'It's a long story.'

Brassica leaned forward. 'Well I ain't going anywhere.' She checked her watch. 'Not while later, anyway, and he'll wait 'cos he's a regular. So fill me in. You never know...mebbe I can help.'

Mariander drained her glass. The cider seemed to be filling the space where her lunch should have been.

'All right, then,' she said. 'You fancy another, Brassica?'

They found Kenneth in the stable, knee-deep in manure. He was wearing a red teeshirt bearing the legend: THE MANSE, P.L.C....GIVE TIME. GIVE MONEY. GIVE SANCTUARY. He looked tanned and fit and happy.

'Aha!' Perilla beamed. 'Not only mucking in, but mucking out!'

'You all right, Kenny?' Betty asked anxiously. 'I've made you a cake, and there's some letters come today.'

Kenneth discarded his shovel, which slid down the wall, and fell over with a resounding clang. In the shadows at the back of the stable, something stirred

'Settle down, Hercules!' Perilla bellowed. 'I'd come out of there if I were you, Kenny. He gets tetchy if he's disturbed.'

'Ooh, you do as she says, Kenny!' Betty, ready for anything, was clutching at her shopping-bag.

'Carthorse, is it?' Granny felt the ground shudder as something large and angry advanced purposefully towards them.

'You don't want to know,' Perilla said firmly. 'Let's go and have that drink.' Behind them, a terrific thud shook the stable, and part of the roof fell off.

They went along a courtyard and back through a long hallway. Betty stared, open-mouthed: Granny knew how she felt. It was all do with them big old paintings and the wood-panelled walls and the parquet floors--and yet, somehow, it wasn't *grand*.

The whole place was Old Money, and Perilla could've lived the high life all right--if she'd wanted. But Granny knew that she wasn't that sort. Couldn't settle if she wasn't giving something back.

There were birds and animals and things you couldn't begin to guess at everywhere, because Perilla wouldn't't've had it any other way, and yet there wasn't any mess...

She turned, winked, and then, as though reading Betty's mind, which of course she was--said: 'We've got a working-agreement. I don't turn 'em away, they don't foul the premises. Seems to work.'

'Is this *all* hers?' Betty was gawping at a couple of hairy creatures hanging from

one of the chandeliers by their tails, apparently fast asleep.

'Been in the family generations,' Granny whispered back. 'This is only part of the house...West wing, I believe...Perilla always says it's a bugger to heat--and there's acres of land. She nearly sold up once, when her husband run off, but that ain't Perilla's style. All credit to her, though, she's reared them boys and made a go of the place...'

At the last count, Granny recalled, there'd been a Riding-School and stables, a Garden-Centre, a Farm-Produce Shop, and some sort of Field-Centre for the Guildschool kids, all on top of the Sanctuary. It was the Sanctuary had really caught folks' imagination, though, because Perilla never turned an animal away.

She'd been on the telly, and in all the papers, appealing for volunteers, and got so many she'd had to have all them special teeshirts made. And then there'd been folks sponsoring animals and suchlike…

They sat in a sun-filled conservatory fronting onto the Garden-Centre. Perilla opened some biscuits, and started pouring glasses of lemonade, but soon had to delegate because her mobile-phone kept ringing.

Betty gave a small scream as a sort of animated hosepipe sucked the biscuit out of her hand and disappeared under the table with it. Luckily Perilla saw it happen.

'AMELIA! You naughty girl!' Chuckling at the expression on Betty's face, she shoved the mobile-phone away somewhere inside her teeshirt.

'Just can't stop snaffling, can you! Come on out of it!'

And she hauled out something still reminded Granny of a hosepipe, only with four legs and a pair of beady black eyes. Perilla scratched its back.

'Anteater, technically,' she said, 'except that nobody's told *her*. She can't stand ants…gobbles everything else, though.

Kenneth was opening the mail Betty had brought. The first letter apparently pleased him no end.

'Got a date for me medical!' he whooped, startling Amelia, who hoovered up the rest of the biscuits and disappeared under the table.

'Oh, Kenny! You ain't going on with that Disability nonsense, are you? Betty said crossly.

Perilla touched his hand. 'You don't have to you know, Kenneth,' she said quietly. 'You're already more than earning your keep here.'

'But I want to! Can't you see,' he said pleadingly, 'that a man needs his bit of independence?'

'Well I still think you're barmy,' Betty mumbled.

'Anyway.' He smiled at Perilla. 'She's a right slave-driver, that one! Come Wolf-weeks, I'll be glad of a rest. Get an allowance, at least I'll have a bit of cash to enjoy it with.'

Oh, yes? Granny thought. *Doing what? Going down the Rat & Pitchfork?*

'So when is this medical?' Betty asked. 'Only I'll press your suit. The one you didn't chew up,' she added unnecessarily.

Kenneth glanced at the letter. 'Awhile yet,' he said, 'it's the twenty-thir...oh, bugger.' He paled beneath his tan.

They looked at one another. 'Don't tell me,' Betty said. 'It's your Wolf-week, ain't it. Well, they can change the appointment, can't they?'

Kenneth glanced at the letter, then shook his head. 'IF YOU DO NOT KEEP THIS APPOINTMENT,' he read, 'YOUR APPLICATION WILL BE CONSIDERED INVALID. NO CORRESPONDENCE CAN BE ENTERED INTO REGARDING YOUR CLAIM.' He screwed the letter up into a very small ball. 'Well that's it, then.'

'Yes but, hold on,' Granny objected. 'If you're applying for disability...stop me if I'm wrong...on account of being a werewolf, well, *won't they want to see you while you are one?*...or am I missing something here?'

'She's right, you know,' Perilla said.

'Yes, but...' Kenneth began, 'I can't just stroll into the Bartlesham Benefits Office being Warg!...they got a NO DOGS sign, for a start!'

'He means,' Betty explained, 'that somebody'd cry wolf. And like as not, shoot him.'

'Only one thing for it then,' Perilla said. 'I'll have to go with you, Kenneth, speak for you, be your, well...handler.'

'Sort of like a guide-dog, only the other way round,' Granny said helpfully.

'Well, if you can get him in and out of that place without him chewing it to bits, good luck to you,' Betty retorted.

'Least I'll be able to have a go,' Kenneth said cheekily. 'This other letter's from the dentist. I'll have me new teeth by then.'

'I've always liked you, Brassica,' Mariander hiccupped. 'Folks have mis-judged you.'

'Like you too, Mari,' Brassica replied, 'even if you are kin to a Grandmistress.'

'Ne'er mind,' Mariander said, 'you're just as good as me, and don't let anyone tell you different.'

'So you're a widder,' Brassica said, 'Although I heard he was an Outsider. How's them girls of yours these days?'

'Well, course, they're grown-up now,' Mariander replied. 'Thuja's a teacher, and Sepia's a doctor. And there's grandchildren, boy and a girl.'

'Must be nice,' Brassica said. 'I was never blessed, meself. Well, I did have a baby once, but it died on me.' She laughed bitterly. 'Bloody thing went to sleep and didn't wake up.'

'Oh, Brassica, I never knew. I'm sorry.'

'Don't be. I was only a kid. Good job it happened.'

'Here, no, Brassica...you don't mean that.'

'Oh, but I do. Look at me. Ain't cut out for motherhood, am I? Anyway, what's past is past...let's have another drink, eh?'

Mariander watched her make her way to the bar...poor Brassica. No need to ask about that teddy-bear tattoo on her arm...

They'd had a surprisingly good time. 'The Wormwood Arms' certainly was a lively place.

They'd played a game of darts with two of Brassica's 'gentlemen', and had a go on the pool-table. And then there'd been a gang of rowdy lads being rude about Brassica's bum until she'd beaten them at arm-wrestling, which had meant free drinks all round...

'Well come on then, Mari!' Brassica said. 'Let's go get that Bevis Tate! Jew know he got photos your sister?'

'Oh, yes,' Mariander said, grimly. 'I'll be wanting a little word with him about that.

Brassica grinned. 'Hey, Baz!'

The landlord went on polishing the special Saturday-night baseball bat he kept under the counter. 'Yeah?'

'You got one of them paranoid cameras we could borrow?'

Baz considered. 'Well, yeah, only it's a bit unstable, hur hur!'

'Not much bloody use then,' Brassica snapped.

'Joke!' Baz said. 'Joke! You want it, I'll fetch it.'

Five minutes later, armed with notebook, pen and camera, Brassica and Mariander lurched out onto Dowell Street, and soon after that, they were banging on Midmaster Tate's front door.

Bevis Tate blinked uncomprehendingly at the two giggling, hiccupping women on his doorstep. Even without his glasses, he could see that one of them was falling--most indecorously...out of her dress, and the other apparently suffering from some kind of vertigo.

What did they want? Women didn't come to Bevis Tate's house. He never knew how to *talk* to women. Were they selling something?

'Afternoon,' said the one with the chest. 'How's life?'

'What...' he found some sort of voice...'can I do for you ladies?'

They spoke simultaneously. 'Raffle-tickets.'

'Sponsored blanket-knit.'

'Ah.' Money seemed to be required. 'I'll...go and fetch my...'

'What?' said the semi-dressed one. 'Not gonna ask us in?' She pouted like a peevish goldfish. 'And there's me without me cardi.'

'Well, really, I...'

'Takes a while, sponsoring,' said the wobbly one, veering dangerously close to his precious potted Andomis plant. 'Need to sit down while you're doin' it. And anyway, it's for the Illis Preem Infirmary.'

'I suppose you'd better come in, then.' He felt a moment's annoyance that someone else had been Organising behind his back. Sponsored blanket-knit, indeed! Why hadn't he thought of that? Strange, these women surely reeked of alcohol! Perhaps they needed it in order to keep on knitting?

They settled themselves in his sitting-room: their presence making him uncomfortable. Well, the sooner he gave them whatever it was they'd come for and got rid of them, the better.

He found his glasses, put them on, and immediately recognised the bosom overflowing what had always been Mother's chair...and of which Mother would definitely not have approved.

'I know you!' he snapped. 'You're that Bray woman who hangs around Bull Alley...er, or so I've heard. You were up at Brim Knap when the Grandmaster Passed On. And...' he blushed scarlet, 'You were in that dreadful Public-House during the week! And as for you...' the other one was gazing intently at the photographs around the wall, 'you're Grandmistress Beamish' sister! Am I expected to believe that the two of you are out doing Good Works for the Infirmary?'

Mariander bridled. 'And why,' she snapped, 'shouldn't we be?'

Bevis Tate looked from one to the other. 'I, erm, well I suppose...'

They were staring fixedly at Edna thc inflatable warthog, currently occupying a small chair by the window, until he got round to mending her with the puncture-kit. Why hadn't he put her away, out of sight?

He flushed again, whereupon the women snorted like a couple of overheated sows, and collapsed, giggling, into Mother's cushions. Disgusting. He'd have to disinfect the lot when they'd gone.

'Nah!' Brassica sniggered, once she'd got her breath back. 'Course we ain't! Not today, anyhow. But we heard you was lonely-'catching the warthog's eye, she choked on the words.

'--so lonely you'd got photos of me sister plastered all round your walls,' Mariander finished. And suddenly she wasn't laughing any more. 'Just like the ones at Bartlesham Police-Station. And I want the negatives,' she concluded.

'Um. Um.' He hadn't expected this. What could he say? He thought he'd been careful. How much did that cursed Grandmistress know?

Meanwhile Brassica, who never could sit still, and who moreover had a raging thirst on her, was off in search of a cup of tea. Bevis Tate was too pre-occupied to notice her opening the dark-room door until she upset the tray of chemicals with a resounding crash.

'You stupid woman!' he howled. 'You've let the light in!'

'Ooh, BEVIS!' Brassica bawled, 'come up and show us your enlargements...

'And then let's see what develops!' Mariander snorted.

'Now look here!' Tukesley Meredith would never have allowed this...this undignified innuendo. 'I must ask you both to leave. Or else I shall be obliged to call a policeman.'

'Why not get that nice Sergeant Gilmore?' Mariander smirked. 'Good friend of mine, he is. And I bet he'd be very interested in your...inflatable friend over there. Just hand over them negatives, along with all the rest you got of Bryony, and we'll go quietly.'

'This is preposterous!' Bevis Tate snorted. 'You force your way in here, making far-fetched demands...'

'Oh, I wouldn't say they was far-fetched, exactly.' Brassica had emerged from the darkroom, 'would you, Mari?'

'No, I wouldn't.' Mariander smiled sweetly. 'I'd say they was more along the lines of blackmail. Ready, Brassica?'

'When you are.' She moved faster than he'd have believed possible, pinning him to the chair... he felt himself suffocating under the weight of her bosoms...and, oh no, she was kissing him with her gin-stinking lips...

'Say cheese!' The flash unit went off before his horrified eyes.

'Very good! Now let's have a few more,' Mariander was saying, 'and yes, with the warthog, different angles, please, Brassica, and more leg...come on, Bevis, wet those lips...pout, and SMILE! Try and look as though you're enjoying yourself!'

He screwed his eyes tight shut, and the last thing he saw was Edna's insufferable, rubbery grin...when the ordeal finally ended, she released him and he lay for a long time with his eyes shut, fighting for breath.

'Here y'are!' Mariander was prodding him in the chest. 'Cupper tea!'

'Looks as though he needs it,' Brassica said. 'Hey Bevis, wake up and get a load of these!'

Reluctantly, he opened his eyes, sat up, and with bad grace took the proffered cup and saucer. Brassica waved the polaroid prints at him.

'Good, ain't they! You could've made an alternative career in Porn Movies, Bevis!'

The thing was, as he kept telling himself whenever the memory of those photographs came back to haunt him, that it wasn't the way it looked. *He* knew that, and so did these two tormenting women...but unhappily, he had to admit, the rest of the world didn't.

Brassica's face wasn't visible in any of the pictures, but his was...set in a mask of terror, which, to the uninitiated would look remarkably like ecstasy...

'All right,' he growled. 'I'll get your wretched negatives. Since you insist.'

'*And* all them prints,' Brassica said. 'Once worked with a photographer.' She treated Bevis to a broad wink. 'As I'm sure you've deduced. And even *I* know you can start again making negatives out of prints...'

'Gosh, Brassica,' Mariander murmured, 'what a good job you come along.'

When Granny got home, there was *another* ruddy enormous bunch of flowers from Tobin...Larksweet, this time. Really, she was running out of things to put 'em in. Have to be a milk-bottle again.

She hadn't told Mariander about the Proposal, because she knew what her reaction'd be. And also because the GRANNY'S homoeopathic remedies were going well...she and her sister made a good team. No point rocking the boat.

But she almost wished she *had* said something, because she couldn't half have done with a sympathetic ear...someone who'd listen without judging.

There was another note, too: FERNS IS GREEN/AND LARKSWEETS WHITE/ GET THAT KETTLE ON TONIGHT.

Wasn't bad for Tobin!--almost poetry! Didn't sound as if he was giving up, though. But then, did she want him to?

'I'll just take a look in your back room,' Brassica said. 'Well well, and what have we here?'

'I do a bit of modelling,' Bevis Tate said, sulkily.

'What?' Mariander pushed her way past, ' Artistic stuff? In the nuddy, you mean?'

151

'Nah,' Brassica said, 'he just faffs about with ships not in bottles, and bits of stone and that...whoops!'

Midmaster Tate covered his eyes. 'You haven't!' he moaned. 'Not my Bartlesham Cathedral matchbox!'

Brassica laughed unpleasantly. 'Course I haven't! But I will, if you don't hurry up and remember where you put them negatives!'

'Well, nice doing business with you.' Mariander smiled as the flames curled the last of the celluloid. She picked up her handbag, ready to go.

'Just a minute!' Bevis Tate snapped. 'Aren't you forgetting about your side of the bargain?'

'What? These photos?' Brassica shoved the polaroids down her cleavage.'I think mebbe we'll just hang onto these a bit longer...til we can be sure you're trustworthy, sort of thing.'

'And until you leave our Bryony alone,' Mariander added. 'No more spying, or stirring things up. And, make no mistake, we'll be watching you.' Her mind drilled the words into his. *And You'll never be Grandmaster, neither. Do I make myself clear?*

Bevis Tate ground his teeth, knowing he was beaten. For the time being. Mother had been right all along: you simply couldn't trust women.

'Anyhow,' Brassica winked, 'Pleasure doing business with you. Give us a call on me mobile if you fancy a quickie...here's the number.'

Mariander dug him playfully in the ribs. 'She means it, too! Do owt for a tenner, Brassica will! And I do mean <u>owt</u>!'

Bevis Tate couldn't believe it: hope surged within him. Perhaps something could, after all, be salvaged from this disastrous evening.

'In that case!' he called hoarsely after Brassica's disappearing form, 'would you consider concluding the grouting above my kitchen sink?'

Gibbous moon, and the Wolf-Patrol is back on duty in the Panda car, down by the water-meadows.

The back seat's littered with cola-cans and pizza-boxes, and Steve's poring over a list of previous wolf-sightings, trying to discern a pattern.

'Seems to like being around people.'

'Yeah, right.' Rog. aims the stun-gun through the open window, and narrows his eyes. *Is that an owl over there? Looks like a vulture!*

'So I reckon we should be patrolling towns and villages.'

'Whatever...I'll have it this time!' *He will, too.* 'Cos you know what I think?'

'Huh?'

There is *something. Definitely.*

Stalking along the riverbank, underneath the trees. Breathing hard and drooling with blood-lust and snapping twigs with its huge, clawed paws...he closes the window just in time to save himself from the large black-and-white cow lumbering by to relieve her sudden thirst. Glaring at him balefully, she pauses to scratch her rump on the car-bonnet, demolishing one of the headlights in the process.

'I reckon,' Steve continues, oblivious, 'that our wolf was hand-reared and released back into the wild. But its cub-memories are strong and it keeps returning like...salmon crossing oceans to spawn.

Rog. regards him sourly. 'You've been watching them wildlife programmes again, haven't you.'

The moon is full, boring old Kenneth left at home, and Warg is up and running, well, galumphing, anyway. The night is his.

Or maybe not, because here comes Killer Calhoun, silent as a tracking stoat despite the big black boots. And tonight's the night--he's going to have that werewolf, just see if he don't, because it's High Moon.

Warg, oblivious, is chasing his tail, stupid with moonlight and never a sniff of danger.

The Bounty-Hunter shuns moonlight, hugging the shadows. He does Skulking very well, born to it, really. Him and the Night are One, sort of thing. Blodwyn lies coiled in his fist, lest the moon betray her presence. Not as that one'd notice--easy tracking. No contest, and no fun at all.

Warg is rolling in a cow-pat. Luxuriating in its feel and smell and texture, he is spreading his substance about his person, according to ancient memory, so as to share it with the Pack upon his return.

Which, in his case, means Betty, who will be considerably less than enthusiastic, but he'll worry about that later.

For the time being, everything Betty and that Perilla don't like, he's gonna do, so there! BIG BAD WOLF, eh!

As he rolls and tastes and gobbles...full of nutrients, cow-dung!...the Bounty-Hunter wrinkles his nose in disgust.

Phorr...smell him from here, can't he, disgusting habits some folks have. He fingers the skinning-knife: need a damn good scrub that pelt will, 'fore he can send it off to the Lab...best take him now, while he's busy...

But the werewolf, startled by a shifting cow he thinks is about to attack him, is up and through the fence...not over it, through it...and off down the road, leaving Killer Calhoun, cursing and stumbling, to negotiate the nettles and cow-pats and follow the trail.

Couldn't miss them big manurey pawprints, though, even without the moon. Straight down the lane and into the village, and that's bad because you never know who'll be watching. But no-one is as he creeps onto Main Street, and there's the werewolf-- but what's the ffaffyn thing doing? Call hisself a wolf? Bugger that size oughter be ripping the throats out of livestock, not the guts out of litter-bins!

Warg's in his element, tearing up paper, gobbling down leftovers, flattening aluminium cans, being BAD. These new teeth are the best things ever happened to him! Yep, he reckons he might tackle the odd tractor-tyre now that he's got 'em, mebbe even mangle that wrought-iron gate outside of the Smithy...

Blodwyn's ready and tingling, and there's no-one about. There'll never be a better time. Now. Gotta be now, while its head's in the bin and its teeth are occupied. He'll stick it with the knife so's Blod can get its neck, because Killer Calhoun never takes chances, which is how he's survived so long...

For once in his life, though, Warg gets up and moves, and that's what saves him. Not that he's built for running as such, but he does manage a bit of a bound once that smell gets in his nostrils.

Right through the bottom of the bin, stronger than anything, it comes swirling. But it's not the reek of danger that he smells, or even the stench of approaching death passing across his nostrils because, werewolf or not, Warg doesn't do Instinct.

It draws him just the same, though, and as the Bounty-Hunter steps out of the shadows, he goes for it--straight down Main Street towards them chips.

Tobin came round, as promised, and Granny put the kettle on.

Then they sat opposite one another in the fireside chairs, and Merged. Merging was, strictly speaking, frowned upon by the Guild, unless you were wed--but Granny figured she and Tobin were a bit old to be bound by them sorts of rules, and anyway, who was to know?

When dusk fell, their mental streams flowed and diverged and mingled into something far more exquisite than physical lovemaking....and as the sun rose over the Beechwood, Tobin lay back in his chair and smiled.

'How was it for you, Bryony?'

How was it? The best and the sweetest she'd ever known. But she couldn't tell him, because that wasn't her way. Granny got up slowly. Her legs felt wobbly.

'Weren't too bad,' she said, grudgingly. 'In fact, I think I better put the kettle on.'

Mariander came home with the milk, and a thumping headache.

155

Another of Brassica's gentlemen had given her a lift, held her upright and waited courteously until she'd located her keys, the door and the keyhole and fathomed out how to connect two out of three of them.

And all the time Brassica had sat in the car making loud, ribald comments about folks what couldn't hold their drink. Then having seen her fall safely over her own doorstep, they'd roared off down Brimbleby Way, with Brassica shrieking goodbyes.

Hilary Bottomley awoke to the sounds of slamming, shouting and hooting.

Why was everything so *noisy* in the country? If it wasn't the dawn-chorus, it was cattle mooing, tractors ploughing or church-bells clanging every fifteen minutes…really, mornings had never been like this in the city.

Irritably, she yanked the duvet off Aubrey's half of the bed, trying in vain to recapture that dream she'd been having, involving a wolf and--two policemen with a gun…and then she remembered. Everything.

They'd *shot* her! That's what they'd done! There she'd been, assisting the police with their enquiries, and they'd shot her, planted her, like evidence, in the front garden, and abandoned her to the neighbours!

Right, there was going to be Trouble now. She'd sue the lot of them, and they'd all be sorry. She'd be straight off to Police Headquarters, and complain, preferably to the Chief Constable himself. And Aubrey could take her.

She'd been nudging and hissing for a full minute before it occurred to her that he wasn't there. Indignation swelled in her bosom…how *dare* he be absent when she needed him!

Snatching her dressing-gown, she went downstairs to confront him. There was a strange, rhythmic noise, not unlike a motorbike engine, coming from the lounge. But Hilary wasn't scared. She could cope with anything now. She was strong again, much more like her old self, and she wasn't going to be intimidated by any intruder…

She flung the door open, and an astonishing sight met her eyes. On the settee, legs in the air, swollen tummy uppermost, lay Truffle. And beside her, *with his shoes on,* and clutching an empty whisky-bottle, was Aubrey, unshaven, fully-dressed and snoring like an adenoidal pug.

A fug of smoke hung over everything; in fact the whole room stank like a low-class bar. And the mess! Well, if this was what happened when she had a few off-days, some firm discipline was needed!

And the television was on! A video was playing...Aubrey had the cover in the hand that wasn't holding the whisky bottle. She peered at it. TRADE SECRETS it was called.

With mounting horror, she forced her reluctant eyes towards the screen. A young couple, the man wearing nothing but a peaked cap, were doing something very rude indeed. In black and white.

'OOH, Mr. Postman,' the girl moaned, throatily, 'bring me your special delivery!'

She searched frantically for the remote-control, but it was nowhere to be seen. Not only could she not switch the beastly thing off, she couldn't even turn the volume down! Well, Aubrey was going to suffer for this!

She felt quite sick. Better let some fresh air in before she did anything else. Flinging the curtains open, she blinked. As if she hadn't enough to contend with, there was a bus parked outside next door. And what looked like a coach-party of chattering women getting out of it.

'Run and get the camcorder, Nathalie. We must record this moment for posterity.'

Mr. Nash arranged the dentures on the small velvet cushion. When it was done to his satisfaction, his assistant filmed him making his entrance into the surgery, and presenting them to Mr. Potter.

Mr. Potter appeared overwhelmed.

'And what the *blithers,*' Perilla exploded, are *these*?'

Mr. Nash was wounded. 'Designer-Dentures,' he explained. 'Last a lifetime. After all, you *did* say money wasn't a problem.'

157

'I know.' Perilla prodded the teeth. 'But hang it all, Peregrine, there's such a thing as *taste!*'

Kenneth's dentures were a masterpiece in plastic, porcelain and gold. With inset rubies, carnelians and emeralds. The sort of item that stuck in the memory. And just the kind any first-hand witness would be able to describe with no trouble at all. Even in the dark.

'You! Driver! Get this bus out of my neighbourhood! And what on earth are you women doing here?'

Hilary Bottomley found herself being scrutinised by three stout, imposing women. She had that same uncomfortable feeling as when she'd first met the Mariander Woman's sister.

'What's it to you?' said the largest, sticking her chest out like a pouter-pigeon.

'I live next door!' Hilary snapped. 'Not that it's any of your business! And Brimbleby Way is an Exclusive Executive Development, not a coach-park!'

'Ooh, hark at her!' said one of the others, who had her arms full of carrier-bags. 'Madam hoity-toity!'

Hilary felt a hot flush starting. It was at times like these that one's husband should have been there, defending one.

'Anyway.' They turned away dismissively. 'Ain't got time to stand here chatting. Got to get in there if we want the pick of the goods!'

'Am I to understand,' Hilary said faintly, 'that my next-door neighbour is...selling things from home?'

'Sight, *you* don't know much, do you?' snorted the one with the carriers. 'Homoeopathic Beauty Products & Remedies! She and her sister make 'em. Ain't you heard of 'GRANNY'S?' Well, nice meeting you, gotta go. Our Mariander's expecting

'You mean--'Hilary gasped, 'that you're all *relatives*?'

'Just us three,' said the biggest one. 'Sisters-in-law, ain't we. The rest's friends and neighbours we've rounded up.'

And so saying, Zinnia, Begonia and Poinsettia marched off down the drive after the rest of the party.

'Ooh, Kenny, you do look a picture.'

Warg rolled his eyes piteously, baring his new teeth in a snarl.

The dentures fitted perfectly. What didn't fit, however, was the coat Betty had knitted him. It was made of orange mohair, it restricted the movement of his tail, and it itched.

'You'll be getting a chill on your kidneys now that the nights are drawing in,' she'd told him, lovingly fastening the matching ribbons round his tummy and under his chin.

Perilla, trying not to laugh, ignored the mute appeal in Warg's eyes.

'And very nice too.' She nodded approvingly. 'Just right for his medical. NO! STOP that biting! You'll unravel it, silly boy!'

Chervil, who was preparing to spend the night up a chestnut tree, demonstrating against the proposed new ring-road, furled his SAVE OUR NUTS banner and muttered:

'That's right! Take his freedom, take his dignity, break his spirit and dress him up like a toy poodle! Not,' he added hastily, 'that toy-poodles are any less valid than wolves...'

'Oh, yes, Chervil.' Betty rooted about in her shopping-bag. 'I almost forgot.' The ski-hat was a perfect match with Warg's coat.

'Had a bit of wool left over,' she explained. 'Well, try it on! Keep you nice and warm while you're out protesting!'

When Betty had gone, wishing Kenneth all the best for his medical, Perilla undid the ribbons on the mohair coat. 'Don't worry. I think,' she told him,' that we can lose this monstrosity somewhere between here and the Benefits Office--make a nice nest-lining for some cold little bird, don't you think?'

'Mrs. Bottomley.' Sergeant Gilmore swallowed hard. 'I've been expecting you...what's that you say? Slow down please!...there's a horrid big bus parked outside your property and you want it moved NOW?'

He began to doodle, savagely. For some reason he kept drawing a woman with a dagger buried in her neck.

'*If* you'd care to look outside, I think you'll find that the vehicle in question has now departed. How do I know? Because, Madam...' here Sergeant Gilmore permitted himself a smirk...'Mrs. Barnes has *permission*. 'Pardon?--permission to use the area as a dropping-off and picking-up point. Some of the ladies on board,' he added, reproachfully, 'are *disabled*.'

At which point he had to hold the receiver away from his ear. 'Well, really, there's no need to adopt *that* tone. I *very* much doubt you could have seen the passengers fighting their way off the bus...are you questioning that charming Mrs. Barnes' integrity?'

Picking up his pen, he embellished the doodle with a stake through the heart and a noose round the neck. There was a short, delicious silence, and then she started again. Sergeant Gilmore sighed.

'Trading without a licence? Not my department, I'm afraid...*and* a formal complaint? By all means. One of my officers did *what* last week?' He tapped the telephone to get rid of the sudden interference. 'Could you repeat that?'

He felt one of his migraines coming on. He was getting too old for all this public-relations stuff. He was going to have to lie down. And stay lying down until this woman had been, given a statement, and gone.

'Then I'm afraid you'll have to come down to Headquarters,' he said wearily.

'I fully intend to!' snapped the voice in his ear, 'just as soon as my husband has sobered...I mean, finished carpeting the outhouse.'

'You can't bring that dog in here!' The receptionist was young, and very pretty. Warg bared his dentures in an ingratiating smile, and offered a paw. The girl recoiled from his jewel-encrusted grin.

'It's not a dog,' Perilla explained patiently, 'it's a wolf, and only a quarter of one at that...he's a whatsit...lycanthrope, theriomorph...anyway, he's here for a medical.'

'The Veterinary Centre,' said the receptionist, firmly resisting Warg's charm, 'is on Lower Kinegate.'

Perilla sighed. 'Warg Potter, 10a.m.'

The girl scanned her appointments book. 'There's only a *Kenneth* Potter,' she said frostily.

'Oh, Sight, I haven't time for all this!' Perilla snapped. 'Got a pedigree Larrupino buffalo to groom before teatime! Come on, Warg, we're going in! HEEL!'

'You can't go in there!' The girl wasn't quick enough. Warg cocked a triumphant leg on the reception-desk in passing. The doctor, scribbling on a note-pad, didn't look up.

'Take a seat, take a seat, with you in a moment,' he mumbled.

'Warg, LIE DOWN!' Perilla hissed. Warg did.

'Now then.' The doctor drew a thick, complicated-looking form towards him. He still had his head down. 'Mr. Potter, isn't it?'

Perilla cleared her throat. 'Well, yes and no,' she said. 'He asked me along as his...interpreter, if you like.'

'Oh?' The doctor finally looked up, pen poised. 'Deaf-mute, is he?' From under the desk, Warg growled.

'Not at all,' Perilla said hastily, 'just needs a little support from time to time.'

'And if I might ask,' the doctor looked puzzled, 'where is he exactly?'

'He's, er, happier on the floor,' Perilla said, trying to ignore the rhythmic grating as Warg, who'd got bored, began gnawing the desk-leg. She yanked hard on his choke-chain.

The doctor cheered up. This was more like it. Someone with a *genuine* disability, and possibly a phobia as well!

'Now Mr. Potter,' he said, 'let's begin with some questions. Name, address and date of birth, got all that...hmm...do you ever hear voices?'

Warg growled again. 'No, he doesn't,' Perilla said after a moment.

'Fine. Well, do you believe or have you ever believed, that you can bend metal objects or control electrical equipment?'

'Excuse me,' Perilla said, 'but what information *have* you got on Mr. Potter, exactly?'

The doctor grunted. 'Not much. Application for Disability Living-Allowance, on the grounds of--what's this? Lunar Lycanthropy?'

'Sounds about right.'

'I'll have to check.' The doctor pulled a well-thumbed reference-book from the shelf on the wall. 'Here we are...list of recognised disabilities...no, it's not in here. What is it, exactly?'

At that precise moment, Warg standing up to his full height, regurgitated a mouthful of half-digested wood-splinters onto the carpet. The doctor's mouth fell open.

'Means he's a werewolf of course,' Perilla said brightly.

Mariander felt a lot better after counting all the money she'd made. As a hang-over remedy, it even beat Sandwillow tea.

Bernard's sisters had been threatening to come for so long, she'd given up expecting them, never mind a whole coach-load! Still, she shouldn't complain, because they'd bought up everything the two of them had produced, even the Pondweed Phlegm-Dissolver and the Gutswort Eyebrow-Gel! Just wait til she told Bryony!

'All right if we picnic in your lounge?' Zinnia was clutching a plastic sandwich-box and a thermos-flask. 'only the bus ain't due back til four.'

'And then mebbe we could go up that pub we passed on the way in,' Begonia said. 'Rat & Spade', or summat...they've got a sign up says they've got a pool-table *and* one of them karaoke machines!'

Mariander winced. She'd just sworn off pubs for the rest of her life.

Poinsettia slapped her on the back. 'Ah, come on, Mari! Live a little! Can't wallow in widowhood for the rest of your life! Not what our Bernard would've wanted, is it girls?'

A chorus of agreement came from the lounge. 'See?' Poinsettia grinned encouragingly, 'we'll make sure you have a good time! It'll be a laugh, and it won't cost you a penny, 'cos the drinks are on us!'

Mariander smiled weakly and said: 'Ta very much.' After all, what else could she say?

'No mobility problems, then.' The doctor, watching Warg hurtle round the room after Perilla's tennis-ball, placed a tick on the form in front of him. 'How is he on stairs?'

Then to Perilla's astonishment, he opened a large cupboard and wheeled out a set of wooden steps.

'Just walk him up and down these, please.'

Warg, who'd just settled down to disembowel the tennis-ball plodded sulkily up and down the steps. He did it six times in all.

The wolf rolled his eyes. 'It's all right, Kenny,' Perilla said, 'I'll show you how it's done.' And leaping onto the machine, she took off at a cracking pace.

'Nothing to it!' she snorted after three vigorous minutes. 'How am I doing?'

'Remarkable!' said the doctor. 'One would almost think you played rugby!'

Once Perilla had prised the half-eaten telephone directory from Warg's jaws and heaved him onto the treadmill, he got a faraway look in his eyes, and settled into a steady, purposeful lope. And he wouldn't get off until Perilla pulled the plug out.

'Magnificent!' the doctor remarked. 'Now just a quick examination before completing the questionnaire...'

He looked in Warg's ears, shone a little light into his eyes, and asked politely if he'd mind opening his mouth. He went very quiet when he saw the dentures, but Perilla put that down to jealousy.

'Would you mind holding his tail up?' he asked her. 'And if you could just cough when I tell you, Mr. Potter...'

Turning his head, Warg gave him a Look. Just the one, but then, that was all he needed.

'Ah,' said the doctor. 'Well. Um. Perhaps not. I think we can dispense with that one...on to the questions then.' He pressed some buttons on his computer keyboard. 'Did either of your parents suffer from heart-disease? Tuberculosis? Arthritis...?'

Perilla looked helplessly from Warg to the doctor and back.

'Well I dunno!' she retorted. 'Don't ask me, I never met 'em! Although looking at him, I'd say there was a mild hip-dysplasia somewhere in the bloodline...'

'..cataracts, diabetes, diverticulitis,' the doctor continued, prodding more buttons.

'Look, what *is* the point of this?' Perilla snapped. 'You'd do better asking about parvo, leptospirosis and hardpad!'

'The point,' the doctor said tetchily, 'is to ascertain whether or not a disability exists. And whilst Mr. Potter's is undoubtedly an unusual case, I have seen nothing so far to indicate the slightest degree of disability.'

'What? *What*? You're completely missing the point!' Perilla shouted. 'Oh, Warg, you naughty boy, NOT that wire...!'

There was a small bang and a shower of sparks, then the computer-screen went blank. The doctor gazed at in disbelief.

'My records!' He cried brokenly. 'All gone!'

'Oh, bugger!' Perilla said. 'Well, forget the Disability-allowance, Kenny. Come on, HEEL, we'd best be going.'

She paused on the way out. 'You're a short-sighted bloody fool!' she told the doctor. 'You had the chance to give Warg here some independence, and maybe a bit of dignity. His future was in your hands, and you blew it.

All you saw was raw energy, endurance, and probably one heck of a bite. In your eyes, he's a perfect physical specimen...40 kilos of lung and muscle-power in wolf's clothing...but that's the whole point.' Warg's sad-eyed gaze caught and held her own.

'It's not his choice. Can't you see that *is* his disability?'

The doctor sat on in silence, surveying the dark, blank screen. Then as an afterthought he called: 'See your G.P., Mr. Potter! I'm sure he'll be able to prescribe some depilatory cream!'

Bernard's sisters must have got her home somehow, although she couldn't remember anything about it afterwards. And they must've poured some Sandwillow tea into her, because after two cups, she felt almost right as sunrise again.

'Ah, Mariander!' Zinnia beamed, 'back with us, are you? We was just saying, where's your Bryony got to? Always good for a laugh, she is, and we ain't seen her since the funeral...how's about if we pay her a call seeing, as we're here?'

Mariander groaned. Not Bryony as well! She'd quite enough on with Bernard's sisters! On the other hand, she knew if she refused, they'd find out where her sister lived and go round anyway. She could've said Bryony would be out, but she didn't feel up to lying, let alone mindblocking...

'Oh, all right,' she grumbled. 'Just give us a minute to put me face on. Here, we're not taking thc whole coachload, are we? Bryony's cottage ain't that big!'

'Them? Nah,' Begonia said. 'Left 'em playing darts with some old men. We'll get the bus to pick 'em up at the pub. Well, come on then, we off?'

Where did they get all that *energy*? A pity Bernard hadn't inherited some of it!

Wearily, Mariander put her coat on, while Grufty, anticipating another walk, fetched his lead.

She *knew* they'd had at least four drinks more than her in the 'Rat & Pitchfork'. She couldn't think where they put it.

They were still townies at heart, though. Village-folk wouldn't've looked twice at 'Shepherd's Cott', gawped at the blacksmith, who was busy with a pair of wrought-iron gates and shrieked 'Look at the pectorals on *that*!'...nor commented on 'Willy's Place' when they got to it.

Mariander sneaked a look at her watch: still an hour and a half til the bus was due back. P'raps Bryony would be feeling sociable. Mebbe she'd've made a cake--and then again, mebbe they'd all win the Lottery and stop speaking to their neighbours-...

Tobin's van was parked outside the cottage. Still sniffing round, eh. Her mind reached ahead, seeing how the land lay...

'No! Don't go in there!' Too late. The sisters were squeezing themselves into the porch...why ever didn't Bryony lock her front door? Mariander trailed after them, knowing full well what she'd find.

They'd pushed the fireside chairs together, if you please. They both had their slippers on, and they were holding hands. They looked warm and comfortable and-...together. And judging by the soppy smiles on their faces, they were...somewhere else. Out of reach. Merging.

'Well, I never!' Zinnia gasped.

'Who'd've thought it?' giggled Begonia.

'The ole devils!' Poinsettia breathed admiringly.

'Oh, Bryony,' Mariander sighed. 'How *could* you?'

Bevis Tate crept along Heifer Way, ready for a spot of burglary on

Brassica's house. He knew he could proceed because he'd seen her, not five minutes previously, in Bull Alley with one of her gentlemen.

Gentlemen! What a misnomer! He sometimes thought of himself as the Last Living Gentleman...not that he ever seemed to encounter any ladies these days...Brassica and the Grandmistress' sister had certainly not behaved in a ladylike manner. But he would have his revenge. And he'd recover those disgusting, incriminating photographs if it was the last thing he ever did.

He found No. 15; exactly the drab, squalid little hovel he'd been expecting, applied his mind to the locked front door, and slipped inside.

'Don't sulk,' Perilla said. 'At least you tried. Not the end of the world, is it? Training's coming along nicely, and we'll carry on as we are...you earning your keep, plus pocket-money, of course. And I'm sure Betty'll do what she can.' She patted his head, gently. 'You won't want for anything, Kenny.'

Warg lay on the passenger-seat, thoroughly fed-up. Knowing he'd blown his chance of disability-benefit wasn't a nice thought. And Perilla wasn't helping. She just didn't *understand* how much he hated being *kept...*

Back at the Manse, she went off to de-tangle the buffalo, leaving him to his own devices. The warm sun gave him no pleasure, but the clear sky did. The moon would be brilliant that night...cold and full and beautiful. Hunter's moon. *His* moon. He felt a shiver of anticipation.

Might as well nip down the paddock and cock his leg up. He couldn't see the sheep...probably down the bottom end, chewing over their grievances.

They'd crept up behind him, quieter than he'd ever have imagined, and caught him in mid-stream. Before he knew it, they'd surrounded him, pulling horrible faces and bleating:

Haa-lf-man haa-lf-wolf, don't smell like ei--ther!

Were-wimp, Were-wimp, run home to your maa-mmy!

Tears filled his eyes as he slunk off under the fence. They were right. He didn't belong. He *was* a half-creature, an embarrassing hybrid-misfit *and* a sponger, living off women...and the training was a waste of time. He hated it, hated having to find the self- control Perilla expected of him...there was no place for him here, or anywhere, come to that. Nobody cared, and no-one would miss him if he went...when he went...and why not? The sooner the better. Tonight, with the moon on him, he'd go. Go, and never come back.

After all, even a werewolf has his pride.

Mariander and the sisters filed out again, going back the way they'd come. There didn't seem any point in staying, seeing as Bryony was otherwise occupied...nobody had much to say.

The sisters didn't so much as glance at the NAKED CHARITY BUNGEE-JUMP poster, let alone pass comment on the blacksmith's assistant's biceps, *or* his awesome gluteae maximae.

They were just turning into Mariander's drive when Aubrey Bottomley came out of his garage, wearing overalls and rubber gloves, and lugging two black bin-liners which he added to the pile beside his car.

The thought crossed Mariander's mind that he'd finally done his missus in and chopped her up...but no, there she was, peeking through the curtains as usual.

Turning, Aubrey shouted defiantly: 'It's that stupid girl in the shop, I tell you, gave me the wrong video!'

Aubrey looked under the weather: in fact, glancing into his mind, she found distinct traces of the morning after the night before. Oh well, that made two of 'em...except hers was the afternoon after the lunchtime *and* night before...

The bus came, and the sisters, still pre-occupied, climbed aboard. 'Well, bye-bye, Mari,' Zinnia, who was last on, called out. 'Interesting day...who says it's quiet in the country, eh! And you wanter watch your Bryony...I ain't never seen Merging like that in anyone over twenty! It's a wonder her head didn't fall off!'

Certainly was, Mariander thought grimly, trying to ignore Sham's perfect impression of a roomful of cackling women. But then it occurred to her...was she mebbe a teeny bit jealous, never having done it herself on account of wedding an Outsider? Could be. But that still didn't stop her worrying about Bryony getting hurt again.

Granny came back slowly. She felt wonderful, young again and sort of revitalised, but drained as well, as if she'd just run to Bartlesham and back.

Tobin stretched his legs, and smiled his little-boy smile. 'All right?'

Gently, she felt her mind, smoothing its edges, prodding its corners. Still there, and no cobwebs that she could detect.

'Reckon I'm good for another few years yet--think I'll just sit quiet a moment, all the same. Your turn to make the tea.'

'Righto. Got any cake, Bry? I'm starving.' He winked. 'All that Merging don't half give you an appetite.'

'Tobin...'she hesitated.

'Yeah?'

'When you was wed...all them years with Dolly...how did you manage...without it?'

He shrugged. 'Like anything else, I suppose...it's what you get used to. Course, you can always go off into a little reverie on your own, but it ain't the same, is it? And it must've bothered you, too--kind of a celibacy, ain't it?'

Granny stared into the fire. 'S'pose we're lucky, then. Some folks go a lifetime without ever having what we got...even Seers...'

He touched her hand. 'And don't you forget it, gel. Now I think I'll make that tea. Hello, what's this?' He stooped to pick something up from the floor. 'Is it yours, Bryony?'

It was a large headscarf, red and black with big poppies on. And she'd seen it somewhere before...

'Oh, Sight, Tobin,' she groaned. 'It's Begonia's scarf...you know, one of That Bernard's sisters I told you about? It looks like we've had visitors while we was...well. And if Mariander weren't there, she'll soon know all about it.'

And then she knew she'd be for it, good and proper.

Perilla heaved a sigh of relief once the buffalo was hosed down, trimmed and groomed and off in a truck on its way to the Annual Big Bovine Show at Tuckmister.

Not that it'd played up, but there'd been so much of it to get round...and then the basilisk'd started shedding scales. It'd just been one of those days. And it wasn't til she sat down with a cigar and a can of cold beer that she realised she hadn't seen Warg/Kenneth for hours.

Brassica's house disgusted him. It smelt of cabbage and curry...or possibly curried cabbage...and there was wet underwear draped brazenly over every radiator. Exactly what he would have expected.

Nevertheless, he steeled himself to do what he had come to do, and professionally, at that. He wore surgical gloves, so as not to leave finger-prints, and black clothes in order to blend with the dusk which would soon be falling, and so slip away unseen.

He began downstairs, searching the cupboards and emptying all the kitchen drawers. He found nothing, least of all anything edible. But then he hadn't really expected a woman of Brassica's low cunning to secrete incriminating photographs in any obvious place.

There wasn't a dining-room...not that he envisaged her and her 'gentlemen' enjoying dinner-parties, because, to his mind, she definitely fell into the fast-food-in-front-of-the-television-category.

The coalhouse, unsurprisingly, yielded nothing, not even coal. Upstairs, then. What horrors awaited him there?

The bathroom cabinet was full of things which might have brought a blush to his cheeks, had he known what half of them were *for*...Women's Things, obviously.

There were strange rubber objects, hair-dyes and pills and peculiar-smelling linaments...one of them labelled AROUSER BODY-RUB...and, right at the back, as though long-forgotten, something called a PREDICTOR-KIT...but still no photographs. Her bedroom reeked of a heavy, cloying scent that gave him an instant headache, and made his nose run. The double-bed itself was almost buried beneath a layer of dolls and soft toys...poodles and teddy-bears and rabbits and porcelain schoolgirls and crinolined ladies...

There were frilly curtains at the window, and a dressing-table with a matching lamp. There seemed to be a great many drawers to investigate: very well then. He would start with the bedside ones.

A promising-looking envelope revealed nothing but a bundle of faded love-letters: he tossed them aside. Brassica's romances, such as they might have been, were of no interest whatsoever.

She seemed to have a vast appetite for works of romantic fiction: the drawers were crammed with them. He supposed they provided an escape from the grim reality of her sordid life. He was about to discard the books, when something protruding from one of them caught his eye. A large envelope! At last!

He opened it carefully. Inside lay, not the anticipated photographs, but a strangely unexpected collection. A child's hairbrush. A pair of white, knitted bootees, and a curl of flaxen hair. He gaped, trying to understand.

'Well, well.' Brassica's voice startled him from the shadows on the landing. 'Ain't this cosy.'

Full moon riding the clouds over the valley.

Full moon, silvering the trees and the water and the geese settling on the wheatfields. Sheep coughing and owls crying and griffon-calls splitting the night--KARK! KARK!

And down by the sleeping river, the mournful, demoralised howl of a wolf who knows that nobody loves him.

'Any of you lot seen Kenn...I mean Warg?' Perilla was starting to get worried. Why hadn't she kept an eye on him?

The ewes, chewing steadily, shifted their hooves and gave her their vacant, glassy stare. She knew that look. Ovine Obstinacy. Their minds confirmed it.

'You wicked old girls, you *have* seen him. All right, one more chance. I'll count up to three, and then I'll get heavy...arn, tarn...*tarn and a half*...tethera...'

Oh, all right. Mimph carried on chewing. *He* was *here. But he went.*

Perilla groaned. Just as she'd thought.

'You upset him, didn't you? Made him cry, drove him away? You rotten lot. Which way did he go? Right, I'll deal with you later.'

She ran back up the paddock. 'Jeg! Chervil! Get the griffons and hurry! Warg's on the run!'

He wished she'd shout at him, scream, throw things...anything but fix him with that terrible just-you-wait smile.

He was, of course, at a severe disadvantage, down on his knees amongst the contents of the drawers. She stood over him, bursting out of that mini-dress and those thigh-boots.

Stood so close he could see the lines where her lipstick had bled and her powder had caked; smell the gin and the cigarette-smoke--

'*Gentlemen* do sometimes come up here,' Brassica said, 'but only by invitation...lets *you* out on both counts, don't it? And you won't find no photos in there...I'll have that, if you don't mind. Sentimental value.' Numbly, he passed the envelope across.

'Well, Midmaster Tate.' Lighting a cigarette, she blew smoke in his face. He felt his mind lurch as she gave it a vicious twist. 'You've broke into my house and gone through my belongings...made a right mess downstairs, or didn't you notice?...and I think you need a lesson in manners. Hey, SCALLION! Up here a minute!'

'Better make sure he hasn't gone to his sister's.' Perilla swung the jeep down the drive. 'And then, if not, we'll collect Bryony...he trusts her, and the more minds on his trail, the better.'

'We really gonna use the griffons?' Jeg asked doubtfully. 'They've never flown free before...what if they don't come back?'

'We'll just have to take that chance,' Perilla said. 'I've got a feeling the hunt'll be on for Warg tonight.'

Steve's heart pounded as he pushed through the reeds, stun-gun at the ready. Whatever the thing was doing, it was making one helluva noise. You'd have thought a creature of the wild would at least have learnt to be silent...

Unfortunately for the couple on the riverbank, silence wasn't a necessary part of the proceedings. And Steve had shot them both before they'd reached a satisfactory conclusion.

He daren't look. This was the end.

This Scallion, obviously one of Brassica's Special Gentleman, could only be the huge tattooed psychopath of his worst imaginings...the one who would make him regret his temerity in ever entering Brassica's house, let alone her bed-chamber…

He recognised the likelihood that his body would never be found, and that, gagged and manacled, he would be horribly tortured by Brassica and her cohort, who would be got up in terrifying hoods and boots and black leather underwear- Oh, Sight…

He had no wife, no children, no cats. But what would become of his models? Would they be treasured, appreciated, displayed in an appropriate setting, such as the one-day Seers' Museum, as stipulated in his will?

Come to that, would anyone ever actually find them, or had he neglected to give Ritro Bowers his spare key?

Following another five minutes' hyperventilation and feverish imagining, it dawned upon him that nothing whatsoever had happened. And then, the anticipation being worse than the reality, he risked a peep.

Brassica was still smiling her dreadful smile. 'Take Midmaster Tate away, Scallion,' she was saying, 'and give him a good seeing-to.'

And then he saw the girl standing beside her: built like an ox, all leather and studs…quite a lot of them attached to various parts of her face…black hair, white skin and black lipstick, admittedly, but a girl, nevertheless.

And her smile, when she parted the black lips, was even worse than Brassica's.'My pleasure,' she purred.

Brassica leered at him. 'Scallion's got lots of mirrors,' she informed him, 'and hidden cameras…so plenty of photos, eh? And this time we'll make sure you *never* find 'em.'

'Escaped?' Betty went white. 'But how could he? I thought he'd be safe with you…'

'My fault.' Perilla shook her head. 'Too much on, I'm afraid, and only one pair of hands. And poor old Kenny didn't get his Disability-Allowance after all…afraid I wasn't terribly sympathetic. And then those blessed sheep have been getting at him as well…'

'We've got to find him!' Betty cried. 'And I'm coming with you! Stay here, Krystle, there's a good girl.' She scrambled into the jeep, shrieked and scrambled out again. 'Ooh! Whatever's them horrible things?'

'Griffons,' Chervil said. 'Shortly to be exploited by callous humans who ought to know better.'

'Really.' Betty peered doubtfully inside the jeep. The griffons rattled their jesses. 'So what they doing here, then?'

'We're hoping they'll help us find Warg,' Jeg explained. 'Sort of like night-hawks hunting.'

'And we're going to fetch Bryony,' Perilla added. 'Don't worry, we'll soon have him back safe and sound.' She only wished she felt as confident as she sounded.

Scallion lifted Bevis Tate up by his lapels: she was a very big girl. 'Come on then, Shorty. Time to get moving...where'd you park the motor?'

Brassica snorted. 'See him in a car! Got one of them poncey mopeds, ain't he? Big girl's blouse.'

Bevis Tate gave them his I-am-what-I-am-and-proud-of-it look. After all, he still had his dignity.

'Well then, you've been misinformed,' he retorted. 'Because I have recently Upgraded my transport facility!'

'Oh yeah?' Scallion gave him another of her black smiles. 'Show us.'

Wasn't often you saw a motorbike and sidecar outside of a museum these days, Brassica reflected. Sight knew where he'd got 'em from. Made it easier to kidnap him, though.

'Right, then. In you get,' she told him, 'I'll drive.'

Bevis Tate started to object. Scallion raised a jet-black eyebrow.

'Don't fuss!' Brassica grinned. 'I was young once, you know! But you go first...it's a few years since I rode one of these things.'

Midmaster Tate was bundled, struggling, into his own sidecar, and locked in. Then to his consternation, Brassica donned his crash-helmet, hitched up her impossible skirt, and climbed aboard his bike.

And then the other one, the Scallion person, swept up on a huge, gleaming customised monster of a motorbike. Pausing only to shout: 'Kick ass, Brassica!' she pulled down her visor and roared off.

'Sight, Perilla, how long's he been gone?' Somehow Granny managed to clip Grufty's lead on, poke up the fire, button her coat and shut the front door all at the same time.

Outside she paused to shout down the garden: 'Get a MOVE ON in that PRIVY, Tobin! We've gotta go look for Warg! He's just popped round for a cupper tea,' she explained to anyone who might be listening. No-one was.

To her consternation, though, Perilla had tears in her eyes, and Granny realised the woman was worried sick about Warg.

'Hey! Calm down,' she whispered, 'we'll get him back.'

'Sorry.' Perilla wiped a grubby sleeve across her face. 'Really quite fond of old Kenny,' she mumbled. 'And Warg, too, come to that.'

'I know,' Granny said gently. 'Oh, nice of you to join us, Tobin! Been reading the paper again, have you?...well, you'd best get Aggie warmed up, and we'll follow on. Where we heading, anyway?'

'Good question.' Perilla stooped to hide her tears and re-tie the laces of her basketball boots. 'No point buzzing round like blue-arced flies, is there? Got to have a sort of H.Q., so to speak...work from there, report back, and so on-'

'Yes, yes, I get your drift,' Granny said, 'but where you...'

At that moment one of the griffons uttered a tremendous shriek, and Grufty took off, with Granny hanging onto his lead for dear life. It was only thanks to Tobin that he stopped at all.

'Was that,' Granny wheezed, when she started getting her breath back, 'what I *thought* it was?'

'Aw, don't be hard on 'em, Bryony,' Perilla said. 'They're excited, bless 'em. It's the night-sounds and smells and...CHERVIL! Let 'em out for a leak, will you...' she turned back to Granny. 'It's the motion of the jeep, shakes their bladders up if you don't watch it.'

Granny watched, fascinated, as Betty emerged, followed by Jeg and Chervil. Each of the lads wore a falconer's gauntlet upon his right hand and arm; and when Granny got a good look at the griffons' talons, she could see why they were needed.

The birds' eyes gleamed amber with excitement: they kept trying experimental little jumps and flapping the great wings in their anxiety to be off. Only Chervil looked as if he'd rather have been at home in bed.

'Honestly, Mother,' he snapped, glaring at Granny and Tobin, 'why not invite the whole of Bartleshire to join the hunt?'

'Don't be a smartarse, Chervil,' Perilla said, 'you're impressing nobody. You know we need as many pairs of eyes as possible.'

'Yes but where we *going*?' Betty asked.

'Who's got the keenest eyes of us lot?' Perilla said, 'The griffons, of course. So, as it's their first time flying, we need high ground. I'd thought of Brim Knap, but it's too far from the sort of places Kenny frequents. No, if I know him, he'll be prowling about feeling sorry for himself, so we need to get somewhere central.'

'I still don't get it,' Betty said. 'This high place you said about?'

'Exactly,' Perilla said. 'Top of the old Fossetby fire-station training-tower do you?'

The 'Rat & Pitchfork' playground lay quiet in the moonlight.

The two winos sat side by side on children's swings, watching a huge grey wolf root through the contents of the litter-bin. It was making a real mess, too.

'Brian,' one of them said, looking thoughtfully at the bottle he'd just drunk from, 'where did you get this stuff, exactly'

'Decorator's skip in Bartlesham, back of Arkle Street, Nev. Think it's some sort of paint-thinners...not bad is it?'

'Not bad at all.'

The wolf, totally ignoring them, had its nose inside an icecream-less cornet, its whole attention bent on scavenging as much as possible in as short a time as possible. 'In fact, come morning, I reckon I'll get us a drop more.'

Warg wasn't having a good time; in fact he was feeling hard done-to.

He almost wished he hadn't run away, because he was hungry and lonely and unloved. All he'd found to eat had been some saffron rice and a piece of cold naan bread outside the Tearoom, followed by a bag of soggy, vinegar-soaked chips near the Village-Hall.

Perilla would've given him a good supper, and some newspaper to shred. She'd have scratched his ears and tickled his tummy and spoken to him kindly...kindly, but firmly. *And* she'd have told them bastard sheep where to get off, as well. A fine woman, Perilla...attractive, too, if you went for the commanding type...and he did. Oh, God, yes he did. She was everything he'd ever looked for. But he couldn't go back now, couldn't tell her how he felt...

What was more, he craved a really good chew...and he daren't, in case he damaged his nice new teeth. Because fear of what Perilla would say if he did was stronger than his urges. Even his freedom was a sham. Now he really *was* a were-wimp.

'*Me*?' Chervil gasped. 'Me, go up there? You've gotta be joking!' The derelict training-tower loomed dark above them, fully 20 metres high.

Perilla turned to face the others. 'This, ladies and gentlemen, I might remind you, is the lad who last week shinned up a threatened chestnut-tree in order to protest about the Gossett By-Pass, *and* it was raining! Now get up there Chervil, and no arguing!'

'*I'm* going, anyway.' Adjusting the griffon on his gauntlet, Jeg set off up the training-tower. 'Just wait' till I tell 'em at school!'

'You won't, my lad,' Perilla warned. 'Not a word to anyone! Just keep that griffon quiet, and watch your footing, this thing's rusty. Got your lures? And the scent-items? O.K., blow the whistle when you're on top.'

'Do you really think we should've come?' Betty asked anxiously. 'I mean, this is still fire-station property.'

'Course we should!' Perilla said. 'After all, where else are we going to get an over-view of the whole area? Tell me something, Betty...is there any particular place Kenny might have gone? Anywhere he heads for when he's feeling a bit down, I mean?'

'Ooh, I dunno,' Betty said. 'Our Kenny'd be in B & Q, else down the Bookie's--but from what he's said about being Warg-- not that that's much...anywhere he can find something to chew, I should think.'

'Thanks. Well, that cuts it down a lot,' Perilla said. 'Right, don't talk to me unless it's urgent...need to concentrate my mind. And by the way, where the Sight have Tobin and Bryony got to?'

Aggie wasn't well. Tobin was distraught. Couldn't understand it. Never let him down in fifty years, he muttered, tenderly running his hands over her battery, gently checking her plugs and points.

Granny sat in the passenger-seat, fuming, fretting and forgotten. He'd never fussed over *her* like that. And there they were, pulled off the Bull Ring and time getting on.

After a great deal of tinkering, Tobin came round to Granny' window, with a very red face.

'Er, sorry, Bryony,' he mumbled. 'Seem to be out of petrol. Pity it couldn't've happened somewhere a bit more romantic, hehheh!'

'Oh, Tobin, no! Now of all times!'

'Not to worry. Bound to have a can in the back.'

'I'll come and help you look,' Granny said, 'you've that much clutter in there, you'll never lay hands on it.'

'Not true!' Tobin said. 'Place for everything, I always say!'

178

After a fruitless ten minutes of Tobin muttering feverishly: 'I *know* there's one in here somewhere,' Granny shoved aside a family of garden-gnomes and a pair of skis.

'What's this thing?' She'd unearthed a huge orange rubber ball, with a face on it. On top were two thick horns, or possibly ears, shaped like handles.

'What?' Tobin swept aside a suit of armour, a fully-inflated paddling-pool and two metal-detectors. 'Space-hopper, ain't it. You're meant to sit on it, grab hold of its lugs, and bounce...good fun when you've had a few bevies...or so I'm told...'

'Right.' Granny hauled the space-hopper onto the pavement. It seemed firm enough. 'No choice, is there...it's this or nothing. Catch us up if you find any petrol.'

'Bryony!' Tobin was appalled. 'You can't! It's for kids! You'll come a cropper!'

Granny gave an experimental bounce. 'You're as old as you feel, Tobin--anyhow, it seems all right to me. You got any better suggestions? No? Thought not. Well, so long!' And climbing aboard, she grasped the handles and hopped off along the Bullring.

Rog. and Steve, distancing themselves from their latest victims...(having first removed the darts)...headed out towards Garm-on-Brim, where there'd been a possible wolf-sighting.

An enormous black-and-silver motorbike passed them, going the other way, and Steve's eyes came out on stalks.

'Did you see *that*?' he squawked.

Rog. grunted. 'Yeah. Nice bike.'

'No,' Steve sighed, 'I meant the babe riding it!'

Moments later, he shouted: 'U-turn, Rog! This I've gotta see up close!'

The old bird in the unflattering skirt was peering perplexedly at the motor-bike's engine-casing. And there was another wrinkly in the sidecar as well: when he spotted them he started banging on the window and shouting.

Steve shouted back. ''Now then! Out for a spin, were you, you and the old man?'

The woman turned, took her helmet off, and gave them a lipsticky smile. 'Ooh, hello, it's the Boys in Blue! What a godsend! We seem to've broke down. Don't suppose you know where they keep the engines in these things, do you, dearie?'

Rog. recognised that cheerful, raddled face from many long nights pounding the Bartlesham beat. 'Oh, it's you, Brassica,' he said. 'Can you do it in a sidecar, then?'

'Dunno yet, do I?' Brassica said. 'Cheeky sod. Look, can you get this thing going or not?'

'That depends. Got a licence, have you?'

'Course I have.' Brassica winked. 'Back at my place. Come round later, and I'll show it you.'

'We'll take your word for it,' Rog, said hastily. He nodded to the crumbly in the sidecar, who seemed to have redoubled his banging and shouting. 'Your old guy not so hot on engines, then?'

'You must be joking!' She gave Bevis a dismissive wave. 'Ain't so hot on anything, if you get my drift! And he's not *my* ole guy...'m just giving him a bit of a ride out in the country.'

'No change there, then!' Rog. sniggered. 'Seems a bit wound-up, though.'

'Well, thinks he's on a promise, don't he?' Brassica said. 'Look, you gonna get this thing going, or what?'

They dutifully tinkered. Didn't matter that they knew absolutely nothing about engines, it was what The Public expected of policemen.

Brassica leaned on the bike, looking bored, and twice they had to scream at her not to light a fag.

After a few minutes' fiddling, Steve called: 'Try her now!' purely because he couldn't think of anything else to say. But to his surprise, the engine fired.

'Well, ta, boys.' They averted their eyes as Brassica hitched her skirt up and climbed back on the bike. She winked, enjoying their discomfiture. 'And any time you fancy a quickie, you know where to find me.'

They waved her off, giving the old guy a men-to-man-but-I don't-fancy-yours-mate sort of smile.

Bevis Tate slumped down in his seat. No-one could save him now. All that effort for nothing. He'd always believed policemen were trained in observation--but they'd ignored his desperate message, laboriously executed in yellow highlighter on the perspex window.

Unfortunately for Midmaster Tate, he had failed to realise that his frantic legend appeared to the outside world as !DEPPANDIK GNIEB MA I !PLEH

Being Undercover, they were keeping a low profile.

Rog. was fiddling about with the radio, trying to get something funky, so that he had his head down when Granny went past on the space-hopper. Going like the clappers, she was, Steve noted. Got a real bounce on in fact.

Steve's voice stuck in his throat. For some reason, all the local weirdos seemed to be on the move, and he couldn't get his head round it at all.

'Rog.,' he croaked at last.

'Yeah, what now?'

They'd soon catch her up, no problem. And then what? Breathalyse her? And if that proved negative, what could they charge her with? Dangerous hopping? Distracting other road-users? Inappropriate use of a child's toy in contravention of highway regulations? The paperwork would be a nightmare. And then of course, it was *her* again. That mad old bird, the one on the WANTED posters, who lived in the wood and put the evil eye on people who crossed her...all in all, it wasn't worthwhile. Let her hop off wherever the fancy took her, just as long as she didn't cross his path.

'Well, *what*?' Rog, said, with an edge to his voice.

'Never mind,' Steve muttered. 'Doesn't matter. Forget it.'

Brassica hadn't got far before the bike spluttered to a halt again, right in the middle of nowhere. And this time, there wasn't a mechanic in sight.

Oh, well. Just have to hope Scallion'd catch on something'd gone wrong, and come looking. Meantime, she wasn't about to let old Bevis out, however loud he shouted. Lighting a fag, she settled herself to wait.

And Midmaster Tate started on the bag of peppermints he'd found down the side of his seat. They had undoubtedly been there an unconscionably long time, but boredom had now overtaken desperation, and any occupation, however uninspiring, was, to his mind, better than none.

Staring gloomily out of the scratched perspex, he froze upon finding himself confronted by a pair of startlingly yellow eyes.

The winos had got themselves as comfortable as anyone reasonably could on a couple of picnic-benches outside the Brimwold Garden-Centre.

They were therefore in an advantageous position to observe the energetic progress along High Street of the old woman on the big orange ball. She passed within yards of their makeshift bed.

Small details engraved themselves on their vision, and on their memory. Her whitened knuckles, as she steered. Her fiercely-gritted dentures, and the way the white hair moved about her face. The flapping of her long black coat. And that silly smile on the ball's rubber face....Nev. surveyed his almost-empty bottle. 'I reckon this stuff's starting to bite,' he observed.

'Either that,' Brian gazed thoughtfully after the old woman's swiftly-receding figure, 'or they've cut the late-night bus-service again.'

Warg's nose was incredibly sensitive. He could've detected sweets across an ocean--and peppermints were his all-time favourites.

Pity they were locked away in this silly little box...but he'd soon have them out of there. After all, he'd got claws, hadn't he, if not real teeth?

As the thing tore at the window, Bevis Tate could only sit, trapped and cowering, awaiting the end. Death in a sidecar, by some unknown horror. What an alternative to dishonour at the hands of that Scallion girl...At that moment, Brassica, who'd been off in a smokey reverie, opened her eyes, spotted the wolf, and screamed. And if there was one thing Warg couldn't stand, it was women screaming. Spitting out a mouthful of canvas window-edging, he bolted, relinquishing all thoughts of peppermints.

Maybe if he was *really* lucky, he'd find some squashed buns outside Polly's Bakery.

'You really think them griffon-things'll find him?'

'I think,' Granny said slowly, 'they're his best chance. And you know Perilla...she don't give up easy.'

Just then they heard Perilla roar above the wind: 'Okay, Chervil, jesse off and...chocks away! Go, boy, go! Fetch!'

The griffon soars, halts, and hovers, scanning the night-town.

Down there is one whose smell lies in his nostrils...the one who wears two skins, yet has no feathers. The one she is seeking, she who feeds him, she who smoothes his feathers, she who gave him flight. He will not fail her.

Far, far below is an infinitesimal movement, and, borne on the wind, the scent of his prey. Fixing the image, he flattens his wings and dives...

'Mum, Mum, he's coming back!' Jeg's voice squeaked with excitement. 'And he's carrying something!'

'Good boy!' Perilla shouted, waving the lure. 'Come on then, bacon buttie!' Wheeling, the griffon came in to a perfect landing on Jeg's gauntlet. Quickly re-attaching the jesse, Perilla crooned 'Good boy!'

'Cool! Jeg breathed. 'He did it! And what's this he's brought?'

He just managed to catch the offering as the griffon spat it out and, watched greedily by its brother, tore into its reward.

'What's *that*?' Chervil said witheringly. 'Looks like a bundle of fish-and-chip papers to me!'

Jeg's face fell as he examined them. 'Yeah, you're right. And there's nothing else, unless he dropped it...what d'you reckon, Mum?'

Perilla, busy placating the other griffon, glanced at the papers. 'He's brought these because Warg's had 'em,' she said. 'and our *clever* boy smelt him on them, *yes he did...*only faint, maybe, but enough.'

'Well at least we know Warg's in town,' Jeg said.

'Huh!' Chervil snorted. 'Proves nothing. Pick any bin, you can bet Warg's been at it! Face it, Mum, the griffons just haven't had enough practise.'

'Don't be such a snot, Chervil!' Perilla snapped. 'What that bird did was quite remarkable for a first-timer. But he's had enough for one night. We'll send his brother out.'

'Oh, yeah!' Chervil scoffed. 'And maybe he'll bring Warg back...if he can carry him!'

'You wait!' Perilla said. 'That's it, Jeg, give him a good whiff of that collar...he'll find Kenny...and then we'll be able to fetch him home.

The second griffon lofts into the dark sky and hangs motionless.

His talons twitch: the earth thrums with the sound of small prey.

Sudden hunger fires his belly. He sees them, smells them, could take any or all of them if he chose--but they are not for him, not this night--Far below, a movement. His eyes burn red. He shrieks. He dives.

Rog. and Steve had given it one last go. They'd done the riverbank, as advised, and nothing. One more false alarm. Wearily, they climbed back into the car.

Nothing stirred except tethered boats bobbing on the quiet water. Ducks and swans snored gently in the reeds, and on a neighbouring field, Canada geese clustered, emitting the occasional drowsy honk.

Even the boathouse was deserted, and that *was* unusual because on an average night you couldn't move for winos and glue-sniffers and bonking couples...Steve's trigger-finger twitched. He despaired of ever nabbing the wolf, but by the same token, he was keeping a sharp eye out for that midnight-cowboy guy, because past experience had taught him that you couldn't have one without the other.

Steve gave a big sigh. 'What's it all about, eh, Rog.? I mean, just what good are we doing? How many more pointless full moons, eh, mate?'

'Don't let it get to you!' Rog., having broken contact with headquarters, hummed along with the Late-Nite Sloppy Mood Radio Show. Naughty, he knew, but he never could stand all that 'Come in Alpha-Bravo-Tango' stuff.

'We're performing a valuable service here, assuaging the Public's fears and all that. And don't you ever forget it! We'll get the bastard one of these...' he broke off, staring at something on the towpath.

The wolf lay on its back, paws over its eyes, whilst an overfed ginger cat set about it with teeth and claws.

Before they could cry wolf, though, an enormous bird--bit like a hard-looking turkey, only uglier, Rog. said afterwards...swooped silently down, and talons seizing the cat round its ample middle, shot back up into the sky.

Fearfully, the wolf uncurled, shook itself, and then spotted Steve aiming the stun-gun. With a piteous howl, it bolted back along the track with the wolf-patrol in hot pursuit.

'Got here at last, did you?'

Grufty jumped sulkily from the van, but at least Aggie was mobile again. Tobin still looked embarrassed about running out of petrol though.

'Managed all the way on that thing, then?'

Granny patted the space-hopper fondly.

'Quite comfy, once you get the knack,' she said. 'Don't want it back, do you? Come in handy for nipping down the village, that will.'

She didn't see the horror in Tobin's eyes: but then neither did she see him repeatedly puncturing it with his army-knife as he thrust it out of sight in the back of the van.

The griffon paused only to drop the cat onto the platform, where it landed feet-first, spat venomously at the world in general, and shot off down the metal supports like a trapeze-artist with diarrhoea.

'Hey!' Perilla, trying to collect herself, yelled after the griffon, 'No! Bad! Come! Heel! Bacon!'...but if it was within earshot, it had gone suddenly deaf.

The others exchanged glances. Nothing else for it. *Going to have to mind-track.*

'Right, then.' Perilla spoke for them all. 'Let's get moving. I'll lead, and we'll just have to hope we're not too late.'

'Scallion! Thank the Sight you've come back!' Brassica knew she was babbling. 'We've broke down twice, and there's bin a great big wolf trying to get in the sidecar!'

'Yeah, right.' Wondering how many drinks Brassica had had, Scallion blew Bevis Tate a black-lipped kiss and yelled 'HANG IN THERE!' through the perspex.

And the little sod really did look shit-scared! Cool! Just how she liked 'em. He'd be easy meat.

'Okay.' She told Brassica, 'No problem. I'll give you a tow.'

Perilla, her mind locked onto Warg's, set off at a cracking pace: Tobin following at a speed Granny would never've credited Aggie with. Grufty went head over heels, and the load in the back shifted alarmingly.

'Oy!' she warned, 'watch them plant-pots, *and* your passengers!'

Tobin didn't reply because it was taking all his skill to avoid the Fosse Way bollards that'd just jumped out at him. Once past, though, he'd a more or less straight run out to the Brockway, and he could just about see Perilla's tail-lights in the far distance.

Granny relaxed her grip on the dashboard a bit. *'And* you better not've damaged me space-hopper!' she snapped.

186

Hastily changing the subject, Tobin said: 'You give any further thought to my offer, Bryony?'

'Offer? What offer?'

Tobin sighed. 'You know. Getting hitched.'

'I don't believe it!' Granny exploded. 'Ain't that just like a man! How can you, time like this when Warg's in mortal danger?'

That shut him up for a bit, but, watching the dark countryside flash past, she realised that she couldn't put it off forever. Sometime very soon, he'd be expecting an answer.

Killer Calhoun stops, and sniffs the air. YES. He can smell him. He's there, heading straight towards him. Come you here, then, and bring us your pelt.

He can wait. Got all the time in the world, hasn't he. Time for a bit of a rest, and a smoke. And leaning against the lampost, he strikes a match.

Warg was running scared, running for his life, running faster than he'd ever run in his whole life, even in his footballing Kenneth-days.

But he wasn't built for running anymore, and he certainly wasn't getting any younger. Trouble was, he'd got soft, even with all the manual labour.

Too many nights sitting out on Perilla's patio with a glass or two of wine, that's what it was. His paws hurt where he'd got grit in between the toes, and one of his pads was cracked, because he wasn't used to running on tarmac.

He'd broken a claw, too...should have cut them when he'd had his bath. His legs ached, even his tail felt heavy. His throat was dry, his breath came in great heaving gasps, and his heart felt as if it would jump out of his chest.

He was dying to cock his leg up as well. He knew now how it felt to be hunted, and it wasn't much fun. They kept taking potshots at him out of the window--so far they'd missed, but his luck couldn't hold out forever.

And they seemed to be *enjoying* themselves. Sick, that's what they were--whooping and screeching to each other as though the whole thing was some sort of *game*....

Sheer cussedness kept him going, long after he should have dropped. Course, he'd have done better without the moon's light on him, helping their aim, and gone faster if he'd got off the main road and taken to the fields.

The thing was, though, that he daren't. Daren't venture into unfamiliar territory in case the moon let him down by going behind a cloud--because, amongst his other numerous hang-ups, Warg was scared stiff of the dark.

Bevis Tate felt sick. He was being tossed around the sidecar like a lone sardine in a tin with no oil, and hating every minute.

He wondered if this night would ever end, and longed for a return of his earlier boredom, during which he'd been reduced to counting the window-rivets. (There were, he could categorically state, 135.)

He would make a note of it later, because the odd number bothered him.) What had he ever done to deserve such torment? His whole existence had been devoted to his own betterment, and that of others.

Naturally, he had sought to expose Mistress Beamish' shortcomings, but only for the greater good of the Guild--it wasn't fair. It wasn't jolly well fair!

Perilla was finding it hard to drive and keep hold of Warg/Kenneth's mind, which would keep skittering off in all directions.

She could only hope that the boys still had a fix on him, and that Tobin and Bryony were keeping up, because that patrol-car was really moving. All at once, she spotted its tail-lights leaving the Brockway at the Deepinwold junction.

'Oh, Sight!' She thumped the dashboard, startling the griffons, which were still in the process of digesting their bacon sandwiches.

'What's up, Mum?' With difficulty, Jeg prised his griffon off the ceiling. 'Haven't lost Warg, have you?'

'No, it's not that. Hang on in the back there.' Perilla swung the jeep into the lane. 'Might have known, that's all. Silly bugger's only heading back to blithering Brimwold! We've come full circle!'

'Well, so what?'Jeg wanted to know. 'He might out-run them. At least he's on home territory!'

'Yes, but there's...' Perilla frowned. So many thoughts, all getting jumbled up.

'What?' Jeg leaned forward anxiously. 'What is it, Mum?'

'I'm not sure,' Perilla said slowly. 'It's just that I got a whiff of-...something a lot worse than those comedy cops.'

She shook her head. 'No, it's gone. Must've imagined it.' She flashed the thought to Scallion: *Forget about going to your place. Follow them undercover policemen. And that wolf.*

Hilary Bottomley peeped through the blinds to see if the Johnsons' visitors were still there, and if so, whether they were misbehaving in the garden.

She'd been deeply irritated all evening by the evidence of other people's enjoyment...barbecue-smells, clinking glasses, shrill laughter and so on--to which she was not party, nor even *at* the party. So annoyed, in fact, that she'd retired to bed with one of her Heads, and then been unable to sleep.

She could not for the life of her understand why she and Aubrey were never invited anywhere, when they had so much to offer, kept such an exquisite home, and were so supportive of Neighbourhood Watch.

How well she remembered that Mrs. Jackson's coffee-morning soon after she'd moved into Brimbleby Way. One would have thought that, as a newcomer, the woman would have been grateful to her for taking the trouble to buff up her coffee-table, especially as she'd been using her own hankie!

But no, Hilary had got the distinct impression that she'd done the wrong thing, although she would never understand why--but then, others' standards would, she feared, never reach the level of her own. Well, the Johnsons' little get-together appeared to be over now, and that at least was a relief.

Such a pity she hadn't been able to get a look at the departing guests, because no doubt they'd have been too intoxicated to drive, in which case it would clearly have been her duty to telephone the police in order to alleviate an accident...she expected there'd be cans and bottles and other disgusting debris all over the pavement in the morning. Her keen gaze scanned the area outside the Johnsons', stopping dead when it reached the street-light.

There was someone there, leaning nonchalantly against the lamp-post, as though waiting for a bus. And even Hilary's flawed logic told her that this was no belated party-guest, because the Johnsons had entertained only adult neighbours...twelve of them, she'd counted, as well as noting names...whereas this person was, most definitely, a child.

A child in a cowboy-outfit, all in black, the colour favoured by burglars, and, worst of all, *smoking!* She could see the smoke curling upwards towards the light, but nothing else was visible because of the over-sized black hat that came down almost to the shoulders.

It was the smoking that did it, that and the slouching. Both, in her opinion, the prime causes of moral decay and obvious characteristics of delinquent slum-children. And where were the parents, she'd like to know? No doubt waiting round the corner to receive the booty from their offspring's burglary, or else sleeping off their drunken excesses in their hovel. Well, she was not putting up with it one moment longer!

Firmly buttoning up her dressing-gown, Hilary stormed off down the stairs. And so annoyed was she that it never once crossed her mind to contact Neighbourhood Watch, or even to wake Aubrey--not that he'd have been rousable anyway, because he'd recently started sleeping in the guest-room, and taking sedatives on the grounds that his nerves were bad....

Wrenching open the front door, she screamed furiously: 'YOU! What are you doing out at this time of night? '

The small figure turned, slowly, unconcernedly, smoke-haze like a halo round its hat. And then, with an swift and unexpected movement, whipped open its long black coat. Hilary screamed.

'Hold onto those griffons!' Perilla shouted, slamming the jeep into 4-wheel drive, and careering into an adjacent field. 'Might just head 'em off this way.'

Betty, who'd sat sobbing into Tobin's hankie, uttered a small scream as they flew over what felt remarkably like a low wall. The griffons, still digesting, merely looked down their beaks, as griffons do.

They see-sawed across the field, headlights illuminating groups of startled cattle, which Perilla somehow contrived to miss. It was an uncomfortable ride, suffered in silence by all but Chervil, who after a particularly violent lurch, yelled: 'Oh, Mother! This griffon's leaking! All over

'Urgh, gross,' Jeg said.

'Sight's sake, Chervil,' Perilla said, through gritted teeth, 'you know perfectly well what he's doing! He's regurgitating his buttie, that's all. Give him a minute, he'll eat it again!'

'Hey, Mum, I think we've beaten 'em!' Jeg was watching the play of headlights in the lane.

'No we haven't,' Betty said. 'They're still in front--that's Tobin coming up the lane. But I dunno who that is behind *him...*'

In the next moment, a huge black motorbike raced past, apparently towing an old-fashioned motorcycle and sidecar.

'Hey, cool bike!' Jeg said. 'Can I have one, Mum?'

'Shut up, Jeg!' Perilla snapped, pulling back into the lane. 'And keep a hold of Warg...and you! Chervil! Forget about your blithering jeans! Calm him down if you can get through...tell him we're on our way and everything's going to be all right, sort of thing.'

She really did wish she believed it herself.

She'd tried bursting their tyres, but she just hadn't been able to concentrate. Going too fast, and too many minds in the way.

'Getting like the Brockway along here,' Granny observed. 'And who was *that* on the motorbike?'

Tobin squinted into the mirror. 'No idea. It was female though.'

'How do you make that out?'

'Do us a favour, Bryony, I may be getting on, but I still got eyes! And even I know they don't make men's leathers *that* shape!'

'Well, now that you've had a good look,' Granny said, 'you'll notice that we're heading back into Brimwold.'

With the last of his strength, Warg crawled up Apple Row, knowing that they weren't far behind.

Well, this is it he told himself. *And all because of that ole moon.*

Whitewashed cottages gleamed in the pale light. He supposed he could have run into one of the front gardens, but then he'd be boxed in, and he'd had enough of being hunted and cornered.

No, when the end came, he'd face them in the open--for the first and last time, like a true werewolf.

Perilla slammed the brakes on, and the jeep slewed sideways in the muddy lane.

'Lost him! Bloody lost him!' She smacked the steering-wheel in frustration. 'His mind's closed down! Anybody else get a fix on him?'

They shook their heads. Nobody had.

Granny closed her eyes tight and concentrated, but it wasn't any use.

'Warg's gone in and shut his door,' she told Tobin sadly. 'I've lost him. And so has them two chasing him, which is good, but...'

Tobin felt the worry cloud her mind, like a shadow across the moon.

'Ain't them bothers me,' she said. 'It's...'

'I know,' Tobin interrupted. 'I caught it too.'

They eyed each other.

'Then you don't need me to tell you,' Granny said, 'that there's something else out there. Something bad.'

Ffaffyn well lost him! Killer Calhoun spat a furious jet of tobacco onto the pavement. Couldn't smell werewolf no more, which meant he was on the move, and, more 'n likely, getting away.

'Time we was going, Blod.' He fastened her back into his coat: taken all his strength it had to stop her going for the silly cow that'd come at him, screaming and shouting: he allowed himself a grin. Seen her off, but, hadn't they!

Oh, well: back on the trail. Done it before, do it again. However long it took. Because Killer Calhoun never gave up.

'I think we've got him.' Rog. slowed down as they neared the cottages. 'Over there! And did you see them *teeth*? Take aim, partner!'

'I am, I am!' Steve was half out of the window, stun-gun at his shoulder. 'END OF THE ROAD, PAL!' he shouted, victory in his voice. And then: 'Oh, sod it. It is, as well!'

'You what?' Rog. sighed. It was all going wrong again.

Steve lowered the gun. 'Dead end. Cul-de-sac, whatever--he's gone down there, between the cottages, and...'

'No problem! Come on! Let's have him!'

And Rog. was off and running before Steve could warn him about the little old lady in the nightie and the dressing-gown. The one standing on her doorstep, brandishing a shot-gun.

'Are you sure you're up to this, Mrs. Bottomley?'

Hilary had specifically requested a policewoman, and W.P.C. Clarkson had drawn the short straw. Everyone at the Station knew about Hilary Bottomley's endless telephone calls, and the constant complaints.

It was the shock, she'd explained to Aubrey, which only another woman would understand. She had allowed him to run

193

her into Bartlesham, but under no circumstances would she allow him to accompany her into the interview-room.

She swallowed, bravely. 'Quite sure,' she said. 'Now--what did you want to know?'

The W.P.C. consulted her notes. 'You were upstairs when you first noticed him. What was he doing?'

'Smoking,' Hilary said firmly, and with just the right amount of distaste. 'Really, these shopkeepers want prosecuting, selling to underage-'

'Yeah, right, they do,' interrupted the policewoman. 'And so you went downstairs and confronted him? Bit unwise, that, if I might say so.'

Hilary twisted her handkerchief. 'Well, I was just so *cross!* And anyway, I had every reason to believe it was a *child* out there, not a fully-developed...'her voice wobbled, but she recovered well.

'Anyway, I'm not afraid to stand up and be counted! And if more citizens did the same, it might be safe to walk our streets again!'

The W.P.C. wondered wearily if the woman was on H.R.T....had to be that or multi-vitamins, because of all that righteous indignation.

'Okay.' She made a note. 'And then you shouted at him. Did he reply?'

Hilary drew on reserves of strength she never knew existed: thanking God that Mother wasn't there to hear such things.

'He did not. At that very moment,' she said firmly, 'he turned round and...opened his coat.'

'Okay, Mrs. Bottomley,' the policewoman said comfortingly, 'don't worry, you're doing fine. But now--and I've got to ask this, but Stress-Counselling is available should you feel the need...what did you actually *see?*'

Hilary shuddered. 'It was horrible, horrible...'

'I'm sure it was.' *And I wouldn't like to bet who was more scared!* the W.P.C. was thinking, 'just tell me in your own words,' she prompted.

'He was sort of *swinging* it!' Hilary squeaked. 'About three feet long it was, and made of metal!'

'I don't care who you are, you ain't going down me back passage!' shrieked the old woman, who had an amazingly loud voice for the size of her.

She had her rollers in and her teeth out, neither of which made her one bit less scary. What *was* it with the pensioners in this village? Steve wondered. Nobody in their right minds'd mess with *them*...what really did it, though, was the shotgun, a big, no-nonsense double-barrelled job that might or might not have been loaded. not that it mattered, because it didn't wobble once.

'And make no mistake, I know how to use it!' she snapped, as though reading their minds--funny how many of them seemed to do that-- 'SO GET THEM HANDS UP!'

They did. 'But we're policemen, honest!'

It sounded lame even to Steve, because they were virtually in plainclothes, apart from the Wolf-logo sweatshirts and baseball-caps, and driving an unmarked car. But how could he ever hope to explain the concept of Undercover Wolf-Patrols to an irate old woman bent on blowing holes in his midriff?

Worse, he wasn't even armed any more because, under threat from a real gun, he'd been forced to lay his own weapon on the cottage doorstep, like an offering.

'Pinch me goosegogs, would you!' She carried on as though she hadn't heard. 'And nick me cabbages, eh? Well, I'm sick of it! Buggers like you! Townie allotment-rustlers!'

'Yes, but there's a...' Rog. waved his arms helplessly. This was useless. And the longer they stood there, the further away the wolf was getting.

She glared. 'Eh? What's that you say? What you mumbling about?' She waggled the gun furiously. 'SPEAK UP, WILL YOU!'

'I SAID...' What *was* the point? Steve gave up. 'SORRY!' he roared. 'SORRY! YES WE DONE IT! IT'S A FAIR COP!'

'YEAH!' Rog. bellowed, entering into the spirit of the thing. 'DON'T TELL THE FUZZ AND WE'LL GO STRAIGHT HONEST!'

She'd heard *that*, all right. She smiled, grimly. 'Right then! Now bugger off before I changes me mind and calls the Law! And don't you come back!'

Steve made one last, unwise grab for the stun-gun. Her reactions were incredible: she'd stamped on his fingers before he knew it. And even with her slippers on, it came keen.

'You LEAVE THAT HERE!' she roared. 'I'll be using it on the next lot comes after me marrows!'

Warg sank down, exhausted: his legs just wouldn't go any more.

He'd found an allotment-shed: locked, but no problem there with his indestructible teeth…which had a sun-lounger in it.

As a bed, it wasn't a patch on the one Perilla'd got him from the pet-shop, mainly because it kept collapsing in the middle as soon as he climbed aboard. And there wasn't even a blanket.

But it was a whole lot better than sleeping rough in a ditch. He couldn't eat, of course, because they'd still be hunting him. But he'd lie down, rest and close his eyes…just for a while…and then he'd head for home.

'Back to the Manse, then,' Perilla said glumly. 'There's nothing else for it. And we'll just have to hope Warg's got the sense to do the same.'

'She's still there,' Rog. observed, 'keeping watch and taking aim. She's rock-steady! There's no chance of getting down that alleyway.'

'Mebbe she'll go down with hypothermia,' Steve mumbled through the mouthful of fingers he was sucking better. 'Vicious old bat! I could have her for assault!'

'Leave it, Steve.' Rog. started the engine. 'Sometimes you've just gotta cut your losses.'

'What, like the never-forget-this-comes-out-of-The-Force's-overstretched-budget-laddie-stun-gun? How'm I going to explain *that* one, eh?'

'Oh, chill out. We'll think of something--meantime, where are we heading? There's hours of the shift left yet!'

Steve shrugged. 'Search me. Where would you go if you were a wolf on the run?'

'Well, there is *one* place,' Rog. said, reversing carefully out of Apple Row.

'Where? Where? Cut the crap, Rog., and tell me!'

'Where all the waifs and strays end up, of course--that bloody animal-sanctuary!'

'Cobblers!' barked A.C.C. Root. 'I dunno, juvenile flashers in cowboy-suits!'

With a straight face, Sergeant Gilmore said: 'Kids do grow up fast these days, Sir. And you did ask to be kept informed of any strange nocturnal goings-on, especially in the Brimwold area.'

The A.C.C. snorted. 'Bloody women! All the bloody same when they get to that funny age! Hormones, Sergeant, hormones. If it's not peeping-toms, it's bloody shoplifting! My missus went like that…got her a budgie. Odd, that..bloody thing swears all the bloody time! Anyway…' he tapped the report on his desk..'get it checked out, Sergeant. Runaway kids sleeping rough, that sort of thing. Any more on this alleged wolf while we're at it?'

'Just the odd sighting, Sir, here and there. Usually around the villages, and always at full moon.'

A.C.C. Root shook his head. 'Full moon, eh? Beats me what they're all on, out in the sticks. But whatever it is, I could use some of it!'

'Put the lights out!' Steve hissed. 'And slow down. In fact, pull the car off the road, and we'll go on foot. If he's out there, he's gotta come this way…we'll nab him before he gets inside.'

'What with?' Rog. slowed to a snail's pace: the gates to the
Manse stood open, the drive lay in darkness. 'Our bare hands? No
more stun-gun, or had you forgotten?'

'I dunno, do I? But I'll get the bloody thing, whatever!'

Rog. glanced at Steve's rumpled hair, the red face, the set jaw
and the wild, stary eyes scanning every bush.

'You're obsessed, you are,' he sighed.

'D'you see what I see?' Perilla was squinting down the drive.

In all the excitement, she'd forgotten to put the floodlights
on, but her eyes were keen enough to spot movement amongst the
bushes.

'Well, well,' she muttered. 'I do believe we've got visitors.'

Steve felt naked without the stun-gun.

He broke a big overhanging branch off one of Perilla's horse-
chestnut trees, and advanced up the drive after Rog., trying not to
crunch the gravel.

And just where the shadows lay deepest, a voice in his left
ear said: 'Drop the branch and turn around. Unless maybe you
feel lucky. Do you feel lucky? Well, go ahead, make my day--'cos
I warn you, I've got a griffon and I'm not afraid to use it!'

He turned, slowly, bowels churning, to find himself
confronted by a young lad holding onto one of them mean-
looking turkey-type things. There was a small, fat dog snarling up
at him, and another kid standing over Rog., with an even uglier
piece of poultry on his arm. The birds' eyes gleamed in the
darkness like they were ready for some action.

'They're not exactly *hungry*,' the lad went on, ''cos they've
had their bacon-butties--but they can always manage a chunk of
nice, warm flesh...' the creatures shrieked horribly, as though in
agreement.

'Better do as he says, Steve.' Rog. actually had his hands up!
Steve lowered his branch, but, because he couldn't quite get his
head round what he was seeing, didn't actually let go of it.

Anyway, he wanted something to defend himself with if those vultures came at him...

Rage and frustration swept over him. Months of his life he'd given to the Wolf-Patrol, and he wasn't about to go back to being Harry-the-Sodding- Hedgehog. He might've lost the stun-gun, but he wasn't giving up now!

'Yeah!' he snarled. 'Yeah, I *do* feel lucky! And I'm going to have that wolf if it's the last thing I do...'he swung the branch in a wide, defiant arc.

That was when the floodlights suddenly came on, and this big, tough-looking female came striding down the drive and looked him up and down. Slowly. And, somehow, made him feel like the naughtiest boy there ever was. Confused, he lowered the branch, but that didn't mean he was giving in!

After a while, the woman sighed, muttered, 'Death-wish, eh?' and gave a long, low whistle.

From somewhere up the drive there was rustling and trampling and a lot of heavy breathing, and then, clear on the still night air, the jingling of small bells. And Rog. distinctly heard one of the lads say: 'Aw, Mum!'

'Let 'em out, Bryony!' the woman called, followed by: 'Right, girls, fell the bugger!'

Steve never had a chance. Gimmer and the flock had him pinned face-down on the gravel before he could say shepherd's pie. They discovered a previously unrealised taste for shoes and buttons--but flesh, when they got down to it, was much more fun, and softer on the mouth as well.

Rog. stood with his hands well up, wondering just where Steve got his foolhardy streak from. Some things just weren't worth dying for.

And who were all these weirdos? His heart lurched as he recognised the mad old witch who lived in the Beechwood-- might've guessed she'd be in there somewhere...

'And I always thought sheep was herbivorous!' Granny observed. 'Just shows how wrong you can be!'

'Gerroffme, you great lumps of mutton!' Steve was screaming.

Perilla regarded him coldly.

'You deserve everything you get,' she told him. 'Hunting that poor wolf all over Bartleshire! Well, now it's your turn! How's it feel to be cornered, eh?'

Steve screamed again, something about 'only-doing-our-job!', and Perilla snorted.

Betty, who was glaring in the general direction of Steve, burst into tears for the second time that evening and sobbed: 'How could you! Oh, Kenny, Kenny, me little brother!'

Rog., looking baffled, lowered his hands a fraction.

'Here, what's she on about, little brother? She potty, or what?'

'Only slightly,' Perilla snapped, glaring at Betty. 'Comes of imagining you've been brought up by wolves in the wild, *doesn't it, Betty?* Anyway,' biting the end off a large cigar, she addressed Steve through the mass of sheep, 'what are we going to do with you, eh?'

'Let us go!' Rog. pleaded. Anything to get away from these nutters and back to civilisation. 'And we'll lay off the wolf, honest!'

'Yes, that's all very well.' Perilla paused to strike a match on her boot, 'but how do I know I can trust you? Hmm?'

'You can, you can!' Rog. nodded vigorously. 'We've learnt our lesson! Just call those animals off and we'll be on our way!'

She drilled him with her eyes, and then gave an almost imperceptible hand-signal. Bleating mutinously, the Flock got off Steve who, when he managed to stand up, didn't look any too good.

He was not an inspiring sight. His trainers were gone, along with his socks, his trousers and sweatshirt in tatters, his cap shredded, and his face lividly imprinted with hundreds of little pockmarks where he'd been pressed down onto the gravel.

But it seemed he wasn't beaten even then. With a shock like a punch in the guts, Rog. heard him say, with what dignity he could muster, what with the sheep nipping at his ankles, 'I am...OW...bound to tell you that we are sworn...BUGGER!-...an oath to...OOF...do our duty, and the SODIT...Wolf-Patrol never gives up!'

They all shook their heads, regretfully. Even Rog. found himself joining in. And then Perilla sighed and said: 'Oh dear, oh dear, you don't learn, do you? Right girls, in again!'

Even Steve, however, had his breaking-point. 'No!' he screamed, trying to protect his pitted head with his tattered sleeves, 'not the sheep!

Anything but the sheep!'

'Knew you'd see sense,' Perilla grinned. 'All right, girls, OFF! Thing is, though, we simply can't believe a word you say, can we?'

'Oh, I think we can come to some arrangement,' Granny said from somewhere behind Steve, twisting his mind and prickling the hairs on the back of his neck.

And then she was in front of him, looking him straight in the eyes, and in the mind, and letting him know that if he ever so much as *glanced* at that wolf again, she'd be coming after him, and he'd be ever so ever so sorry...

'Right,' Perilla said briskly. 'Too cold to stand here chatting. Things to do, animals to bed down...and you gentlemen can bugger orf now. What'd'you reckon about the car, Bryony?...do all four tyres and the spare?'

'Done 'em,' Tobin said quietly, 'while you was messing around with them sheep. Headlights,, mirrors, radio, the lot...'

Rog. let out a stifled yelp, and Perilla said: 'Yes? Got a problem with that, have we? No? Then let me wish you a pleasant walk home in the moonlight. And don't come again, will you?'

Warg stirred and stretched: comfortable, he was not. And when he tried to get up, everything sort of locked.

Age, that's what it was. Well, he'd have to take it steady: getting too old and stiff for all this rushing about. But at least he'd given them chasing him the slip.

Just let me get home safe he promised himself, *and I'll stay in for the rest of me life.* Not that he meant a word of it: after all, he said the same thing every single time.

'Do we go out after him,' Jeg said, 'or leave him to come home?'

'Honestly, talk about thick!' Chervil snorted. 'Surely even *you* can see the danger's over? And incidentally, Mother, wasn't that all a bit uncivilised, setting the sheep on those men? I mean, what about their Human Rights?'

'Chervil,' Perilla said tiredly, 'if you haven't anything useful to contribute, I suggest you go and polish the basilisk...he hasn't moved for at least six days, and he's collecting dust on that bookshelf.'

When he'd gone off, sniffing disgustedly, she turned to the others and said: 'Well, what's the consensus? Wait here, or try and track him?'

Jeg said: 'Stay here, and he'll come home. He always does.'

'The lad's right about those men,' Granny said. 'I can guarantee we won't have no more trouble with *them*...but what about that other thing? The one that's after him and ain't open to persuasion?'

Perilla said: 'Oh. You felt it too.'

'Me n' all,' said a voice from the bushes. 'And to my mind, it's a bit of a sod.'

'Brassica!' Granny said. 'How the Sight did you get here?'

'It's a long story,' Brassica said, 'and it's been a bloody sight longer day. Let's just say it all started when that Bevis Tate broke into me house..''

'That was you!' Granny said, 'on his motorbike! Well, where's he got to, then?'

'Little turd!' Brassica snarled. 'Let's just say that Scallion's sorting him out-you do remember Scallion, Bryony?'

How could she ever forget! Scallion'd struck terror into many a grown man right from being little...and Granny felt a big smile coming on at the thought of her Sorting Out Bevis Tate. Just what he needed, and exactly what he deserved.

'Look, this is all very cosy,' Perilla said, 'but it's getting us nowhere. Anybody feel this...malign influence at the moment? More to the point, is anyone picking up on Warg?'

'Who's Warg then?' Brassica said with interest. 'Your new chap, is he? About time you got yourself a man, Perilla, after that creepy sod you married...'

'Don't matter,' Granny said hastily. 'Let's just say he's in danger, and we want him back safe. And no, I ain't getting a thing off him.'

'Me neither,' Tobin said, 'not a peep from either of 'em.'

Jeg shook his head. 'It's like Warg's switched off,' he said.

'Well then,' Perilla said, 'We'll have to hope that the whatever-it-is has lost Warg's trail. I'd suggest we all have some supper, go to bed, and keep our minds tuned in.'

'Fine by me,' Tobin said. 'I'm for bed. Totally worn out with all this excitement, I am. Lots of double rooms in this place, are there?'

Granny fixed him with a Look. 'Don't you go getting no funny ideas, Tobin Hackett,' she snapped. ''Cos I'll be Sitting Up and keeping me mind out for Warg. Once I've had me supper, of course. I'm gagging for a cupper tea.'

'And it was *this* big!' Rog. paced the room, arms outstretched.

'And then some,' Steve added, 'with these massive steel teeth...'

'...with which it shredded all your clothes,' Sergeant Gilmore suggested.

'Oh, no.' Steve protested without thinking. '*That* was the sheep. You never saw such a vicious bunch in your life!' He knew he wasn't being terribly convincing. '*She* made 'em do it, Sarge, the horsey woman. Honest, I thought my time was up! Don't ever let anyone tell you sheep are gentle!'

The Sarge raised an eyebrow. 'I'll bear it in mind, lad, next time me and the missus are crossing a meadow--back to the ill-fated Patrol car, then. This here wolf punctured *all four tyres and the spare* with the aforementioned silver teeth, I take it?'

'No, Sarge, no,' Steve said. 'That was the scary old woman's boyfriend. And he said he'd done the lights and the radio as well...I dread to think what's happened under the bonnet. And you know, it was like he'd done it with his mind or something, because he never went near the car! I was watching!'

'And that's when you lost the Stun-Gun,' Sergeant Gilmore said heavily. 'That innovative and-dare I Mention it--valuable item of specialist equipment what we'll never hear the end of once the Chief Constable gets to hear about it.'

Steve shook his head. '*No* Sarge, that was the other old woman, the one in the dressing-gown and slippers.'

Sergeant Gilmore nodded sagely. 'The little old Granny who somehow wrested it from your hapless grasp and forced you into submission? Breed 'em tough out Brimwold way, so I've heard.'

'But you don't understand!' Rog. protested. 'She had a shotgun, great big double-barrelled job it was! She was protecting her gooseberries, and she meant business!'

Sergeant Gilmore hadn't had a migraine for more than a year, and thought he'd done well. But he knew, sure as death, that he'd got one coming on now. His head was pounding. Lights flashed before his eyes. But he'd got to get to the bottom of this before he went to lie down in a darkened room...

Rubbing the bridge of his nose, in an effort to delay the attack, he said: 'So what exactly happened when you got up this animal-sanctuary? And how did those people get the better of you?'

'Well...' Steve actually looked a bit embarrassed. 'It was this young lad threatened me with his big, ugly bird...'

'Hold on a minute, son. I cannot believe what I am hearing. Are you saying that some unchivalrous lout employed his *girlfriend* to menace you? Because if so, then Society has certainly gone a long way down the slippery slope....'

'No, Sarge, no, it was a great big vulture-thing with a curved beak and a horrible look in its eye. It would've had me, sure as...'

'Sure as sheep, eh, son?'

'Well, yeah...but I didn't give in, Sarge! I fought back...until them bloody sheep knocked me down.'

Sergeant Gilmore shook his pounding head in a bewildered sort of way. 'Well, of course, a spot of ovine assault would do it every time! After which you heroically fled, as well as you were able, shoes being but a distant memory--' Steve winced as his blisters throbbed....until you fortuitously obtained a lift back into Bartlesham?'

They nodded silently. Even Rog. and Steve knew when Sergeant Gilmore's sarcasm had gone into overdrive.

'Tell you what, you two.' He patted one of Steve's mangled sleeves. 'This is beyond me. Got one of me heads, and I'm off to the Restroom. But you've had a bit of a night of it, so off the canteen, get yourselves a cupper tea to clear your heads--and then STRAIGHT BACK HERE AND WRITE IT ALL UP, ONLY WITHOUT ALL THE WOLVES WITH BIG STEEL TEETH AND MACHINE_TOTING LITTLE OLD LADIES! I'll expect a copy from each of you on my desk before midday--understood?'

'Can't go on avoiding it,' Tobin said as they crossed the corridor into the East Wing. 'You owe me an answer, Bryony.'

'I know,' Granny said, stepping carefully over a colony of Great Crested Newts Perilla had popped into a washing-up bowl for safekeeping because their pond had been excavated for a new housing-development, 'and I been thinking it over. Even though I said I'd tell you at Summer's End, I've made up me mind. I'm set in me ways, Tobin, and don't know as I'd want to stop pleasing myself.'

'Ain't asking you to!' Tobin paused by a large oak kist overshadowed by a gloomy old tapestry. 'Sit down here a minute, Bry. Sight's sake, let's talk it over. I'd look after you, you know that.'

'That's just what I'm afraid of,' Granny grunted, sinking down onto the polished wood. 'Because mebbe I've still got things to do.'

'But we're neither of us getting no younger!' Tobin protested. 'And we've all gotta slow down sometime!'

'Is that so?' Granny snapped. 'Well, don't you go taking to your bed on my account, Tobin Hackett...you may've retired from your fancy farm, but I ain't given up yet!'

'Like what? Not all that Grandmistress stuff, surely! Pack it in, Bryony, stand down and make way for someone younger. You and me could be going out living it up!'

'I ain't one for dance-halls and fancy restaurants, as well you know.'

'Well, all right then, we'll stay in and have fun!'

'What, with Guildings and Joinings and Passings to organize? And Bingo and sing-songs and Summering and Wintering Ceremonies? Old Tukesley kept 'em all going, and so shall I. Tradition's important!'

'Not *that* important,' Tobin said gently. 'Gotta move with the times. Things change, Bryony.'

She looked at him for a long moment and then said, sadly: 'And some things don't, Tobin...like you for instance. Never was much of a Seer, were you? Wouldn't stand up for what you believed in. Well, some of us care, and go on caring until we drop. Guilding ain't a hobby, it's a way of life!'

'Ah, Bryony,' Tobin had gone pale. 'Don't create. What if I said I'd let you carry on with it all?'

'That's just it, Tobin,' Granny said. 'You'd-let-me. Just that. And you'd come to resent it, don't you see? That I wasn't one-hundred-percent yours? And sooner or later we'd fall out over it, and part...and I'd rather have you as me friend than me enemy.'

'So the answer's no? You're going to throw it all away for the sake of the Guild?'

Granny stared long and hard at the dust on the tapestry. 'Put it like that, Tobin,' she replied, 'then, yes, I s'pose I am.'

She hadn't meant to drop off, but it had been a long day, and, although she'd never admit it to a soul, that space-hopping did rather take it out of a body.

Perilla, too, was tireder than she realised, what with night-driving and mind-searching and especially all that shinning up and down the training-tower, which was silly, really, because it surely wasn't any harder than rugby-training....yet by the time she'd settled the Telsian dragons, which had only just arrived...usual thing, rescued from the sewers after being flushed down people's loos...fed the baby bat she carried round in her vest, next to her bosom, and got the locusts bedded down, she felt completely done in.

Jeg and Chervil, in accord for once, weren't in the mood for sleep. They were playing loud music and getting silly on some Drescombe scrumpy that Perilla didn't know they knew about.

'The look on that guy's face when saw the griffon!' Jeg snorted. 'What a classic!'

Brassica was well away and snoring after a bedtime nip or two from the small flask she carried to chase away the demons; Betty dreamed fitfully about Kenneth meeting a nice young lady and settling down, Grufty drooled in anticipation of Perilla's magnificent breakfast, and Tobin dreamed sadly of what might have been if he hadn't let Bryony go all them years ago...

Despite all Perilla's training, terror drove Warg straight through the front door, without bothering to open it, along the dark corridors and into his Kenneth-room, where he flung himself on the bed and howled into the duvet because there was something horrid after him that made his pelt crawl....

Of course, he really should've got in his basket, the reinforced plastic one with the nasty, anti-chew coating that Perilla'd had specially-made to break him of the habit, but there was something comforting about the Kenneth-room. It was normal, manly, *human*...the way his life ought to have been, had been, before all this moon-madness...granted, Perilla had done her best to help. Unlimited supplies of newspaper and his new steel-and-porcelain teeth had almost cured him of chewing things he shouldn't, and he didn't think he howled half as much as he used to.

Quite often now, when he got Urges, he could sort of hear her special Training-Voice going NO,NO, NO!...and then he'd feel Bad.

But not for long, because the pull of the moon was just too strong, and he knew he'd never be free of it. If only he'd had them jabs, if only he'd left that dog alone. If only he hadn't got bitten...

Sad old git, that's what he was turning into, always looking back. What good would that do him? And what use was he to anyone?

He thought about all them who'd tried to help him: Granny, Perilla, Jeg, Chervil and poor old Betty...what a life *she'd* had, putting up with his Monthlie...and how he'd let them all down. Maybe they'd be better off without him.

He wondered if Perilla was awake and worrying about him...but then why should she? Bitter tears ran down his muzzle, soaking his fur. Funny, that. Until he'd been Changed, he'd never even known that wolves could cry....perhaps the whole thing would be taken out of his hands...paws...before very long, anyway. Because once the whatever-it-was tracked him down, that'd be the end.

Shunning moonlight, Killer Calhoun hugs the shadowed margins of the Manse, his very boots steaming with excitement.

So *that's* where the bugger's gone to ground, in the ffaffyn animal-sanctuary! He might've known...squinting, he makes out the wolf-sized hole in the privet hedge. Smells him, too..half-man, half-wolf: that rank, fear-filled stink that he'd know anywhere on earth...

.....and something else. He raises his head, scenting the night-wind. *Ffaffyn supernaturals!*...smell 'em anywhere. Could be Roc, could be Wyvern or Griffon, could be any or all of 'em...well, well. Seemed he'd struck lucky. Beneath the hat, his eyes glitter red with bloodlust. Mebbe this'll turn out to be his lucky night.

In his clenched fist, Blodwyn senses them too, lunging and tugging, wanting them.

Down, girl. You shall have 'em soon enough. He licks his lips, fingering the long knife-sheath, imagining: Roc-skin, wide and white as the Llangolygoch Falls, and Wyvern, with its toasting-fork tail....but most of all, he craves Werewolf-hide. Only ever had one of them, just one in a whole lifetime. It hadn't been enough. And mebbe he won't send this one to the Lab, because after all this time, he reckons he deserves a bit of fun...

Mebbe him and Blod'll...play with it instead, take its skin while it's still screaming...make a cracking rug, that will...

…..but he'll never get it, stood there wool-gathering, will he. Best be off after it, while the scent's fresh.

In the Great Hall, Yaw the donkey paused in his sleepless clopping and twitched his ears, lifted his muzzle and brayed fit to bust.

Along the corridor, in the Minstrels' Gallery, the Griffon brothers stopped in mid-preen, beaks agape. Their leonine bodies tensed, poised, despite their recent outing, for action, preferably of the aggressive kind. They shrieked, as only griffons can, and high on his library shelf, the basilisk opened one eye.

Killer Calhoun stopped to take his hat off: he had to. Couldn't see a blamed thing with it on, even though he'd bought the smallest size *and* stuffed it with newspaper.

He shoved it behind the drinking-fountain in the courtyard: he'd come back for it later. Pretty soon, he reckoned, he'd be needing both hands. One for the knife, and the other for Blodwyn.

Granny woke suddenly and completely, knowing through the deep, dark silence that Warg was in trouble.

But where the Sight was he? Where were Tobin, Perilla and the boys? And even if she managed to wake Grufty, how would she ever find her way round this maze of a place?

Killer Calhoun creeps along the dark corridors, Blodwyn at the ready.

Silent and deadly he moves, likes gas down a mine-shaft, allowing, of course, for his age and the biker boots. Not so light on his feet, maybe, but a deal less hot-headed than he used to be.

Tracking the werewolf, slow and thorough, scanning, sniffing, missing nothing. Good warm trail, strong scent, easy following. Blodwyn pulls, sensing warm necks. Shadowed statues and painted ancestors look askance at their passing.

Cracking night-vision he's got, finely-honed by years of chasing nocturnal supernaturals, and a good nose on him, too. And all right, his teeth mightn't be his own, but they can't half bite. Only his hearing lets him down, though he'd never in a lifetime admit it. Folks will keep on bloody whispering, that's what it is, but that's their ffaffyn problem...after all, can't have a bounty-hunter with a hearing-aid, can you?

True, but then if he had, he wouldn't have missed the soft, insistent scratching on the parquet behind him.

Warg cowers at shadows in the Kenneth room. He listens, straining the long, hairy ears....but there's only his thumping heart, and the chattering of his steel-and-porcelain dentures.

He's not safe, though, it's still after him, the one that wants his pelt, and there's nowhere left to hide. And before he can stop himself, he raises his muzzle and unleashes all his pain and desolation in one long, agonized howl.

Killer Calhoun has cornered a *something* in the Billiard Room. Not the werewolf, but it's shit-scared, and it'll do to be going on with. And Blodwyn's yanking so hard he can hardly hold her....likes a good, solid neck, Bloddy does.

Go on then, girlie...take it now and bring it back to your Da. And he lets her go, unleashing her, so to speak, and she whips forward, wrapping herself round her prey's neck, locking and throttling, but not too much, just the way he's taught her.

And grabbing hold of Blodwyn again, the Bounty Hunter draws his victim slowly, inexorably back towards the skinning-knife, its screams, choked and muted, are music to his soul. Oh, but this one'll suffer, all right...

But then he hears it, howling, long and crazed and full of fear, and he gets a whiff, strong and close, of werewolf-musk, and it's no contest. Gotta let the ffaffyn thing go if he wants the top prize.

Course, Bloddy's all for finishing it off, but much as he'd like to oblige, there's no time to do it slow and proper...it's the werewolf or nothing.

But Blodwyn won't let go of her prey, she's got it on the floor, worrying it, throttling it slowly, link by link. Killer Calhoun sighs. That's young and headstrong for you, isn't it, forgetting all her training, *mauling the meat and getting personal.* Can't have that, no bloody good at a time like this. He's even left the whistle at home, not thinking to need it. Oh, well, back to basics…

'COME BY!' he bawls, in his best, carrying-over-the-hills voice, 'LEAVE IT, YOU BUGGER!'…and even then he has to heave her off.

God, but she's strong. Full-grown now, of course…with one last, vicious twist, she releases, and something falls, gasping, into the shadows. Pity about that one, still, you gotta be professional…course, Blod's got a sulk on now. Can't be helped, though.

'Come on, girl,' he whispers, coiling her round his hand. 'Find that there werewolf, and we'll *both* have us some fun.'

He could feel it, sure as moonrise, coming for him. Terror made his fur prickle.

The Kenneth-room, once a nursery, was crammed with child-sized furniture, too small to hide in, or under. A painted rocking-horse creaked faintly in front of the window, as though wanting to be off across the moonlit fields, and Warg held his breath. Was that a footstep out in the corridor?

A family of porcelain dolls regarded him with glittering eyes in waxy faces: he could have sworn one of them smirked. Panic hit him again: he gazed around in desperation. There just had to be *somewhere.…* and then he heard, it really heard it, not just in his head. Something coming down the corridor, halting at the door…terror drove him into the nearest toy-box. He didn't fit, but then he wasn't in any fir state to consider geometry.

The door, taking forever, creaked open. And into the stifling, terrifying silence, a voice said: 'My. My. Mr. Werewolf, *what* a big tail you got! All the better to grab you by!'

And Granny stumbles along dark corridors, yelling and banging on doors and pushing her mind out towards somebody, anybody.

Bit by agonizing bit, he's being extracted from the toybox, every hair in his tail protesting. His claws scrabble desperately for a paw-hold, but there's nothing, not even a splinter, on the worn wooden surface.

And the strength of the puller is truly astounding because Warg is no light-weight. The lid bangs his head, several times, painfully, as the last bit of him's hauled out, eyes tight shut because he daren't face whatever's waiting in the darkness.

And then comes the dee gurgling sound, like sludge moving through sewer-pipes.

'Well, dang me!' says a gravelly voice. 'Mighty fine specimen we got here, yes siree. Okay there, Bloddy girl...GO!'

After which, getting away becomes very much a second option for Warg. His first involves breathing.

Well, if she couldn't rouse anyone else, she'd have to do it on her own.

Granny puffed along the corridor, Grufty waddling behind, and she cursed the darkness, and legs that wouldn't go like they used to. Where the Sight was Perilla, and why wasn't she awake? She almost wished she'd let Tobin share her room, because she hadn't a clue where his was.

She could feel every ounce of Warg's pain and terror, but she'd be buggered if she could get through any of it to comfort him....and if she didn't get a move on, it'd be too late to ever help him again.

Warg's world kept coming and going, in and out of focus. Every so often, he'd manage a short, rasping breath, only to have it snatched away again by whatever was choking the life out of him.

Odd sounds drifted across his brain…half-heard words, cruel and taunting, that part of him realized would probably be the last he ever heard.

Ffaffyn werewolf, not so brave now, eh boyo?

And then he felt himself being pulled again, that terrible pressure on his neck.

Come you here and let's have that skin off you, nice and slow…

So this is where it ends, he thought sadly, *just like Betty always said it would if I didn't stay in of a night. She was right, and I was wrong.*

He felt bad about Betty, wondered how she'd cope with the broken-down bungalow when he was gone…and the bills and everything. Well, nothing he could do about it now, or anything else for that matter.

Fact was, he hadn't even got the breath to cry. He could only brace himself against the coming pain.

No need to guess where he was…Granny's head was near bursting with all the pain he was going through.

'WARG!'she bellowed. 'Hang ON! I'm COMING!'….before kicking the door in, because that was what you did when you were rescuing someone and wanted to scare off their attacker, and anyway, she'd still got her big ole boots on.

Whatever she'd been expecting, though, hadn't included the sight of the griffons, black against the open window, perched on the rocking-horse and gobbling down something she didn't want to dwell on….and they weren't half making some disgusting noises doing it.

Warg was flat out, clutching his throat and breathing hoarsely, his mind beyond terror. He was hurting, but at least he was alive. And he'd mend, that much she knew, although he'd need a deal of love and kindness along the way.

She didn't go to him, though, because backed up against the toybox was the evil little bugger that'd put him there, all dressed in black and with some sort of chain-thing wrapped around his hand, as well as a mind full of poison. And she smelt that evil again, and knew this was the one that'd been training Warg.

But she wasn't worried he'd have a go at her, because he didn't look any too good. He'd got a sort of glazed, gobsmacked face on him, because, said his mind, it couldn't cope with coming off second-best for the first time ever.

There was a fair bit of blood running down his neck, she realise, and as the moon caught him full in the face, she saw the odd-looking outlines of his cheeks: what was it about 'em? And then it hit her: too smooth! No ears! Them griffons'd gone for the sticking-out bits!

'Well, well.' Folding her arms, she looked him up and down, dwelling particularly on the bloodstained lugholes. 'Stopped wearing your glasses then, have you?'

Roaring with rage and pain, Killer Calhoun went past Granny like an express train, knocking the breath clean out of her. The chain in his hand lashed out once, in passing, and she felt a searing pain on her cheek. What kind of a thing was *that?* She'd never seen its like before.

The griffons, who'd moved straight into their regurgitation phase, glanced up, belched noisily, and settled back onto the rocking-horse.

Granny leaned against the door-frame, fighting to get her breath back. She could feel blood on her cheek where that...thing'd got her, but, more importantly, she could hear Warg's wheezing breaths, so at least he was still around. She'd go and sort him out, just as soon as she could manage to breathe and walk at the same time.

One of the griffons brought up something unmentionable and sat, immobile, with whatever was dangling from its beak. After a few moments, it began bolting it down with evident pleasure.

Granny looked away, fighting the urge to gag. But then, what right had she to judge? Took all sorts, didn't it? And when all was said and done, them griffons had saved Warg's life, so who was she to begrudge them a couple of ears?

'All right, all right,' she wheezed, 'I ain't nagging. You two've done enough for a lifetime, and that little turd'll get his comeuppance. Enjoy your, er, second dinner.'

Killer Calhoun ran blindly, alternately wiping blood off his neck and tears of frustration out of his eyes, Blodwyn trailing sullenly from his hand.

Them ffaffyn great bird-things'd got him, the bastards, and he'd lost the werewolf! He couldn't believe it. He must be slipping…and that knowledge hurt more than the places where his ears had been.

Call hisself a bounty-hunter when he'd got caught like that! Well, it wouldn't happen again, that was for sure. Out in the paddock, he stopped to get his bearings. And that proved his second mistake of the night, because The Flock was abroad, woken by all the commotion.

Led by old Gimmer, they came pounding up the field. And having surrounded the newcomer, stood glaring, blowing down their noses.

At which Blodwyn reared up, quivering, and it took all Killer Calhoun's strength to hold onto her…always had a thing about sheep, hadn't she, long as he'd known her…

'NO!' he hissed. 'DOWN, Bloddie! I'll tell you when!'

And then Perilla, resplendent in baseball boots, men's pyjamas and what would, in times gone by, have been described as a smoking-jacket, appeared, waving a lantern-torch and boomed: 'What the blithers is going on?'

Tobin, looking scared but determined, hovered behind. After all, he'd already been through the worst bit…waking her up and getting her out of bed. Definitely not a woman he'd want to cross, Perilla.

The Flock, ready for a good rumble, pressed tightly around the intruder. Old Gimmer bared her worn teeth, daring him to Start Something. She'd sort the bugger out, by heck she would.

Killer Calhoun whirled, unsure which way to face. Goldarn it if they hadn't got him surrounded! After a bit, he dropped into a sort of gunslinger's crouch, only without the gun, but with Blodwyn coiled and ready round his throwing arm. He'd been in worse corners'n this! Nothin' him and his pardner couldn't face together…

'Hey!' Perilla bawled. 'You with no ears! Can you hear me? What're you doing frightening m' sheep, eh?'

The Flock sniggered. Them, frightened! Hah! Just let 'em at him! Any minute now she'd give the word, and they'd go in--

Killer Calhoun said nothing. But he did sneer, which, under the circumstances wasn't any too clever.

Then Perilla looked into his mind, and her eyes went cold. 'Been after the werewolf, haven't you? Only my boys got to you first, I see. Pity they left you your...'

She was interrupted by one of the younger ewes, which, fed up with niceties, took a chunk out of the bounty-hunter's buttock-- just to start the action, really...whereupon Blodwyn, goaded beyond endurance, forgot all her training and lunged.

'NO!' screamed Killer Calhoun, feeling his hand go dead where she'd wrapped herself round it, 'Not the ffaffyn SHEEP, you silly bugger!...get the WOMAN!'

Blodwyn wasn't having it, though...sheep's necks were what she lusted after, and sheep's necks she would get...she'd gone crazy, just like the first time he'd seen her, flailing and lashing until there was no holding her. Seemed like she'd forgotten everything he'd ever taught her and gone back to the Wild.

The ewes, who'd jumped nimbly out of the way at the first sign of trouble, watched her contortions with interest. Killer Calhoun wrestled with her, intent on aiming her at the woman, but she was that mad she was literally tying herself in knots. And she didn't give up, neither, she'd gone beyond reason, and he knew he had to best her, now or never.

But pain and blood-loss had weakened him more than he'd realised. And he had to stop her. It weren't no good her strangling ffaffyn sheep just because they were winding her up--wasn't there where the danger lay...with the last of his strength, he yanked her back, feeling her power and her fury, but knowing that he'd beaten her. And as he stumbled and fell, there was no fight left in him, and no rage in her.

He lay on his back, winded, staring up at the stars through a mass of sheep, Blodwyn quiet beside him. She uncoiled and came to him, then, her Master, and beautiful she was as no woman ever could be: his breath caught at the cold, lovely glint of her beneath the moon--his Bloddy.

'Get you here, then, girl,' he murmured, 'and no hard feelings, 'cos after all, your Da knows best.'

Soft as a whisper, she snaked around his neck, smooth as a string of pearls, caressing his throat like a lover. And then, oh bugger, tightened...

'That's that, then,' Perilla grunted.

He didn't *look* much of anything, lying there, not enough of him to frighten anybody. But Perilla knew from his poisonous mind what he was, what he'd been, and she wouldn't be crying any tears over him. And she supposed she'd have to report it, bloody nuisance, policemen all over the place, scaring the animals...then again, mebbe she wouldn't bother.

The remains of Blodwyn lay beside him, three short lengths of broken chain, snapped courtesy of Tobin and Perilla's mindpower. And the thing's'd left scorchmarks on the earth...well, she'd bury them later, good and deep. Have to remember not to let the sheep graze there.

The ewes were sulking because they'd been cheated out of Having A Go.

'Sorry, girls,' Perilla told them. 'Can't be helped. 'Know you're pissed orf, but some you win, some you lose.'

They'd never disobey, that much she knew, but their eyes pleaded: *Couldn't we have a bit of a trample? Just a little one?*

'No,' Perilla told them firmly. 'Appreciate the thought, but, scum though he is, he's gone. And two wrongs don't make a right. Besides which, we'd better be finding Kenny and Bryony. One of 'em'll be wanting a cuddle, and the other one some good, strong tea.'

Mariander knew nothing about the night's events until she ran into Betty alongside the 'Pennypincher' bacon-counter. And when she did hear about it, she got good and mad.

'That's typical Bryony, never thinking to call, and specially seeing as how she'd got me dog with her! She's always been the same, keeping things to herself!'

'Well, it *was* a bit of an emergency,' Betty said apologetically, 'what with the Wolf-Patrol and then that horrible little man after our Kenny...d'you know, Perilla reckons he was a *bounty-hunter!*' She shuddered. 'Can you believe it? My poor little brother was nothing but a hide to him!'

Mariander shook her head. 'Sounds horrible. How is Kenneth, by the way?'

'Well, you know,' Betty said, 'bit shook up, and his throat's sore, but your Bryony's give him some of her linctus and lozenges, and Perilla's really making a fuss of him.' She lowered her voice to a whisper. 'And I could be wrong, but I get the impression she's a bit sweet on him!'

'Really.' Mariander squinted at the instructions on a can of air-freshener, muttering: 'Waste of money! Bunch of Brightwort'd do just as well!...' before adding, 'that's nice for 'em both then.'

'Mind you,' Betty said thoughtfully, 'the women always did like our Kenny. Even last night, with the state he was in, that old tarty one couldn't keep her hands off him...I still dunno who *she* was...must ask your Bryony...'

Mariander's hackles, which Betty thought she'd smoothed down, seemed all of a sudden to have gone up again.

'Tell me she didn't have stilettos on?' she hissed. 'Or a short skirt, fishnets, bleached hair, lot of eyes and lips?'

'Well...er, yes, yes, she did,' Betty stammered. 'You know the sort, loud and good-hearted, but wouldn't mix with polite company--'

'I *knew* it!' Mariander shouted, snatching up a packet of frozen sausages and hurling them into her basket, frightening old Mrs. Gray who was innocently inspecting the black puddings.

'Brassica-bloody-Bray!'And muttering furiously she stomped across to Household Products, Betty trailing nervously behind.

Well, that does it!' Mariander snapped, grabbing a pair of rubber gloves and waving them furiously. 'Everyone's been on this jaunt but me--and what was I doing? Sitting in mixing up facepacks, wasn't I! Well, thank you all very much! And *Brassica Bray*, if you please! Did she have an old man with her as well?'

Well, not that I saw.' Betty was beginning to wish she'd never broached the subject. She gave Mariander a sidelong look. 'Why? Been pinching your boyfriends, has she?'

'No she hasn't! I just....wondered what she'd done with him that's all! Well, obliged for the information, Betty. And now I'll be off round Bryony's to hear her side of it!'

'Oh dear,' Betty murmured. 'Looks as if I've dropped Bryony in it good and proper.'

Bevis Tate was having the time of his life, because Scallion possessed everything he had ever desired. With the woman of his dreams, his wildest fantasies were indeed being realised. Life was truly all his birthdays come at once.

She possessed a shredder, a fax-machine, a photocopier, a scanner and a state-of-the-art computer to which he was allowed free access...('except when me and me mates have a games evening.')

She had provided him with reams of high-quality paper, packets of coloured dotsstars and stick-on numbers, all the folders and document-holders he could possibly require, and, best of all, a mobile phone, and an electronic organiser with word-processing facility.

He had acquired millions of rubber bands and paper-clips-- the decent, plastic-covered ones, not the inferior metal sort...and marker-pens in every conceivable hue.

She had showered him with ledgers and card-files and notebooks, and a handsome dark-green filing-cabinet. And she had given him carte-blanche to re-organize, and to inaugurate a new appointments-system.

Because his employer was, after all, a busy young lady, with a great many clients to accommodate. An expanding business, the Massage-Industry: Scallion had, for a very long time, been in need of someone efficient to organise her affairs--and Bevis Tate was he.

The remuneration was not overly generous, but his life, once the new system was in place, would be very largely his own, to model or photograph as he chose. (Indeed, he was already planning a three-dimensional computer representation of inter-linked paper-clips as a kind of tribute to Office Technology.)

But best of all, his accommodation was commodious, allowing him space for a dark-room. Without a trace of regret, he had put his house on the market, having accepted that he would never now live in Fossetby Mill, and caring not one whit, and drafted his letter of resignation to the Guild.

He intended staying where his talent was appreciated.

After Tobin had gone, dropping her and Grufty and the space-hopper off at the top of Mariander's road, Granny felt as though a load had been lifted off her chest: knowing, without a shred of doubt that she'd done the right thing.

Oh, he'd sulk for a while, and reckon his heart was broken, but he'd get over it...because Romance, she told herself, was one thing, and friendship, which definitely lasted a deal longer, was quite another.

And if she'd wed Tobin, she knew that their friendship would've winked out like the last spark in the grate.

Getting into the car, Hilary Bottomley glanced up just as the Beamish woman, with her smelly little dog waddling and panting behind, came bouncing along Brimbleby Way on a sort of huge orange rubber ball which, she could have sworn, had an evil smile on its face.

Even Aubrey gaped, and he'd never believed *anything* she'd told him about that woman.

Trapped in her carrying-cage on the back seat, Truffle, sensing Grufty, lifted her muzzle and howled like a miniature timber-wolf, whereupon the old woman's dog stopped dead, tail at half-mast, ears pricked, listening. And then he sat down and howled back.

'BE QUIET, you wretched dog!' Hilary snapped. Quick, Aubrey, before he upsets her any more! We mustn't be late at the vet's. Remember, there's a lot of money riding on these puppies!'

Mariander stared speechlessly at the space-hopper, which was criss-crossed with puncture repair patches.

'Now that you've *finally* got round to calling,' she said, eventually, 'why couldn't you just walk, or catch a bus like everyone else? Tobin's van not good enough any more?'

Granny ran her fingers through her disordered hair. 'You're only jealous,' she snapped. 'Good exercise, is that. And as for Tobin--well, that's another matter. Ain't that right, Grufty--what's up, old lad?'

'Grufty, come back! Where you going? Oh, so that's it...well, just to tell you something you *didn't* know,' Mariander said, 'It looks like he's spotted Truffle. They've just took her off to the vet's. It must be her time.'

Hilary Bottomley swept into Mr. Simmons' surgery, having insisted, against his advice, on a caesarian delivery for her Queen Courvalier bitch. She certainly didn't want any nasty mess in *her* home.

Refused permission to go in and supervise--they'd actually advised her to go home and ring up later!!...even though she offered to scrub up like they did on 'T.V. Vet'...she settled herself indignantly in the waiting-room with a pile of 'Home Beautiful' magazines.

Aubrey had said he'd wait in the car, and even though she strongly suspected him of smoking and tuning in to the cricket, she really couldn't be bothered to argue when their future finances were at stake. She immersed herself, instead, in a feature on Lord Frinkenbury's drawing-room.

Well, once the puppies were sold, she'd be able to afford a smallish cut-glass chandelier of her own. And keeping it polished would give Aubrey something to do other than hang around that woodyard with those undesirables--as if she didn't know what he got up down there!

Mr. Simmons seemed to be taking a remarkably long time delivering those puppies! She banged impatiently on the door, but there was no response, other than what she could have sworn was an outbreak of unseemly giggling!

Five minutes later, however, the veterinary nurse put her head round the door. She looked flushed, and seemed, for some extraordinary reason, to be smirking.

'Would you...like to come in and...see the puppies?'

'And about time, too!' Flinging down her magazine, Hilary Bottomley strode into the surgery.

'Ah, Mrs. Bottomley.' Mr. Simmons peeled off his surgical gloves. His white coat, she noted with distaste, was splashed with blood.

'Congratulations!' he snorted, shoulders heaving. What *was* the matter with the man? Had he been drinking?

Truffle lay on the table, under a brightly-lit lamp, sleeping deeply. A livid scar, neatly-stitched, ran across her shaven side. And next to her lay two small, blind creatures, still wet with unmentionable substances: she thought them absolutely revolting.

'Two?' Hilary said sharply, seeing the chandelier shrink before her eyes. 'Two? Is that all she could manage?'

The vet. gave her an odd look. 'They're fine big puppies, though,' he replied, 'and both boys. Pick them up and feel the weight of them!'

He thrust them at her: Hilary recoiled. 'Urgh! NO, thank you, they're all slimy!' She peered closer. The vet. and his assistant eyed her with interest.

'Wait a moment!' Hilary's eyes narrowed. 'These are nothing like her, or her...husband! Unless...' she looked enquiringly at Mr. Simmons, 'they're going to change a great deal?' But Mr. Simmons shook his head, firmly, enjoying the joke Nature had played on this terrible woman. Fine, strong puppies, definitely, but Pedigree Queen Courvaliers, they were not.

Hilary peered closer. Her eyes widened as she took in the full horror of the situation. 'But they look exactly like-- AUBREY! AUBREY!'

And as she ran shrieking into the car-park, Mr. Simmons and his nurse gave full vent to their laughter.

Bartleshire needed 12 off two overs to beat Drimsett: tension ran high as Cottleshaw, who'd been suffering from severe hay-fever, went in to bat.

Aubrey unfortunately missed the outcome, because at that moment, his wife appeared, screaming like a banshee, and dragged him off into the vet's surgery. Where he was forced to agree that Truffle's puppies looked nothing like their father, but very much like-

'You stupid man!' she raged at the vet., as though, he said afterwards, he'd deliberately swapped the pups at birth.

'Well, I don't want them, or her either, come to that! You can drown the lot of them for all I care! And don't bother sending me a bill, because I shan't pay it!' And so saying, she swept out, dragging Aubrey, who at least had the grace to look embarrassed, in her wake.

'Please!' He called desperately behind him, 'look after her!'

'Well!' Mr. Simmons picked up the wriggling puppies. ' Write that one off to experience, eh? Good, well-boned puppies, these, if not exactly handsome--what I suppose you'd call tough mongrel-stock. I'd love to know how the father got past that woman. People like her shouldn't have dogs, anyway.'

He restored the youngsters to their sleeping mother. 'Better knock out a FREE TO GOOD HOMES notice, then, Joanne.'

Granny poked up the fire: the nights were starting to draw in.

Casting a professional eye over the bowls of fast-cooling turnip face-pack, she got her coat on, patted Truffle's head, and read the pups the Riot Act.

'Now don't you be chewing anything!' she warned, 'else there'll be no supper tonight!'

Not that she meant a word of it, because they were at that chewy stage. She watched them trying to climb out of their box, solid, sturdy little things, both of 'em the image of their Dad. Half-weaned or not, poor old Truffle spent hours filling them up and the rest of her time hauling them out of danger by their scruffs. She was a born mother, all right.

Course, she'd only be keeping the one...the bossy adventurous little Tyke with That Look in its eye; but Truffle and

the other pup were going to live with Tassie and Gorrie Bough, where she knew full well they'd be spoilt rotten. Funny the way things worked out for the best....

The sun's warmth lingered. There'd been showers, and everything had that just-washed smell. It wasn't quite dark: rooks racketing round the Beechwood, quarrelling about anything and everything. Good night for dog-training, she reflected, although she wouldn't've minded betting Grufty'd forgot everything he'd ever learned.

Well, they *had* all been a bit busy of late, what with Kenneth's troubles, and then that bounty-hunter getting his comeuppance.

In the end, they'd buried him, good and deep, and weighted down, in the clay at the bottom of Perilla's disused quarry, where nobody'd ever find him. Hadn't seemed worth the bother of reporting his death--and who'd've believed it, anyhow?

As for the Wolf-Patrol; the Police'd sent a breakdown-truck next morning to pick up the car...and a right mess it was, too, Granny'd felt really proud, seeing as how they'd wrecked it in the dark.

Of course, Perilla'd denied all knowledge of what'd gone on with the sheep and the griffons, and everybody'd backed her up. And as there wasn't a scrap of evidence, it'd came down to their word against the policemen's...she didn't envy them one bit, writing their report.

When Mariander opened her door, Grufty thumped his tail once and carried on demolishing whatever it was he'd dug out of the flower-bed. Up on the mantelpiece, Sham perfected the delicious slurping chomp he'd added to his repertoire.

Granny poked a corner of Grufty's mind: wasn't much in it, as usual, beyond thoughts of food. And he certainly wasn't worrying about passing any Proficiency-Test. Mariander eyed him resignedly.

'Expect he'll do his best,' she sighed.

On their was round to Betty's, Mariander glanced up at the pale, full moon.

'I wonder how it's going with Warg,' she mused. 'Still living in sin with Perilla, is he?'

'Far as I know. Ain't heard a thing from either of 'em...but then we've been a bit too busy with the Remedies, haven't we?'

'Mmmm. Funny how "Pennypincher" agreed to sell 'em, weren't it? Shouldn't't've thought it was their kind of thing.'

'Oh, well,' Granny said vaguely, 'done their Market-Research, obviously. Meeting the Customer's needs and all that.'

'And of course, nothing whatsoever to do with any Hard Sell from one of the manufacturers,' Mariander said.

Granny smiled. 'Course not.'

Betty's cottage was transformed: Perilla's workmen had done a fair old job on it.

When Granny had first seen it, it'd sort of...squatted, like a Bog-Toad in amongst the rubble and potholes and junk, but now! It had new window-frames, not to mention windows, and the walls had been whitewashed, just like when old Tarrill'd lived there. The garden was neat, and there was gravel on the drive and tubs of flowers everywhere. There was a smart new front door, and a little brass bell hung beside it.

And Betty herself looked that different...years younger. Even Krystle had a spring in her step and a light in her eyes that hadn't bin there when she'd first been rescued.

'I'll just get me cardi,' Betty said, and as she went back inside, the hall smelt of furniture-polish and fresh baking. Grufty sniffed hopefully.

The Village-Hall was crowded: especially the bit with Bernard's sisters in it.

Granny regarded them with horror, especially Zinnia, who was wearing an outsize teeshirt with: SAVE THE WHALE! I'LL HAVE IT FOR PUDDING!--on it, which she knew'd go down a treat with Perilla. Some things you just didn't joke about.

There was noise, but subdued noise, as though everyone was on their best behaviour.

'MARI!' Granny hissed, 'did you invite...'

'Yes I did,' Mariander said firmly. 'It's a night out for 'em, and anyway, you forgotten how much of our stuff they bought, them and their friends? And besides, they're off to the 'Rat & Pitchfork' afterwards after to play darts with...some men they know.'

'Well, they just better keep quiet, is all,' Granny hissed, giving the sisters a falsely-cheery wave.

There wasn't so much as a curled lip from any of the dogs, who all sat primly at their owners' sides. Those who passed the Test would receive certificates, and an option to progress to Intermediate level. But the failures, as everyone knew, would stay behind...in the Puppy Class.

Perilla bustled in, magnificent in leopard-print leggings and matching halter-neck top, over which quite a lot of Perilla protruded. Chervil followed, wearing his I'm-too-good-for-all-this expression, and then Jeg.

But there was no sign of Kenneth...or, Granny realised, Warg, as he would currently be. She just hoped Perilla had got him somewhere secure so's he wouldn't be off in the moonlight, biting lumps out of things....Jeg and Chervil, having covered a trestle-table with what looked remarkably like an old velvet curtain, proceeded to set out rosettes and certificates. Perilla clapped her hands for order, and a terrified hush descended on everyone except the sisters, who cheered loudly.

Perilla fixed them with a Look. 'RIGHT, let's begin!' she bawled. 'First dog out here, Annie!'

One by one, in alphabetical order, the dogs went through their paces, until at last it was Grufty's turn.

'Come on then lad,' Granny said, 'and let's get this right first time.'

'Buggered up that car good and proper, didn't you? Vehicle-maintenance are still putting it back together. *And* mislaid an expensive weapon to boot!--have you anything to say for yourselves before I instigate disciplinary-procedures?'

Rog. and Steve studied their boots. Of course, there was quite a lot they *could* have said. They could, for instance, have fingered the old woman, the stroppy one with the slippers and the allotment, but what was the point? She'd only have hidden the stun-gun, or buried it or sold it or something, and then they'd be accused of harrassing old-age pensioners and lying to save their careers....

.....and as for the car, the one that looked like the loser in a collision with a juggernaut, well who was going to believe that a bunch of weirdos had done all that damage with their *minds?*

'No, sir,' they muttered in unison.

'Then I'll thank you to hand over those caps.'

Assistant Chief Constable Root took the baseball-caps with the wolf-logos--at least, he took Rog's, and what was left of Steve's...and tossed them contemptuously into his stainless-steel litter-bin.

And then, standing up to his full height, he ceremonially ripped the matching epaulettes from their sweatshirts...(not that Steve's took much detaching.)

'The Wolf-Patrol,' he intoned, 'is hereby officially disbanded...and a bloody good job, too. Waste of resources. Complete load of cobblers from start to finish. And as for you two...'

'Bloody Harry-the-hedgehog again,' Steve muttered.

'What?' A.C.C. Root barked. 'Oh, no, my lad. Not a bit of it. Traffic-control outside the Shamford Dishcloth & Teatowel Museum & Tearooms ought to do it. Dismissed!'

When they'd gone, he turned to Sergeant Gilmore, who'd been officially recording the proceedings.

'You realise there'll have to be an Internal Inquiry?' He winked.

'Which I very much doubt will uncover anything untoward...if we understand one another?'

'Perfectly, Sir. Er...'Sergeant Gilmore hesitated. '....about those letters of complaint from the Public, in particular, one Mrs. Bottomley who says she's suing us for her lost reputation?'

'What, that crackpot claiming to have been shot by our officers? Lose the lot, Sergeant, lose 'em. I'm sure I can rely on your ingenuity. If necessary, arrange a very small outbreak of unaccountable arson in your filing-cabinet.'

'I reckon we did all right, Grufty,' Granny told him as, hot and tired, they sat down after their performance.

'Never thought you had it in you, you ole bugger!' Begonia roared.

'Yes, that weren't half bad!' Mariander beamed. Betty agreed.

In truth, Granny had been pleasantly surprised. It hadn't been Grufty who'd laid down beautifully on command and then gone to sleep and refused to get up again.

Hadn't been him who, once off his lead, had totally ignored his owner's command to 'COME!' and then gone straight for the throat of his deadliest enemy, who'd been nose-down, innocently watching a wood-louse cross the floorboards.

It hadn't even, for once in his life, been Grufty who'd come bounding back, all co-operative, then shot straight past and eaten all the prize-sausages off the certificate-table....!

No, all in all, things could've been a whole lot worse.

When everyone had finished, Perilla scribbled a few notes, put her clipboard down, and announced: 'Before I give you the scores, we shall have a Special Obedience Demo--show you how it's done, sort of thing. Bear with me one moment.'

Granny, Betty and Mariander looked at one another, wondering, as Perilla strode out of the hall.

Their hearts leapt as she returned moments later, leading a huge and magnificent wolf. His coat gleamed, and he held his plumed tail proudly, moving with a slow, confident lope that was a pleasure to watch.

A gasp went up from the spectators, particularly the Sisters, one of whom breathed: 'Ooh, I'm all of a flutter! I thought them sorts of animals was extinct!'....as Perilla removed the wolf's check-chain, commanding him to sit. He sat watching her with bright, intelligent eyes.

Granny thought afterwards that the two of 'em looked as if they were linked by invisible wires as they moved around the hall.

Uncanny might've described it, even though one of 'em was a Seer, because they were in perfect accord. And not once did Warg's concentration waver: it was all done with eye-contact and hand-signals.

Even Grufty looked impressed. A storm of applause broke out as Warg and Perilla left the floor. Granny glanced at Betty to see how she was taking it, and saw that her eyes were full of tears.

Having got over their initial fears, everyone wanted to pat the wolf.

'Must be one of her Sanctuary animals,' someone said. 'Amazing how she trains them, isn't it?'

Quite a few people commented on Warg's impressive teeth. Good job, Granny thought, that he didn't open his mouth wide-- obviously under orders from Perilla.

Then she heard someone ask Betty: 'How's that brother of yours? Keeping well, is he? I haven't seen him about for a while.'

'Oh, he's fine,' Betty replied, adding truthfully, 'only he couldn't come tonight because he had to be somewhere else.'

'Just one more thing, before you go, Sir.' Sergeant Gilmore was frowning over a report that had just come in.

'Yes, what is it?' A.C.C. Root was hoping to get stuck into 'Topiary Today' before the missus started watching her trashy soap-opera.

'This disappearance...caretaker chap at County Hall. The lads have been searching the basement, and his flat.'

He wrinkled his nose. 'Turned up some *very* dodgy stuff indeed. Usual loner, and a proper pervert by the look of it. Let's hope he's moved on...we're well shot of *him*. Here's the report, Sir...only I wouldn't read it til after you've had your tea.'

There were only half-a-dozen failures: dogs which needed a bit of firm handling, which Perilla made sure they'd get.

Grufty came third out of all the dogs in the class: he'd only done it, Granny knew, to impress the snooty Salamar which won, paws-down, and *still* wouldn't acknowledge him.

But she still couldn't help feeling ridiculously proud as they went up to collect their certificate, rosette and sausage...(luckily Perilla, who knew about dogs, always carried spares in the Jeep.)

'One more thing!' she yelled over the congratulatory clamour, 'you'll be glad to hear that they're building a hypermarket on the site of the Bartlock Dog-Pound!' She shot Granny a meaningful look.

'And they've moved both dog-wardens, because there are so few strays around here!' Over the cheering and catcalls, she added: So let's keep up the good work because, remember, a well-trained dog is a happy dog! And now, who's coming down the pub?'

'That's us,' Begonia said happily. 'Game of darts, game of pool, and then I'm for the karaoke...eh, girls?'

'Not me,' Betty said, fondling Warg's ears. 'Krystle's waiting by the fire.' She dropped her voice to a whisper.

'Wasn't it wonderful seeing our Kenneth so obedient? He's coming over to stay tonight, aren't you...he's got his own bed now, haven't you, and he won't chew it up this time...*will you?*'

'No more problems, then?' Granny nodded towards the bright moon pouring its light through the high windows.

Warg gazed wistfully upwards, a deep longing in his eyes. He raised his muzzle, opened his mouth, displaying flawless fangs, and cleared his throat.

'NO,' Perilla told him firmly, 'LEAVE IT.'

Warg dropped his head, relief chasing disappointment across his face, and Perilla tickled his chest.

'It's all right,' she told him, 'it's OVER. Big Boy.'

And Granny could have sworn that Warg winked at her--if wolves could wink.

'Right,' Betty said briskly. 'Would you and Mariander and Grufty care for some supper?'

'Well, if you're sure him and Warg won't fight,' Granny said., because Grufty could be very nasty indeed when there was food about. But he gave her a withering glance that said, plain as day: *What me, fight that? Call him a wolf? Hasn't even got his own teeth! He's no wolf, he's people, and always will be!*

Granny felt a smile coming on. 'All right,' she said. 'It's been quite a day. I reckon a bite of supper'd go down a treat.'

EPILOGUE

They say, whoever they are, that, when the moon is full, a great, grey wolf with silver teeth roams the Bartleshire countryside.

Some speak of a werewolf, albeit one who prefers flapjacks to flesh, blackcurrant-juice to blood: a were-wimp who attacks nothing more threatening than litter-bins.

This is a wolf who jumps at shadows and flees from cats, they say, and the sight of his cringing strikes pity in the onlooker, silver teeth notwithstanding.

And others say that, if you stand and listen when the moon is full and the night is still, you will hear his call...mournful, and desolate with his never-ending loneliness. Or, more possibly, indigestion.

But there are those who know better the sound of one howling for effect, because it's The Done Thing, rather than one railing at his Cruel Fate.

Because although the moon will always claim him, here is a wolf with a microchip implant, and therefore a home to go to, when his roaming's done. And be sure that when he *does* go home, he is loved and petted and cossetted in a totally caring way....a man/wolf with his own duvet, and a pillow on which to lay his weary, metamorphosing head....Until the next time.

And then there are still others who say that a bounty-hunter roams the country lanes, in search of skins.

A small man, dressed all in black, he wears biker-boots and a hat so big you can't see his face.

He veers drunkenly all over the place--probably because he can't see out from under the hat...endlessly flailing a long chain that hums like wind in the telephone-wires...And should he, for some reason, remove the outsize hat, you will shrink from eyes that are dead, eyes that have no love in them, nor ever had.

There are weals around his neck, deep and livid, like the marks left by choking chains. And then you will notice something else: he has no ears, only dark, bloodied holes.

And if you should meet this pitiless phantom, don't hang about, and don't get in his way, because he stops for no-one.

Who is he, and where does he come from? And what do we call this fearsome apparition?

Call him anything you like...he can't hear you!

THE END

And coming next......'**Seers' Bones**'.....read it here first...

PROLOGUE

Once more round the bastard field, and then he'd knock off. He'd done more than enough for one day, and the boss was away, so he'd never know. Shane Mason shifted his chewing-gum and adjusted his headphones. When he'd got the music good and loud, he put the digger into gear and moved forward, jerkily, in time with the beat.

Music helped drown out the boredom, because digging wasn't really his thing. Come to that, he wasn't exactly sure what *was*, still, it kept him in beer-money, and Kylie out of his hair. And he did like *ramming* things...he hadn't half enjoyed ripping that ole hedge out yesterday, and the trees the day before...all them panicking birds and things...a pity he hadn't had a shotgun handy.

Just another job, wasn't it, digging things up and tearing them down. Forty houses going up on this field: not that him and Kylie'd ever be able to afford one on the wages Pickard's paid. He spat out of the cab window, lit a fag and consulted his watch: just hit opening-time if he got a move on. Squinting through the smoke, he churned his way along the margin of the field: going great until, with a judder, he hit something.

Cursing and muttering, he jumped down and squatted to examine the ground. Instead of the expected boulder, though, was—Shane wasn't an imaginative lad, but some things still gave him the willies and stopped him sleeping nights. Blood. Dentists. And....

He didn't stop to think about it. Abandoning the digger half in and half-out of the ditch, he ran for his life.

*****

www.ingramcontent.com/pod-product-compliance
Lightning Source LLC
Chambersburg PA
CBHW020654030726
47498CB00002B/508